EXECUTIVE ORDER NO. 9066

THE TERRIBLE INJUSTICE OF 1942

A CAPTIVATING HISTORICAL NOVEL FROM WWII

SOLLACE FREEMAN

Publish Authority

Executive Order No. 9066
ISBN 978-1-954000-75-9 (Paperback)
ISBN 978-1-954000-76-6 (eBook)

Editor: Janie Mills
Cover Design: Raeghan Rebstock

Published 2023 by Publish Authority,
300 Colonial Center Parkway, Suite 100
Roswell, GA USA
PublishAuthority.com

Printed in the United States of America

There are, at any moment, millions of people on this planet who
are the victims of -
Hate
Greed
Hunger for Power
Prejudice
Racism

This book is dedicated to them.

PREFACE

This is a work of historical fiction. The characters and many of the details of the story are not real.

The story was created to remind the readers of the sad chapter in our country's history when racial prejudice and fear took a major toll on the civil liberties of over 127,000 American citizens.

Although fictional, the description of events around the removal of these Japanese Americans from their homes and their transfer to remote internment camps is based on extensive research about these events.

Descriptions of the removal and life in the camps have been created from actual documents from the internees.

Many families and individuals were detained in these primitive living conditions for over three years. They had to abandon their homes, their businesses, and any possessions they could not carry. When they were released, they returned to find that their homes had been destroyed or auctioned off and their businesses taken over. Financial losses were estimated at $400 million. That's estimated to be about $7.5 billion in today's dollars.

It was not until 1988, under President Reagan, that Congress passed the Civil Liberties Act, which provided a $20,000 cash payment to each surviving detainee.

This is the story of one of these families.

PROLOGUE

DECEMBER 7, 1941, WAS A BRIGHT, SUNNY SUNDAY ON THE ISLAND OF OAHU.

The two senior military leaders, Admiral Husband Kimmel, Commander of the US Pacific Fleet, and Lieutenant General Walter Short, Commander of the Hawaiian Department of the US Army, had a golf game planned for later in the day.

Despite numerous warnings from military leadership on the mainland, neither had any concern about imminent hostile action.

For the twelve hundred sailors aboard the USS Oklahoma moored outboard of the Maryland on Battleship Row, a quiet Sunday was expected. By 0700 the captain's gig had already carried a group of them ashore to attend worship services.

At 0755, the first wave of the coordinated attack by Japanese aircraft began. They targeted the largest ships in the harbor and aircraft on Hickam, Wheeler, and Bellows fields. The attack was over by 0910.

Both Kimmel and Short rushed to CINCPAC Headquarters but were unable to control the chaos. Kimmel was struck in the chest by a stray bullet. Short was uninjured.

Following the attack, both were immediately relieved of command, reduced in rank, and returned to the US. Some feel they were scapegoated.

It was a different story aboard the Oklahoma. She was struck by eight torpedoes, opening a huge gash at the waterline on her port side and creating massive internal damage. She capsized in less than ten minutes. Four hundred and twenty-nine members of the crew drowned or were killed by the explosions. Heroic efforts by civilian contractors, led by Julio DeCastro, rescued thirty-two members of the crew by cutting holes in the hull.

In all, two thousand, four hundred and three persons—sailors, soldiers, and civilians died in the attack. One thousand one hundred and seventy-seven of these were on the USS Arizona, where they remain today.

The Navy lost twenty ships, including eight battleships. The Army lost over three hundred planes.

On December 8, President Franklin Roosevelt addressed Congress calling December 7th "...a date which will live in infamy," and called for a declaration of war against Japan.

Forty-three days later, on February 19, 1942, the President issued Executive Order 9066, setting in motion the process that led to the internment described in this story.

1

JEMEZ MOUNTAINS, NEW MEXICO

JULY 14, 1945

The sun was sinking behind the mountains ahead of him, its rays turning the few wispy clouds varying shades of red and orange. The lengthening shadows around him quickly fading into darkness. He'd been riding west for almost two hours. The red '41 Indian Sport Scout with its 750-cc flathead v-twin he'd bought from one of his coworkers purred flawlessly, performing as if it felt at home in the sand and dust of the place.

I'm sure glad I grabbed these gloves from Bill's locker. It's a lot colder out here than I expected.

Since escaping the assembly compound at the Los Alamos site, he'd been riding in the desert, staying off the roads in case the MPs were looking for him. Once they found his note exposing his team's plans to sabotage the A-bomb test, he knew they'd be looking for him.

David, the name he got at the start of his training in

Tokyo almost three years ago, was twenty-six, 5'8", and well-tanned from several months in the desert sun. Although he was half-Japanese, his mother's genes must have been the stronger part of the blend. Except for the jet-black hair, he had none of his father's features or coloring and easily passed as White.

His heart rate was finally returning to normal as the last effects of the adrenalin drained from his system. Since he hadn't seen signs of any pursuers since he left Los Alamos, he was breathing a little easier. Then, as he paused to drink from his canteen, he saw moving lights a few miles back. His fear immediately returned.

Damn, those guys are good! I'd better not get overconfident. If they catch me, it'll be prison or the firing squad.

He jammed his canteen back into the case, kicked the bike into gear, and sped off, going faster in the darkness than he should have.

As he attempted a sharp turn into the narrow canyon, he felt the motorcycle's back wheel skid from under him in the thick dust. It went down hard on his left leg. "Damn," he cried as a sharp pain shot up the side of his left leg and body. His helmet and the noise of the engine muffled his cry. Stars flashed in his eyes, mingling with the starlit sky of the coal-black desert night.

Killing the engine, he lay still for a few moments, collecting his thoughts and mentally checking out his body. Then he carefully pulled himself from under the machine and slowly got to his feet, gingerly testing his leg. *No breaks,* he thought, thankful for the soft ground, as he uprighted the bike.

He pulled a small flashlight from his jacket pocket.

That's when he saw the front fender stuck out sharply from the wheel. Wincing as he balanced on his left leg, he kicked it back with his right foot, making sure it didn't touch the tire. He remounted and kick-started the engine, relieved that it started with the first try.

"Thank you, friend. You're as tough as they said you were."

He gently released pressure on the clutch lever and slowly continued into the canyon. He stopped about ten yards in, walking back to the canyon's entrance. Using his foot and jacket, he erased his tire and skid marks turning into the canyon.

Returning to the bike, scratching over his footprints behind him with a stick he found, he headed deeper into the darkness. The narrow beam of the mostly blacked-out headlight barely illuminated the narrow trail between the rocks.

I think I've lost them. Now, if I can just get to the shack and hide the bike, I'll be okay 'til morning. Then I can get to California and find my family and Hana.

Up ahead, he could just make out the aging, weathered shack in the narrow beam. It backed up almost against the canyon wall under a low outcropping of rock that protected the back half of the structure from the elements.

He pulled to the back. There was just enough space for him to push the bike out of sight, hiding it mostly with a piece of rotten tarp and a fallen branch. He limped to the front, letting himself into the shack through the door hanging by one hinge.

He discovered the structure in early June. While supposedly on a liberty pass from Los Alamos to Taos, he drove his bike into the desert to work out an escape route. He'd heard the locals working construction at the site say the hills were full of old squatter or prospector camps.

"Yeah, them guys from back east would come out here lookin' for a piece of land or a vein of gold. Nobody's out there anymore. Just a lot of busted dreams."

In the light from his flashlight, the shack was as he remembered.

Good to see nobody else has any interest in this place.

There was a chair with a broken back, a rickety table, a makeshift shelf with an empty Folgers coffee can, a frame that once held some sort of crude mattress, a flue that had been attached to a small iron stove, probably taken by scavengers, and thick dust and cobwebs everywhere.

Feeling dizzy, he sat in the chair and realized his pants leg felt cold. Aiming the light at his leg, he saw that the inside of his pants had a large tear. From just above his knee, running down into his boot, was a dark, shiny red stain.

"Damn!" he shouted. "It must have been that fender."

With the light, he followed the trail of dark red splotches in the dust to the door.

I've got to stop the bleeding or die here, probably never to be found.

He swept the light around the cabin and saw the pieces of rope webbing hanging from the bed frame. He started to stand to get a piece and fell backward into the chair, almost passing out.

Whoa, this is really bad. I've gotta fix this now!

Sliding to the floor, he dragged his body to the bed and, using his knife, cut a length of rope. With his waning energy, he broke a leg from the chair. Then, using the technique he'd learned in training, he fashioned a tourniquet that he placed just above the wound and tightened it until the bleeding stopped.

Exhausted by the effort, he propped himself against the bed frame, took a long drink from his canteen, and allowed himself to doze. As he lost consciousness, the events in San Francisco from three years ago that had brought him to this place flooded back into his mind.

"Gerald," he heard his mother's voice say, "go help your father with that luggage. The Army trucks will be here soon."

MARCH 8, 1942 – JANUARY 22, 1946

2

"JAPANTOWN" SAN FRANCISCO, CALIFORNIA

MARCH 8, 1942

It was a chilly Sunday morning. Bunta Horito, a second-generation Japanese American, often called "Nisei," and his bi-racial son, Gerald, "Sansei," or third generation, are sitting at the kitchen table in their home in San Francisco enjoying hot tea. Sandra Horito, Gerald's Caucasian mother, and Rachel, Gerald's twelve year old, sister are still asleep. Bunta's parents, Haruto and Aiko, are asleep in their house next door.

They were taking this quiet opportunity to discuss a growing concern.

"Gerald, I fear for our future," Bunta said. "I'm afraid our family and many others are going to be forced to leave San Francisco and move inland. That means selling our house, getting a second car so the six of us can travel, and having our belongings shipped to some new location. We'll have to find jobs and a place to live. It will be very difficult and stressful, especially for Otosan and Okasan.

"Fortunately, we do not own a business like many of our neighbors. I don't know what they'll do."

"Father, you and I have jobs that benefit the military. The Navy gave me a secret clearance. Mama is not Japanese, Rachel is young, and Ojichan and Obachan are old. We are clearly not a threat. I just can't believe they will make us move."

"Son, I hope you are right. I am just so fearful."

Since 1913, state legislatures on the West Coast had been passing laws restricting Japanese, who were primarily farmers, from owning land.

Then, in 1940, Congress passed the Alien Registration Act, requiring all aliens to register with the government and be fingerprinted. Bunta's parents, Haruto and Aiko, had to register.

Since the attack on Pearl Harbor in December, the racial prejudice aimed at the Japanese had increased in intensity. There was growing concern that the Japanese living in America retained loyalty to the emperor, regardless of how long they had lived here.

On February 14, 1942, Lieutenant General John DeWitt, who led the Army's Western Defense Command, wrote to President Roosevelt,

"[The] Japanese race is an enemy race who, regardless of birthplace, would be ready to die for Japan."

Five days later, on February 19th, Roosevelt issued the

first and only attack on the constitutional rights of American citizens, Executive Order 9066.

The order gave the military the authority to "...prescribe military areas...from which any or all persons may be excluded...." Although it did not specify any ethnic group, General DeWitt announced curfews that included only Japanese.

On March 2nd, he issued Proclamation #1, creating Military Areas 1 and 2, which included most of Washington, Oregon, California, and Arizona. It encouraged "voluntary evacuation."

3
"JAPANTOWN"

WEDNESDAY, APRIL 22, 1942. SIX DAYS TO DEPARTURE

At 6:30 a.m., the Big Ben alarm clock clanged to life, jarring him awake. The sound intruded on the recurring nightmare images of exploding ships and people chasing him with pitchforks. Even with the gentle, cool sea breeze coming into his room, his pillow was damp with sweat. Appearing as part of his dream, the yellow morning light through the billowing curtains cast menacing flame-like shadows on the far wall.

Gerald had not slept well since seeing the images of the Pearl Harbor attack. The burning ships, the swarms of planes, and the face of Gunner's Mate Third Class Charlie White in the explosions on the USS Oklahoma haunted his nights.

Charlie was his best friend throughout their four years at Washington High. Unlike Gerald, who received a BS degree in electrical engineering from San Francisco State University in 1940, Charlie had enlisted in the Navy right after graduation. He sent letters back to his family and schoolmates while in boot camp at the Naval Training Center, San Diego. The letters continued while he was in Gunnery School at Great Lakes, growing less frequent when he joined the fleet. Returning to San Francisco for a week's leave, he almost convinced Gerald to enlist and join him on the Oklahoma when she sailed for Pearl Harbor in October 1941.

Some days, Gerald was overwhelmed with guilt for not having joined him.

At twenty-three, Gerald was the exception to many of his classmates from Washington High. When he graduated at eighteen, he had been accepted to the San Diego School of Engineering, Caltech, and San Francisco State.

While his parents said they would find a way to pay the expenses if he wanted to leave home for college, Gerald knew that would be a huge burden for them.

"Papa, Mama, that is very generous. Thank you for the offer. But I can get just as good an education here in San Francisco as I can at those big-name schools. And besides, I want to work here after graduation, and it'll be easier to find an internship at a local business if I'm living here. So, unless you're trying to get rid of me," he said, smiling and giving his mother a gentle poke, "I'm here, at least for the next four years."

He continued his excellent scholastic record at SFS, and true to his plans, at the end of his sophomore year, was hired as an intern by the company that would eventually hire him permanently.

The only thing that suffered was his social life. After studies, helping his father with maintenance on the two houses and the car, the internship, and running errands for his grandparents, Haruto and Aiko, there was little time left for dating. On weekend evenings after home chores, he'd often go to a movie or a soda shop with classmates. Girls in the group were always flirting, which he enjoyed, but he never got serious with any of them.

After graduation, he was hired by Western Electrical Manufacturing and Supply. Because of his excellent academic career and the connections he had during his internship, he was placed in charge of the production line for their new contract with the Navy. This required a secret clearance, which was issued to him with no concerns.

When the Civilian Exclusion Orders issued by the Army started appearing in the surrounding areas, both his and his father's bosses had told them, "You are working in an area important to the war effort. Hopefully, you will be allowed to continue your work with us. If not, you can work here until you are told you must leave."

When Order #5 covering San Francisco County was posted on April 1st of that year, Bunta was required to report the following day to the Civilian Control Station to receive instructions for the family to be relocated. At that time, he was told that the receiving camp was still being constructed, and his family would be notified when they would have to leave. The family would be able to continue their normal routine until that notification.

Smelling the bacon frying, Gerald got up, took a quick

shower, dressed, and joined his father in the kitchen as his mother put breakfast on the table.

"Good morning, Mama, Papa," he said, giving his mother a quick hug and sliding into his chair. "Rachel's the sleepyhead today, huh? Must be nice to be young.

"There are big doings at the plant today," he said. "The Navy's inspector is visiting to go over our work on the design changes they made last month. I'm really excited to show him what we've come up with. Have you heard anything from your plant's inspection last week, Papa?"

"Yes. The Navy's not pleased with the results of the new dyes they've ordered, so they want us to mix a new batch. That means steam cleaning all the vats, lines, and pumps. None of the production guys are happy. I need to get there earlier than usual. Finish your food. We need to catch the earlier bus."

THEY RODE TOGETHER EACH MORNING, WITH PAPA GETTING OFF first. They had been riding the city bus for almost two years, as had most of the other passengers. Most knew everybody's first name and where they worked. Now, since the Pearl Harbor attack and the issuance of the Exclusion Orders, there were stares and muttered "Jap" directed at Bunta from some of the other passengers. It made the ride very uncomfortable.

How could they be treating Papa this way? They've seen him and spoken to him on this bus for so long. Why are they making the assumption that he's somehow not the same man he was before? It's just not fair.

It was no different on the earlier bus.

Reports of rising verbal hostility in the market areas kept Bunta, except for this bus ride, from leaving the neighborhood. Sandra made the trips to the grocery, and Gerald did the banking and bought gas for the car.

GERALD ARRIVED AT HIS DESK IN THE OFFICE OF THE ELECTRICAL manufacturing company at 8:00 a.m. The orders for the daily quota of electrical switches for the Navy were spread out in front of him. He got busy converting the orders into a production schedule for the plant workers. He felt good about doing this to support the war effort.

At noon, he stood up, heading to the break room for lunch. Suddenly, his way was blocked by a soldier who entered the office without knocking. Gerald's eyes instantly focused on the pistol strapped to the man's waist. His heart skipped a beat.

"Gerald Horito, by authority of Presidential Order 9066, and in compliance with Civilian Exclusion Order #5, your family will be transported to the Tanforan Assembly Center in six days. From there, you will go to the Topaz Relocation Center in Utah.

"Your secret clearance has been revoked. You are ordered to stop what you are doing immediately. Your employer has been informed. You must leave the premises now. Leave your briefcase and lunchbox and go directly to your home. Do not leave your neighborhood until you hear from the Army. You will get further instructions there. Sign here," he said, as he put a one-page document on Gerald's desk. US ARMY was printed in large letters across the top, followed by several typed paragraphs and a place to sign and date at the bottom. He handed Gerald a pen and took a step back, his hand resting on the butt of his pistol.

Gerald quickly signed the document without reading it and left quickly, relieved to be putting distance between himself and the gun.

I cannot believe this is actually happening to me.

Since late February, Gerald was hearing stories at the gas station that members of the Japanese community on the outskirts of San Francisco were being asked by Army personnel to leave the area voluntarily. A small number were doing so. Then, beginning on March 29, using the force of Public Proclamation No. 4 issued by the commander of the Western Defense Command, Lt. General John DeWitt, Army and law enforcement squads began going street to street. They forced people from their homes, loaded them into buses, and took them first to Assembly Centers, then on the long trip to internment camps. Even third-generation American citizens, "Sansei" like Gerald, were caught up in the mass relocation fueled by war hysteria and racism. Now, the soldiers were headed to his street.

"Papa, Mama, is it true? Can they do this to us? Do we have to obey the orders?" Gerald asked loudly, as he burst into the house, finding his parents and younger sister Rachel sitting in the small living room.

"Yes, son," his mother responded, holding her daughter. Both had cheeks wet with tears. "And we can take only what we can carry."

"What will happen to our home, the car, the things we can't take? What about Papa's and my jobs? What about the garden? Are they taking Papa's parents, too? They're not taking yours, are they, Mama?"

His father's parents lived next door. His mother's parents are in Oklahoma City.

"Calm down, son," Bunta said in a low but stern voice. "This is a terrible situation. If we are to be OK, we must be very strong and not panic. I've just come from the clothing factory with three of my coworkers. The foreman said we'd have our jobs when we return, but I don't believe him. What did your boss say?"

"I didn't see him. The soldier said he was told that I was leaving."

"Otosan and Okasan will come with us," his father said. "This will be really hard on them. They're so frail. Grampa and Grams will not have to go to the camp, but I'm sure they'll be watched by the police.

"I don't know yet what to do with our car or our houses. Some people are turning off the utilities and locking the doors and windows. Others are selling everything very cheaply. I just don't know what to do.

"Tomorrow, someone will come to give us specific instructions about the relocation process. Perhaps they will provide guidance about what we should do with our houses and belongings. For now, I think the best thing to do is to begin to bring things to the living room that we want to take with us. Once we have it all in one spot, we can see how much we can carry."

Standing up, he continued. "Now, I need to go check on Otosan and Okasan. I don't think anyone has come to their house yet. Once they know what's happening, they'll be afraid and confused. It'll be very important that we keep them close to us when we leave. We need to be sure we all get put on the same bus. Sandra, I'll be back in about an hour bringing them for supper."

Bunta returned with his parents as Sandra finished putting the meal of rice, miso soup, broiled fish, and tea on the table.

"Good evening, Ojichan, Otosan," Gerald said, bowing while Rachel ran up and hugged them. "It's good to see you. Mama has dinner on the table. Let's go eat." He took his grandmother's arm and led her into the kitchen, the others following.

Bunta's parents, Haruto and Aiko, were nineteen when they met and married in Hawaii in 1883. They had lived in neighboring villages in Japan but did not know each other. They had both migrated to Hawaii in 1881 to look for jobs. In early 1885, they immigrated to California as part of a group hired to work as laborers in the vegetable fields. Their experience as farmers in Hawaii brought them quick success. Within three years, they were making a stable income as tenants for a large landowner, then decided to start a family. Bunta was born in May 1898. By 1900, although laws prevented them from owning land, they could lease about one hundred acres and hire their own labor.

One evening, Bunta spoke to his parents. "Otosan, Okasan, now that I am sixteen, I want to move to town and find a job. I do not wish to be a farmer. Please allow me to make my own life."

"Bunta, in Japan we would not allow this," his father said. "You are too young. But this is America. We moved here to make a new life. We must allow you that freedom too. You may go. Here is a little money to help you get started. Please come see us often."

Three years later, in June 1917, against his parents' strong objection, Bunta married Sandra, a coworker at the clothing factory where they both worked.

4

SANDRA AND BUNTA'S FAMILY.

Sandra, a Caucasian girl from Oklahoma, was one year older than Bunta. She was a free spirit who chaffed at the structured lifestyle of her upper-middle-class professional parents. She was uncomfortable that the couple who were the live-in servants were Negro.

She announced to her parents at breakfast one morning, "Mother, Father, I have decided to quit college and go to San Francisco to find a job. One of my classmates has an older sister who works in the garment industry there, and she has agreed to let me stay with her until I find a job. I have saved three thousand dollars. That will tide me over until I start getting a paycheck. I know you will disapprove of this, but my mind is made up. I will be leaving tomorrow on the bus."

For several moments, there was silence in the room. Then William, Jr. broke the silence. "Sis, you're crazy! You'll never make it out there in that crazy place. You'll come running home with your tail between your legs in three months."

"William, that's no way to talk to your sister," his mother said. "Let's discuss this courteously."

"There's nothing to discuss, Mother. As I said, my mind is made up. I'm eighteen, and I can make my own choices."

"Daughter," her father said, "you are correct. We cannot and will not stop you from this immature, poorly thought through choice. But know this. When you leave this house, do not expect any help from us."

He stood up abruptly from the table and left the room. Her mother followed him. Her brothers stared at their plates, unsure of what to say or even think.

For the rest of the day, Sandra stayed in her room packing her clothes and other things she would take with her. She came down for lunch and supper. Only her mother and younger brother, Frank, ate with her.

"What time are you leaving tomorrow?" her mother asked. "I'll have the chauffeur take you to the bus station."

"The bus leaves at nine-thirty and, thank you. I was going to take a taxi."

At seven-thirty the next morning, Lucas, the chauffeur, knocked softly on her door.

"Miss Sandra, it's Lucas. Yo' momma asked me to come get your luggage. We needs to leave for the station at eight-fifteen. Sarah has yo' breakfast ready."

Sandra opened the door and pointed to the pile of luggage. "Thank you, Lucas. That's everything there. I'll see you at the car a little after eight."

When she got to the car, her mother was standing there, tears on her cheeks. She hugged Sandra and stepped back, holding both her hands.

"Sandra, I do not agree with what you are doing. But you

have always been a strong-minded, independent young woman. I believe you will do well. I wish you every success.

"This will help some. Your father does not know about it." She reached into her pocket and handed her an envelope. "Please wait until you are in the car to open it."

They hugged again. Sandra got into the car as Lucas closed the door behind her. As they were driving off, she turned for one last glance and saw that her father and brothers had joined her mother at the drive.

She waved. They all waved back.

When she opened the envelope, she found it contained twenty-five hundred dollars in cash. Tears filled her eyes.

Judy met her at the bus.

"My God," she said embracing Sandra in a bear hug. "I didn't think you could pull this off. I'll bet your family was fit to be tied. Let's grab the trolley right over there. It'll take us one block from the apartment. Here, let me help you with all that luggage. Damn, girl, you certainly don't travel light!"

It did not take her long, with Judy's help, to find a job.

"I've got a terrific job as a buyer's contact with a clothing manufacturing company. I'm a liaison between the buyer's reps and the production staff. Right now, our biggest buyer is the Navy, and they have some *really cute* reps. I probably shouldn't tell you this, but I've gone out with a couple of them. They're smart, fun, and seem to have plenty of money!

I know my boss is looking for additional help. I'll take you in to fill out an application tomorrow."

"That would be great, Judy. Thanks. Just remember, I'm looking for a job, not a husband," she said with a smile.

Within a week, she was hired in the same job as Judy. When Judy took her into the plant to meet some of the production managers, her life took an unexpected turn.

On the tour, Judy introduced her to Bunta Horito, a Japanese American citizen who had just been promoted to the new position.

I've never believed in love at first sight but, boy, was I wrong!

She sensed that Bunta was taken with her as well. Two days later, he asked her out to a movie. The dates continued.

One evening, when she returned to Judy's, she was met at the door.

"And you said you're not looking for a husband. I think you'd better reconsider that thought. He looks like a keeper. You'd better grab him quickly!"

Sandra blushed. "Friend, I believe you're right."

After three months, as they were walking to Judy's, Bunta said, "Sandra, we need to have a serious talk. "I want to marry you, and I sense you have the same feelings. My problem is, if we get married, that would crush my parents."

"They have given up many of their traditions to come to America, but I'm pretty sure they could not handle me marrying a non-Japanese."

"Bunta, you are right. I do want to marry you, as well. However, I believe my parents would be as opposed as yours.

"But the world is changing in so many ways. I know that your parents, by coming to America, have had to change many of their old beliefs. And once my parents see we are happy, I hope they will accept us."

Two weeks later, they were married.

After the civil ceremony with Judy and one of Bunta's coworkers as witnesses, Judy said, "Sandra, you can stay here until you can find a house. With your combined income, you can certainly afford one. The problem's going to be, where?

"Bunta, I'm sorry to say that it will be almost impossible for you to buy a house in a White neighborhood. And some Japanese neighborhoods would not accept Sandra. I do know one area where there are some mixed couples. But you'll probably have to rent for a while. I'll introduce you to a couple who lives there soon. Have you told your parents yet?"

"You dishonor us by this marriage," Bunta's parents told him. "You married outside your race. To us, you are now dead." Sandra's parents' response was the same. Neither spoke nor had any communication with them, despite getting pictures of their first grandchild when Gerald was born sixteen months later, in October 1918. It was the birth of Rachel in 1930, with her distinctly Japanese features, that finally broke the ice with Bunta's parents but not Sandra's. Bunta sent pictures of her to his parents' home on the farm. They immediately asked him to bring her for a visit. At first, Bunta visited alone with Rachel. The joy his parents showed over their granddaughter brought tears to his eyes. After several visits, they said they wanted to come to his home to meet their grandson and apologize to him and Sandra.

When Bunta brought them to his home, they all gathered

in the small living room that held just enough seats for everyone, with Gerald and his parents on the couch. Sandra held Rachel in her lap. The afternoon sun shone through double-sashed windows, brightening the room as the bay provided a cooling breeze. Except for the framed Kanji symbol for peace that sat on top of a cabinet, everything in the room was typical California decor. When they bought the house, Bunta insisted that they have an American home.

Everyone except Rachel was unsure how to act. She seemed thrilled to have the attention of so many people. Her laughter, squeals, and obvious excitement gave everybody something to focus on.

Bunta's parents could read and understand simple English but could speak only a few words, so he was the translator between them, his wife, and son.

Sandra began. "Mr. and Mrs. Horito, I am honored to have you in our home," Bunta translated. "It has been a wound to my heart for our families not to be together. Today, I hope that wound will be healed. Your courage in coming here is impressive. Thank you."

Once Bunta finished translating, his mother spoke. Bunta translated. "Sandra, it is we who are honored that you welcome us. Our grief at leaving Japan led us to believe we would lose Bunta if he married you. When we could not stop the marriage, we grew angry and acted foolishly, turning our backs on him and you. When he first brought Rachel for a visit, he told us you were the one who insisted he keep the door open for us."

She leaned toward Sandra. "My husband and I have come today to ask your forgiveness for our blindness and to beg you to let us become part of this beautiful family you and Bunta have created."

When Bunta finished translating, Sandra spoke to him quietly. "Would it be okay if I gave her a hug? Do I call her Okasan or Giri no Haha?"

"Yes, a hug would be fine. I believe she would be flattered if you call her Okasan."

He saw his parents smile as they figured out what he and Sandra were discussing. Sandra passed Rachel to Bunta, stood, then walked over to Aiko as both she and Haruto stood. She bowed very slightly, then opened her arms. "Aiko," she started to say, but Aiko interrupted her. "I Okasan" and walked into the embrace.

They visited for another hour, and Sandra served green tea and some small almond cookies. Bunta helped as his parents, Gerald, and Sandra began to know each other.

Later, as they walked to the car together, Aiko turned, taking Sandra's hand.

"Please," she said haltingly, "You, Gerald, come with Bunta. He bring Rachel next month."

The trips to the farm became a monthly event as they caught up on the past thirteen years.

It was not too long during these visits that Sandra spoke to Bunta on the way home.

"Bunta, I am noticing how frail your parents are becoming. I'm concerned with them living so isolated alone on the farm. If a situation came up where one of them needed help, it might not arrive in time. Do you think they might be willing to leave the farm and move closer to us?

"I was thinking the same thing. If we could find something in the neighborhood that had room for them to have a garden, we might persuade them to move. My father has mentioned that they are finding it difficult to maintain the farm like they want to. That, plus seeing how much they enjoy Rachel, might make it easier for them to move. I'll start looking for a house tomorrow."

The next day, Bunta called a couple of realtors. On his second call, he discovered that their next-door neighbors had been talking to that company about possibly moving to Los Angeles. The realtor told Bunta that he'd let them know of his possible interest.

Within two weeks, Bunta and Sandra had made an offer on the house and put down a deposit.

"Now we need to go visit Otosan and Okasan and present to them the possibility of moving next door to us."

THEY ARRIVED AT THE FARMHOUSE ABOUT TEN IN THE MORNING. They had asked to return earlier than the monthly routine. "We have exciting news that we want to discuss with you in person."

Within an hour after arriving, his parents agreed to the move.

Haruto said to them. "This is an answer to our prayers. We have become concerned about our ability to keep this place up but did not want to impose on your family. The house sounds like just what we need. We can certainly help with the purchase using the money we make from the sale of the lease here."

Bunta bought the house next door for them at 1303

Folsom Street the next day. They moved in within a week. Once there, they began daily visits, took trips to visit Gerald at college, started a family garden between the houses, and Aiko taught Sandra and Rachel how to prepare Japanese meals, much to the verbal objections but secret delight of Bunta.

5

"JAPANTOWN"

THURSDAY, APRIL 23, 1942. FIVE DAYS TO DEPARTURE.

Without a job, there was no 6:30 a.m. alarm this morning. Today, it was the loud knocking at the front door at seven that interrupted his nightmare.

Remembering that his father was next door with his grandparents, Gerald quickly got up, threw on some clothes, and headed to the front door. His mother, tying on her robe, barefoot, her hair in curlers, came from her room right behind him.

"Who could that be?" she asked. "Did your father lock himself out? How forgetful he's getting."

The knocking came again, more rapidly and louder this time.

"Mr. Horito, this is the police. Open the door!"

Arriving at the door, Gerald put his hand on the latch, paused, took two deep breaths, opened the door, and quickly stepped back, keeping himself between his mother and the open door.

"Gerald, I'm Sgt. Thomas. Where is your father?"

Gerald recognized the man as the cop who walked the area around the local shopping center.

"He's next door with my grandparents. He's trying to help them understand the order to leave."

Pointing to the uniformed man next to him, Sgt. Thomas said, "This is Lt. Powell with the Army. His unit is responsible for relocating the people in this neighborhood. We've come to explain to you what will happen in the next few days and what your family must do to be ready. We'll come in while you go get your father."

Sandra came out from behind her son.

"No," she said defiantly, blocking the door. "You will wait outside until my husband gets here. We have done nothing wrong. I want you to hear that from him. Gerald, go get your Papa."

She moved slightly to the side so her son could pass through. The men backed down the two steps off the small porch as Gerald brushed past them, turning left toward his grandparents' house. The thick dew wet his slippers. As he got to the common driveway, he saw his father coming toward him, buttoning his shirt, looking very concerned.

"I heard the loud knocking and voices. What's going on? Where's your mother?"

"The police and Army are here. She's blocking the doorway, not letting them in."

Despite the seriousness of the moment, Bunta could not

help smiling as his wife—barefoot and in a robe and curlers —was holding back two armed men.

"That's your mom. She won't let anyone or anything buffalo her. It's one of the main reasons I married her. She's so different from the Japanese women I know."

They arrived at the door.

"Gentlemen, I'm Bunta Horito. This is my wife, Sandra. Sergeant, you know Gerald. Please come and have a seat in the living room." He then walked into the house, followed by his family and the two men. Everybody sat. Bunta turned to the police officer. "Sergeant, please tell me why you are here."

An icy chill entered their bones as they listened to Sgt. Thomas.

"Mr. Horito, Lt. Powell and I are here to enforce the instructions you received at the Civilian Control Station on April 2nd."

"We will transport you and your family to a local Assembly Center in five days while Relocation Centers are being completed. You will be allowed to bring only what you can carry."

Struggling to remain calm, Bunta said, "What of our homes and all the clothes and furnishings? What about my car? What of our jobs?"

"That is not our concern," Lt. Powell replied gruffly. "You are free to dispose of whatever you can't carry any way you can. Neither the federal government nor the State of California assumes any liability or responsibility for what you leave behind."

"Since you and your son work for the Navy, those jobs will not be held open."

An oppressive silence covered the room like a blanket as the enormity and horror of what they'd just heard filled their minds and hearts.

"You know my wife is not Japanese, don't you?" Bunta finally said, breaking the silence. "Does she have to go to the camps as well?"

"Actually, she does not have to go," Lt. Powell said. "She is free to stay here and take care of your houses and belongings. However, with no job and all your friends and neighbors gone, that would be very difficult for her. She should probably go with you. It would be better for everybody."

With those words, the sergeant and the lieutenant stood up.

"That's all we have for now. We will be back in five days to pick you up." Then they left.

Bunta put his arm around Sandra's shoulders as she began to weep. Just then, Rachel came into the room, saw the distress of her parents, and rushed to her mother.

"Mama, Mama, what's happened?"

"The men have just come, sweetie. We'll have to leave soon. But now, let's make some breakfast. We've got a lot to do. Bunta, go see if your parents are up. If they are, bring them here."

RACHEL WAS TWELVE AND IN THE FIFTH GRADE. ALTHOUGH SHE HAD the distinct Japanese features of her father, she was, in temperament, more like her mother. She was very bright and inquisitive, which gave persistence to her independence and determination. At times, she could be a little rebellious, especially when it came to a battle of wills with Sandra over things like clothes and hairstyles.

She would occasionally bring a note from one of her teachers. "Mrs. Horito, please help your daughter understand that challenging something the teacher is saying is disruptive and disrespectful."

"But Mama, she's sometimes wrong. I only challenge her when she is."

"Sweetie, I understand. It must be frustrating to hear someone in authority say something that is incorrect. But to point out her mistake in front of the whole class is discourteous. If you really believe she is wrong, you need to wait until after class to point that out to her. You need to learn more self-control."

"OK, Mama, but it's not right."

"You will learn as you grow up that adults do not always do or say the right thing. It shows maturity to be able to accept that."

SANDRA, GERALD, AND RACHEL HEADED TO THE KITCHEN WHILE Bunta went next door to get his parents. By the time they returned, Sandra had water boiling for tea and oatmeal, and Gerald was cutting bread to put in the toaster.

They gathered around the table, Rachel poured tea, and Sandra began.

"Ojichan, Obachan, the time has come for us to get ready to leave. People will be here in five days to take us away.

"We will be allowed to take only what we can carry. Except for small, precious mementos, we must take only what is practical and will help us... manage." She almost said "survive" but felt that would be too frightening.

"Let us eat and then we will decide what we would like to take, then bring those things to the living room."

Sandra and Bunta served oatmeal and toast. Butter, jam, nuts, and brown sugar were already on the table. Everyone ate in silence, heads down and cheeks wet with silent tears.

When everyone had finished, Sandra cleared the table and Bunta poured more tea for all. Still, no one spoke.

Bunta broke the silence.

"Let's begin by listing those family things most precious to us. Things that will bring us comfort in dark times and help us remember who we are will be the most important.

"We'll put them in two groups: those things we must take and those we can take if we can find a little room after we've packed everything."

Sandra then said, "Clothes will be mostly what we take. And we should bring only Western-style clothes. We do not want to give the authorities any more reason to hate us than they already have.

"I will put together plates, cups, and utensils for making tea and simple food. We may not like what they offer us for meals."

Rachel broke in. "Mama, what can I do?"

"You and Gerald go with your grandparents and help them decide what bedding to bring. Your father will be over in a while to help them decide which documents to take.

"Bunta, let's you and I start on our documents."

•　•　•

BY LUNCHTIME, THE COFFEE TABLE AND THE CARD TABLE, WHICH had been pushed up against the wall, were full of photos, pictures, figurines, and other small pieces of art. Aiko was occupied dividing them into the groups Bunta had suggested.

Sandra had made miso soup with white fish, noodles, and tea. This time, the conversation was brisk, shifting between the difficulty of making choices and anger at those forcing them to make them.

"I don't blame the soldiers and the police. They are only following orders," Gerald pronounced. "Mister Roosevelt and the men in Congress are the ones who are responsible.

"They have allowed the fear of people based on nothing but prejudice to govern their actions. Why don't they come here and talk with us and our leaders and businessmen? They'll see we are no threat."

In a strong voice belying his frailty, Haruto spoke. "This is the kind of evil Aiko and I left Japan to escape. Certainly, we have experienced prejudice and hate in many forms since we have been in America, but never anything like this. It makes no sense and is an insult to our loyalty and love of our adopted country. Even then, I can almost understand it being directed toward our generation. But toward Rachel and Gerald ...." He stopped, unable to continue.

6

"JAPANTOWN"

FRIDAY, APRIL 24, 1942. FOUR DAYS TO DEPARTURE

It was a grey day, chilly for that time of year. It's as if nature was reflecting the feelings in the neighborhood and particularly in the Horito homes.

After a restless night, Bunta, Sandra, Gerald, and Rachel woke earlier than usual.

"I'm going to check on Otosan and Okasan," Bunta said. I'll just be a few minutes. Rachel, please help your mama get breakfast ready."

Bunta walked across the driveway, knocked, and opened the door. "Okasan, Otosan, are you up?"

He was surprised to find them fully dressed and sitting at the kitchen table drinking tea.

"Good morning. You are up early."

"Musuko, please come sit with us. Your mother and I need to talk with you. We have never spoken to you much about our life in Japan and why we left. We both lived in small villages where life was very simple. Everybody knew everybody else, and we looked out for each other.

"But the old ways were disappearing, and there was social uncertainty. People were often confused and sometimes afraid.

"For all of our life, we had adhered to two essential values of all Japanese that enable people to persevere in troubling times. The first is *Shikata ga nai*, which means 'It cannot be helped.' Essentially, it means accepting and enduring silently what you cannot change. The other is *German*, which means 'enduring the seemingly unbearable with patience and dignity.'

"We were prepared to follow these values as our way of life was rapidly changing. But then, the opportunity to migrate to Hawaii was given to us, and we took it.

"Now, however, your mother and I believe that there is no opportunity to escape this looming danger. But, whatever happens, we will be alright. *Gaman* and *Shikata ga nai* will ensure that we are not beaten.

"So, Bunta, you must focus your attention and energies on your wife and children, not on us. They will need all your strength."

"Otosan, Okasan, thank you for those words. I will urge my family to model their behavior on yours. And I assure you we will do all that we can to protect you.

"Now, I need to go get breakfast. There is much to do in the next few days to get ready for Tuesday. Please come over for lunch."

He stood, bowed, and, in a rare gesture, hugged them both.

When he got back home, he gathered Sandra, Gerald, and Rachel.

"I've just had the most open and personal conversation with my parents that I've ever had. As you know, they grew up in the very reserved culture of Japan. Because of that, our relationship and conversations have always been loving. But they have also always been very formal and deal with facts but no emotions. As I've told you, Sandra, the only time I ever felt any anger from them was when we got married.

"But this morning, they gave me an insight into their personal strength that I found to be very revealing."

"I'm so relieved, dear," Sandra replied. "I was concerned that they were not talking to us. I know they must be afraid. Tell me about what they said."

Bunta spoke slowly. "Because of what they shared with me, I now know that mentally and emotionally, they will be able to handle any humiliating or insulting behaviors or situations they experience. However, I continue to be concerned about their physical ability to handle any deprivations or hardships. We must all be particularly attentive to them at all times. At the same time, we would all do well to notice and emulate how they handle tough situations. They will be joining us for lunch. Maybe you can get them to talk about how they are preparing for what's about to happen.

"Now, Sandra, are you ready for us to eat?"

After breakfast, Bunta said, "Now we must figure out the best way to dispose of what we must leave behind: our houses, the car, furniture and kitchen appliances, household items, and clothing."

"Bunta, the first thing I need to do is go to the market for the food and supplies we'll need until they come on Tuesday to take us. I'll go after lunch once I've talked with Obachan."

"Good thinking, Sandra. I was about to rush out and sell the car. I'll start on that this afternoon."

"Gerald, would you go now to talk with some of our neighbors and find out what they plan to do with their houses and contents?" And Rachel, I know that some of your classmates and teachers are not from this neighborhood. Do you know if any of them have telephones? If you have their numbers, you might want to call them to say goodbye and maybe get their addresses so you can write to them.

"When I left work on Wednesday, my boss, Mr. Wilson, gave me his address and asked me to write him. I plan to do so."

Rachel replied. "One of my teachers lives two blocks from here. After lunch, can one of you go with me to see her?" She might have that information."

Grabbing his cap and jacket, Gerald headed for the door. "I'll be back by lunch."

He decided to walk to the end of the block and start knocking on doors as he worked his way back home. That gave him seven houses to visit. He knew most of the people living on their street.

He knocked on the first door. After a couple of minutes, it was opened by a Japanese woman about his grandmother's age.

She studied him for a moment. "You're the Horito boy, aren't you? I play mah-jongg with your grandparents. They are very proud of you. What can I do for you?"

"Yes, ma'am, I'm Gerald. My grandparents say that you and your husband are very difficult to beat," he said, smiling. "Maybe the four of you will have the opportunity to get mah-jongg started when we get to the camps."

She only frowned and sadly shook her head.

"My father asked me to check with some of the neighbors to see what you're going to do with your home and contents when we are forced to leave on Tuesday. What are your plans?"

"My husband talked with the company we bought our house from six years ago. He wanted to sell it back, completely furnished. They told him they were not buying any homes. There were just too many. They were afraid they'd be stuck with property they couldn't sell.

"We have decided to turn off the utilities, lock the doors and windows, and just leave." She paused and wiped her eyes. "We put most of our savings into the down payment. The mortgage will default in a couple of months; then the bank will own it. I'm afraid that is going to happen to a lot of us. I wonder what the banks will do with all that property? It's probably going to cause them great problems. Serves them right. It's community leaders who own those banks. They should never have let this happen!"

"Thank you, and best wishes to you and your husband in the coming difficulties. Perhaps we will see you at the Assembly Center."

He bowed and went down the steps to the next home.

It was somewhat larger and had a car parked in the driveway. This time, a young man about Gerald's age—with a much more distinctive Japanese appearance than his—answered the door.

"Good morning. I'm Gerald Horito. Our house is the

sixth one on your left. I'm doing a survey of our neighbors to find out what you're doing with your house and car."

"Sure. My father works for a company that has offices in Carson City, Nevada. Unfortunately, they don't have a job for him there, or the Army might let us move there. A couple of friends he's worked with are bringing a large truck on Sunday. They will load as much from the house as they can. They'll take that and the car back to Carson City. My father will give them money for storage for a year. They will keep up the insurance and maintenance on the car in exchange for using it.

"Father thinks we should be back in a few months, so he has paid the taxes and insurance on the house through the end of the year. The mortgage is paid off, so we're OK."

"I hope your father is right. However, I'm afraid the government is not going to make all this effort for just a few months. Thank you for this information and best wishes."

At the next house, yellow warning tape was across the front door, and a large sign stating DO NOT ENTER. CRIME SCENE. Gerald moved on to the next house.

When he got to the fourth house, there was a couple about his parents' age sitting in chairs on the front porch. He did not know them but had seen them shopping in town before the bad feelings got too prevalent.

"Good morning. I'm Gerald Horito from down the street. I've seen you shopping."

"Yes, we recognize you. What can we do for you?"

My father has asked me to talk with neighbors about what they plan to do with their home and belongings. Do you know what happened next door?"

The woman spoke. "An older couple lived there. They

had no family that we know of. They kept to themselves. We did not know them. A neighbor from across the street came to check on them and found them in bed, dead. The story is that they took poison."

"How sad," Gerald replied. "They must have been so afraid of the unknown."

"I can understand." the man replied. "We have said that if we didn't have family back East, we might do the same."

"What will you do with your house and car?"

"I went to see a real estate company yesterday. They didn't want the house, but they gave me a card with a man's name and number. They said he's buying houses for cash. They would send him to my house.

"I then went to a Chevrolet dealership. I had a 1939 Coupe that I paid $859 for. They were happy to buy it–for $200!"

I figured that was better than just leaving it in the drive. Besides, that money will probably be very important in the days ahead.

It was the same thing with the house. The man showed up, gave me his business card, and said he'd heard I wanted to sell my home. I don't want to sell He took out the card and showed it to Gerald.

NEED TO SELL YOUR HOME QUICKLY?

I'M YOUR MAN!

Stephen J. Freeman. Esq.

(Associate with Coastal Realty)

LAndscape 4-3400

The man related his conversation with Mr. Freeman.

"As the card says, I'm your man.," he told me,

I looked your house up. It was built in 1930 on the site of a home destroyed in the '89 earthquake. Your family bought it in 1935 for $3,527. You've still got a good-sized mortgage. I'll take over your mortgage and give you $300 for the house and contents.

"I have this contract from your mortgage company that outlines that you are selling your house and contents to Coastal Realty for $300.

"Sign here."

"What could I do?" the neighbor said, head bowed and shoulders shaking from his silent sobs. "We've lived here for seven years. My wife and I both had good jobs, a nice home, and a car."

"And now, all we have to our name when we have to leave is five hundred dollars!

"Damn the government! Damn President Roosevelt!"

He turned and walked back to his wife. He put his arm around her shoulders as they walked silently through the front door into the unknown.

7

"JAPANTOWN"

Gerald decided he was unlikely to find any good solutions among any of the other neighbors, so he returned home.

His mother was just finishing taking shopping bags into the house.

"Where's Papa?" he asked his mother as he came into the house. "I want to tell him what I've learned from some of the neighbors."

"He's over helping Ojichan and Obachan select what they will take with them. He's helping them understand to select first only what they can carry. Then, if there is anything else that they really want, to set those things in a separate place, and we will see if we can add it to what we are carrying.

"Did you learn anything helpful?"

"Helpful, yes. Comforting, no. I'll give Papa the details,

but it looks like there is no way to save anything other than what we carry."

Bunta came in. "Hi, Son. What did you find out?"

"None of the neighbors I talked with know of any way to save our property. They are faced with the realization that we all have only two choices. Abandon everything or sell it for pennies on the dollar. Whatever we get from these sales will at least give us some cash to use when they lock us up.

"I have the name and phone number of a man who will probably buy our houses. I think you can take the car to any dealer as well."

"OK, we'll move on these two sales tomorrow. I'll give you the title to the car. You might get a better deal than I would since you look Anglo. You could say you bought it from a Jap who was sneaking out of town ahead of the roundup. I'll deal with the guy on the house.

"Now, please go bring your grandparents over for lunch."

After lunch, Sandra said, "Now we must get serious about sorting. Obachan, have you and Ojichan finished?"

"Yes," said Aiko, "We have two piles on the kitchen table. One has our important papers, our Family Registration documents from Japan, our immigration documents into the United States, our 1940 Alien Registration Forms, and about $700 in cash. We have a photo of my parents, our farmhouse where Bunta was born, and several family pictures of you, Bunta, and the children. In the other pile, we have clothes, shoes, heavy coats, bathroom items, and two pillows from the couch that we can use on a bed. The documents and money we can carry in our clothing. The other items fit in two small suitcases we can carry for short distances. We did not add anything for your family to carry for us. We are old, and our needs are simple. You must be able to take as much of your own things as you can."

"Thank you, Obachan. Gerald will bring the suitcases over here tomorrow."

"Rachel, I saw the pile of clothes and shoes in your room. Honey, you will need to cut that in at least half. You will need space in your suitcase for some of the books you read for fun and as many of your schoolbooks, pencils, and paper as you can fit in. You have to select your clothes for comfort and durability, not fashion."

"Oh, Mama!" she replied and stomped off to her room.

"Bunta, you and Gerald should see if you can fit in some small tools, a couple of flashlights, and extra batteries. I'm going to put in some things from the kitchen. Some of those new small plastic drinking glasses and plates, knives, forks and spoons for cooking, forks and spoons for eating, and two small pots."

By afternoon, most everything was packed into six suitcases and a few small handbags. Rachel only had to discard an additional three blouses and her favorite pair of school shoes for her suitcase to close—when she sat on it.!

"I have called the man about the houses. He will come by tomorrow morning," Bunta said. "Now, Gerald, here is the car title. Once we've finished our business on the houses, you can take the car to the dealership, sell it, and catch a bus back home."

"Rachel, I think we are at a good place to take a break and go visit your teacher," Sandra said.

"OK, Mama. Let's go."

As they walked to the corner, they were passed by

several cars driving rapidly in the neighborhood. They were full of people, mostly men, with the windows rolled down, honking horns, yelling obscenities and "Dirty Jap! Go back where you came from! We'll make you pay for Pearl Harbor!"

Sandra grabbed Rachel's arm and turned back to the house. Then the cars disappeared, so they continued.

They arrived at the teacher's house, walked up on the porch, knocked on the door, and waited. Shortly, a man opened the door.

"Are you Mr. Nakamura? " Rachel asked. "Your wife is my teacher. I'm Rachel Horito, and this is my mother, Sandra."

"Yes, Rachel. She speaks of you. She says you are the brightest student in her class. Sometimes maybe a little too bright," he said with a smile. "You and your mom come in. Evelyn, you have company," he said, closing the door behind them.

When they left, they had the addresses of several of Rachel's Anglo classmates, and Mrs. Nakamura said she would make sure they knew Rachel was planning to write to them. She also told them it was good they came by today. Tomorrow, she and her husband were going to live with her sister's family in Ohio.

8

"JAPANTOWN"

SATURDAY. THREE DAYS TO DEPARTURE

The problem was, everybody woke up earlier than usual after a fitful night, but nobody wanted to leave the warmth of their bed. When you are facing the unknown and fearing the worst, even the simple pleasure of snuggling under the covers seems to provide an unexpected security.

Finally, Sandra nudged Bunta. "Honey, we've got to get up and face the day. We are bigger than the evil being forced on us. We should go over our packing lists again and see if we've all thought of everything we can possibly carry."

Bunta lay quietly for a few moments. He then rolled over and took Sandra in his arms.

"Sandra, my love, there's a thought that keeps creeping into my brain, and I can't get past it.

It's my fault that you're being subjected to this. I was not a stranger to discrimination and occasional blatant expressions of racial hatred when we met and fell in love. I should have been smart enough and strong enough not to subject you to my world. None of this would be happening to you if I had not been so weak. You would have been so much better off today if you'd married a nice Caucasian man."

Sandra broke his hug, sat bolt upright, and turned to him.

"Bunta Horito, you listen to me! You think I wasn't aware of the strong feelings against the Japanese when I met you? Do you think for a moment that I was not smart enough to see the risks? Me, a girl who left the security of wealth and position, quitting college and all the plans my family had for me? Me, who struck out on her own for a new city with only a little money and the name of person I'd never met who I'd been told would take me in?

"Bunta, your baggage never gave me a moment's pause. Even if I had known then what we are faced with now, I would never have considered not marrying you. I knew that, as a team, nothing could defeat us!"

"So, get that crazy thought out of your mind. You had nothing to do with what's happening to me today."

"Now," she said in a much softer tone, "in what may be the last private time we'll have for a long time, let me show you just how much I love loving you."

With that, her head slipped beneath the covers.

After a period of bliss when all the cares of the world had disappeared in their passion, Sandra said, "Now, lover, we really do have to get up and figure out what to do with our last two days of freedom."

"You're right, as always. I have two houses to sell, and

Gerald's got to make a deal for the car. Let's get the kids up for breakfast. I'll go check on Otosan and Haha while you're getting it ready."

AT BREAKFAST, GERALD SPOKE UP. "PAPA, MAMA, I'M THINKING we should probably go to church tomorrow. I know we haven't gone in a while, me longer than you. But maybe we should go to see if we still have any friends among the Anglos. That might be good to know. If so, maybe they'll let us write them when we get where we're going."

"That's a good idea, Son," Sandra replied. "And after church, we can all take the bus to The Palace of Fine Arts. It's one of my favorite spots in the city."

"Mine too," Rachel added. "I love to draw there."

The doorbell interrupted their conversation.

Bunta stood up. "That's probably the guy about the houses. Sandra, do you want to be part of this conversation?"

"No, it'll be too painful. You and Gerald go."

When they opened the door, they were met by a short man in an ill-fitting brown tweed suit, black-and-white bow tie, slicked back hair, pencil mustache, and two-tone spectator wing tips that matched his tie. There was an unlit cigarette behind his right ear. He was carrying a worn, fat leather briefcase in his left hand. With his right hand, he extended a business card.

GOOD MORNING. STEPHEN J. FREEMAN, ESQUIRE AT YOUR SERVICE. I BUY HOUSES

Oh crap, we're in trouble, thought Gerald. He glanced at his father's expression of dismay.

"Mr. Freeman, I am Bunta Horito, and this is my son, Gerald. Our neighbor down the street gave us your name."

"That's great. You know I'm ready to buy both of your houses and everything you leave behind.

"Let's make this quick. Your two houses are similar to your neighbor's, with about the same mortgage balances. I'll buy this one for $350 dollars and the one next door for $300. I don't really want the contents, but you can't take them with you, so I'll do you a favor and take all those things off your hands."

"Just sign this statement saying you are selling your homes to Coastal Realty, and I'll give you $650 dollars cash. You can stay in the houses until the Army says you have to leave."

Just like that. In less than ten minutes, the deal was done.

They went back into the house to find Sandra and Rachel standing in the living room.

"Is it over?"

Bunta said nothing. He just held up a wad of cash. Sandra slumped into a chair, put her head in her hands, and cried. Rachel, crying too, hugged her mother's shoulders.

GERALD'S TRIP TO THE CAR DEALER PRODUCED ONLY SLIGHTLY better results.

When he arrived at the sales lot, he was met by a young man about his age.

"What can I do for you, friend? Are you here looking to

get a new car? That's a mighty nice one you've got there. I can give you a really good deal on a trade, even though we're kinda swamped with used cars right now. Seems like the Japs are in a sudden mood to sell," he said with a smirk.

Gerald took a deep breath and counted to ten as he was getting out of the car.

It probably wouldn't be a good sales technique to punch this guy in the face.

"No, sir, I'm here to sell. Earlier today, I bought this off a guy who needed to sell. Now I just want to make a little profit."

"Bad timing, friend. As I said, we're swamped with used cars. It is nicer than some of the others we've taken in, and since you're not Japanese, I'll give you $350 cash. Got the title?

"Right here, and it's already signed."

The salesman gave Gerald the money and reached out his hand to shake.

Gerald took the cash, refused the extended hand, and left before he really did punch the guy in the face.

The bus ride home gave him time to cool down. The family now had $1,000 in hand to help with their future.

9

JAPANTOWN TO TANFORAN ASSEMBLY CENTER

MONDAY, APRIL 28, 1942. DEPARTURE DAY

At six a.m., the two Greyhound buses stopped in the middle of their block. From behind a curtain, Gerald watched as three soldiers, two with stripes on their sleeves, carrying rifles, and the third, a young officer wearing a pistol at his waist, stepped from the lead bus to the sidewalk. Behind the buses was an Army truck with a large open bed with sides. Two soldiers stood on the bed.

"They're here," Gerald announced loudly.

The family had been up since four. The six of them ate breakfast in silence, afraid of communicating their fear to each other, the several layers of clothing making their movements awkward. Then, they went into the living room for a final check of the luggage and packages they were taking. These contained the things that would represent their lives for an unknown future.

Bunta spoke. "OK, family. Now, we must comply. Please pick up the small items from the table and put them in your pockets. Then, stand by the pieces of luggage that you decided you can carry. When the soldier knocks on the door, we'll be ready to do what he tells us. It is important that we show neither fear nor anger. Either can only make the situation worse. Once we leave the house, keep close to each other. Our neighbors will be coming onto the street as we do, and we don't want to get separated."

At that moment, there was a sharp knock at the door.

"Is this the Horito family?" the soldier with the rifle demanded.

"Yes, it is."

"Are there five adults and one child here?"

"Yes."

"Here, attach these six tags to the outside of your clothing so they can easily be seen." He handed Bunta six three-by-six-inch manila tags with long strings attached. Each had their family name, the inscription number 20464, followed by the letters A through F, the date, 28 APR 1942, and their destination—Topaz.

"Here are tags for your belongings. From now on, you will go by this number, not your family name. Be sure you remember it." He gave Bunta a bunch of the same blank manila tags.

"Print your number on them clearly and attach them very securely to each item you don't take on the bus. If they come off, your items will be lost. You can carry small packages and handbags on the bus.

"When you have done that, pick up your belongings,

leave your house together, and take everything to the truck. You will then go to the first bus."

Bunta, Sandra, and Gerald put on their tags and helped Rachel, Aiko, and Haruto attach theirs. Then they took the other tags, writing 20464 on them as they attached them to the six large suitcases and six smaller ones that sat on the living room floor.

Pausing in the process, Sandra looked at the assembled luggage.

This is the sum total of our family's lives! How can these people be doing this to other human beings?

"Are we all ready?" Bunta asked. "If so, Gerald, please lead the way and wait at the bottom of the steps until I get there. Rachel, you and your mother take your luggage to the bottom of the steps, then help Obachan and Ojichan with theirs. I'll come last and lock the door on the way out."

Once they were all down the stairs, the soldier who had come to the door shouted,

"All right, move quickly to the truck and hand your luggage to the soldiers. Then go to the bus."

They joined the line of their neighbors, some carrying babies, doing the same thing.

No one spoke. All eyes were on the ground. Defeat and uncertainty filled the air. They gave their luggage to the soldiers on the truck, who added it to the pile and walked to the bus.

The young officer standing at the door checked their tags against a list on his clipboard.

"20464 family, find a seat. We'll be leaving in about thirty minutes."

The bus was half full. They found seats near the middle. Their next-door neighbors were right behind them.

Sandra whispered to the wife, "Do you know where we are going?"

"No," she replied, also in a whisper. "I think they'll tell us soon."

The bus continued to fill up. Some of the young children were crying softly.

Once all the seats were filled, the officer called for their attention.

"We are leaving now for your Assembly Center. Pull down the window curtains and do not raise them or attempt to look out until we arrive. Once we arrive, we will direct you inside the fence, where you will find and collect your belongings. Someone will lead you to your temporary quarters. You will remain at Tanforan until your quarters at the Topaz facility in Utah are completed."

As she pulled the curtain down, Sandra took one last look over her shoulder.

Will we ever see our home again? A deep emptiness settled in her chest.[1]

THE BUS PULLED UP NEXT TO A GATE INSIDE OF A TALL WIRE FENCE. A cordon of armed military police formed a corridor from the bus door to the gate.

The officer stood. "You will exit the bus and go through the gate. On your right are your belongings from the truck. You will locate yours and take them and set them next to the building on the left. Now, exit the bus."

Gerald led the family off the bus and helped his grandparents down the steps. His parents, with Rachel clinging to her mother, followed.

"I'm scared, Mommy."

"I know, sweetie. It'll be OK. Just stay real close to me."

Once inside, they located their luggage and belongings and moved them across the area. Soldiers were busy opening and going through every bag, pulling out liquor, razors, and anything that they considered a weapon.

"Your belongings will be delivered to your quarters. Now, you are to go to that location where you see that large sign in English and Japanese that reads ENTER HERE. That will take you under the grandstand where nurses and doctors will examine you. Once that is done, you will fill out several forms, and each family will be assigned living quarters. You will be led to those locations."

Once they got to the grandstand, two lines were being formed, one for females and the other for males. They were led inside curtained areas.

"Bunta, now I'm scared."

"Don't worry, honey. They said we'd all be housed together. As soon as the nurses and doctors check us out, we'll be put back together to go to our new home."

Once they were finished with the exams, they were led to a room with long tables and chairs. Soldiers were handing several papers and pens to each family.

"When you have completed these forms, bring them to this front table. There, you will be assigned to your quarters. One of the civilian staff will take you there."

"What about our belongings?" Sandra asked.

"They are being delivered now," the officer said. "If they

are not in your quarters when you arrive, you will get them by this evening."

They turned in their papers and headed toward an open door. Outside, there were about twenty-five people standing in a loose group. Gerald could see several families that he knew from the neighborhood. As they drew closer, a man with a large name badge spoke.

"Give me your attention, please. I am Mr. Williams. Please take some of the fruit, biscuits, and water from that table and join me back here. Then I will take you to your quarters.

"The regular barracks are not completed yet, so you will be housed in those large wooden stables. The stalls have been converted into living quarters. Once the barracks are completed, you will be moved into them. Follow me, please."

They walked about fifty yards toward a series of long, low wooden structures, sloping roofs, and divided stall doors on the front, capped by a narrow overhang.

They were, unmistakably, horse stalls.

"My God!" said Sandra. "We are expected to live like animals!"

The shock only worsened when Mr. Williams pointed to one of the doors.

"This is your home. Over there is hay to fill your mattress sacks." He pointed to several large piles under the stable eves, then he turned and left.

Going inside, they discovered that a swinging half-door had divided the stall into two sections. The front one looked about 10' x 7'. The rear one was 10' x 12'. Linoleum had been laid over the floor and whitewash had been hastily brushed on all surfaces, trapping a number of bugs—now a white image of themselves. A single light bulb hung from the ceiling. There were folded army cots stacked in a corner, equaling the number in the family. There was one blanket and one empty mattress sack per person. People over sixty got cotton mattresses. Their belongings were piled against the wall in the front section. The odor of manure and urine was overpowering.

No one spoke. Tears rolled down the cheeks of Aiko and Sandra. Rachel, putting her hand over her mouth, ran back outside and threw up.

Gerald and Bunta quickly set up three of the cots so everyone could sit down.

"The horses lived better than this. There was only one of them to a stall," Sandra said.

"Where are the bathrooms? Where will we eat? Is there a place to wash clothes? How can we keep our belongings off the floor?"

"It looks like it's going to rain," Gerald said. "Let's get these mattresses stuffed before that happens." Then the rain started.

---

1. The internees were being taken to the Tanforan Center, which was a converted horse racetrack located near the San Francisco airport.

    Its purpose was to have a location where those people taken from their homes could quickly be housed while more permanent facilities further inland were completed. It was one of fifteen similar locations occupied from April 28 until October 13, 1942.

    At Tanforan, 8,000 Americans, 64 percent of whom were US citizens, were housed there. About 1,600 were children, with about 110 being under one year old.

The usual length of stay was about four months. They were then transferred by train to the Topaz Relocation or "Internment Center" near Delta, Utah.

There were ten such centers, mostly in the West, where 127,000 innocent Japanese Americans were held until January 1945.

10

MONDAY, APRIL 28, 1942. DAY ONE CONTINUES

At 11:00 a.m., it was still raining hard. Most of the grounds around them had been turned into ankle-deep mud.

Mr. Williams, the man who had brought them here, returned at 11:30. He was wearing an olive-green military slicker with the hood covering his head. His rubber boots came up to his knees. He called for everyone in their stable to come to the door of their stalls.

When all had responded, he, in an official-sounding tone, announced, "I am your Block Captain. You can contact me if you have any questions or problems. Here is the schedule for meals. They will currently be served in the grandstand," he said, pointing back toward the entrance gate. "Signs on the building will point the way to the mess hall. The nearest latrine is that way. He pointed in the opposite direction. "Normally, service for lunch will begin at noon. Today, however, it will begin at one o'clock." He then turned and left.

For Gerald and his family, the nearest latrine was twenty yards from their building and the single mess hall was back at the grandstand about forty yards away. To get to either meant walking in the rain, through the mud, and standing in line. The mess hall could only seat 500 at a time on picnic tables and benches. The food for the first ten days was prepared by Army cooks and followed Army menus.

They went to lunch together. They waited in line for fifty minutes under the shelter of the grandstand.

"I wonder what else they can do to make us more miserable?" Sandra said loudly. Several of the people around her responded in agreement.

When they finally got to the serving line, they were given a segmented metal tray. On it, the servers ladled one-half cup of a meat and vegetable stew from a new-looking garbage can and added two slices of bread, a cup of water, napkins, and utensils. They found seats together, sat down, and stared at their trays. Aiko and Haruto looked at what they were expected to eat. Aiko said "I'd rather starve. We're going back to the stall."

They stood to leave. Sandra said, " Obachan, please wait a moment while Gerald eats his food. Gerald, finish quickly and go with them. We'll be there when we finish."

When they all got back, Gerald said, "Papa, I noticed a pile of scrap lumber as I was coming back here. I think we could get some of it to make some shelves to get our stuff off the floor. I brought a hammer and a tape measure. Perhaps Mr. Williams can find us some nails and maybe a saw."

"Let's go see what we can find, Son. Then I'll look for Mr. Williams."

They brought back two arms full of 1" x 12" boards of varying lengths. Bunta went to look for Mr. Williams. He returned about an hour later with a handful of nails and a small saw.

"The nails cost $2.00, and I have to return the saw by supper tomorrow. Now, let's see if your engineering skills are worth what that degree cost me, he said with a smile.

Gerald figured they had enough boards to build four-foot high shelves in each room. Sandra and Aiko figured those would hold most of what they'd brought, The rest could be kept in suitcases under the cots.

Two hours later, the job was completed. The shelves were filled. They all stood back to admire the additions. Sandra gave Gerald and Bunta a hug.

"You are my heroes. With your skills, you may make this place almost livable.

Bunta and Gerald set up the rest of the cots. Sandra and Rachel added the mattresses, sheets from home, and the blankets. Haruto and Aiko's cots were arranged, leaving a clear passage to the front.

Everyone's spirits were raised a little by the sense of order.

Rachel said, excitedly, "Papa, tomorrow morning, we can go look for lumber to build two small tables."

Sandra said. "Now, this has been a very difficult day. We are all tired and deeply troubled by the future. I think it would be smart to rest awhile on our cots before we have to get in the line for supper. Ojichan Otosan I wish you would go with us. The food is insulting, but it is nourishing. I saw some people drinking tea from tea bags. At least you could do that. Please think about it. Maybe we can figure out something else tomorrow."

They lay quietly, but only Rachel and Aiko slept. The rest wondered how they would survive.

At four, Haruto said, "Let's go find the bathrooms in the grandstand, then we can get in line for supper. The mess hall opens at five."

They got in the line at four thirty and got to the serving line at five-fifteen. This time, the meal was two tablespoons of macaroni, one-half of a boiled potato, and water. Sandra said to the server. "May we please have cups of hot water and tea bags?"

The server went to the back of the kitchen, returning with a metal pitcher of hot water, paper cups, and tea bags.

"Here you go," he said with a broad smile. "Bring the pitcher back when you return the trays and utensils."

"Thank you, Aiko said.

Again, they found seats. This time, Bunta explained to his parents what the food was and encouraged them to eat it. Reluctantly, they took a few bites, especially relishing the hot tea.

Returning to the stall, Sandra suggested they go find the latrines and washrooms. She, Aiko, and Rachel went to the women's buildings while Bunta, Haruto, and Gerald looked for the men's.

As the women entered the latrine, Rachel exclaimed, "Oh my God, Mama, this is terrible. There is no privacy."

At one end were eight toilets, four separated by

partitions. The other four were not. There were no doors. All were occupied as they entered, and there were about ten women and young girls waiting their turn. In front of several of the stalls, someone, probably a family member, stood facing out into the room, partially blocking the view into the stall.

Along the other wall were six handwashing sinks. There was no soap, no towels, and no hot water.

"Rachel, just close your eyes and pretend there is privacy. I'm afraid that not only has our freedom been taken from us, but also our privacy. We must adapt or be miserable. We must remember to bring soap and towels tomorrow."

The men had found the same arrangements in their buildings.

When they returned to the stall, distressed by what they had found, there was a note attached to the door.

THERE IS A CURFEW FROM TEN P.M. UNTIL SIX A.M. LIGHTS MUST BE OUT BY TEN-THIRTY. A SIREN WILL SOUND AT SIX FORTY-FIVE P.M., AT WHICH TIME EVERYONE MUST BE IN THEIR ASSIGNED QUARTERS. A HEAD COUNT WILL BE TAKEN BY THE BLOCK CAPTAIN.

They make us feel like prisoners, Bunta thought as they all headed to their cots to start getting ready to sleep. He spoke.

"Family, please let's all come in here and sit for a few minutes before we go to bed. I would like to say a few things and then any of you can, as well.

"We are in a terrible situation. Not only is it a mockery of everything we were taught to believe as Americans, it is going to be physically very demanding. And it looks like nothing will get better for a long time. The only good thing we have is each other. We must help each other as we learn how to survive in this hellish situation. We cannot let it defeat us. And let's be an example of strength and perseverance for those around us.

"We must be constantly vigilant. Conditions like this often bring out the worst in people. Sandra, you, Obachan, and Rachel should never go out alone. When you do go out, please let me or Gerald know where you are going and when you expect to be back. Each day, we will become more accustomed to our new life. We will discover ways to make survival easier. Does anyone else want to say something?"

Gerald spoke. "Papa, we have to survive this. We have to show those in charge that we are not a threat. We are here not just because of prejudice but also because of fear. If we can show our captors that we are loyal Americans, they will not keep us here."

"Son, I hope you are right. Now, let's give the ladies some privacy so they can get into their nightclothes."

Gerald, Bunta, and Haruto stayed in the larger room while Aiko went to her room and got into her nightgown and into bed. Then they moved to the smaller room while Sandra and Rachel did the same.

Haruto then joined his wife. Rachel and Sandra closed their eyes as Gerald and Bunta made their preparations. When everyone else was in bed, Bunta said, "Good night," and turned off the light.

"Rachel and Gerald, now you will discover how loudly

your father snores, a discomfort our captors did not plan. However, you will get used to it. I did. If it gets really bad, I'll poke him as I often do."

11

TANFORAN ASSEMBLY CENTER

TUESDAY, APRIL 29, 1942. DAY TWO

The sun rose behind the clouds on four thousand people who had just spent the most miserable night of their lives.

Fortunately, despite the rain, the temperature stayed above fifty-three degrees. The rain had stopped around midnight as the winds picked up.

None of that softened the reality of uncomfortable beds, unfamiliar surroundings, the wind through the cracks, and the smell of horse urine and manure.

The walls between the stalls were not soundproof. The sounds of the neighbors filtered through. Bathroom trips meant waking up someone to go with you and dealing with the mud. For Gerald's family, the process of giving privacy for dressing was repeated. Then they joined the lines to the latrine.

They returned just as the 6:45 siren sounded.

"We'll need to get up earlier, " Sandra said.

Just before seven, there was a knock on the door.

"20464 family, please come to the door to be counted."

A civilian, clipboard in hand, stood there. "You are six, correct?"

Bunta nodded yes.

"Once you have finished breakfast, you will go to that building over there," he said, pointing to a pavilion. "You will be given a presentation on camp rules and facilities."

The trip to the mess hall was a little easier as the mud was beginning to dry out. When they arrived, they were served three pancakes with butter and syrup, a bowl of oatmeal, one piece of plain toast, and coffee. Sandra asked the server from the previous night if they could have tea again.

"Yes," he replied, and as long as I'm here, you won't have to ask again."

Rachel's shout of "Oh boy, Mama, pancakes! Cool!" drew a disapproving glance from Aiko. However, this time, everyone cleaned their tray except for the coffee.

When they got to the pavilion, there were already several hundred people sitting on benches. They found seats on one of the last benches in the back. At the front of the room was a table with a podium and a PA system. Mr. Williams, another civilian, and two Army officers sat behind the table. There was a large map of the Center on a board behind them. Mr. Williams stood up.

"Good morning. Today we will first give you an orientation of the Center's campus. The map behind me shows the whole campus. The buildings shown by solid lines are completed. Those with dotted lines are under construction with their completion date written. Then we will go over rules which are designed to keep you safe. Finally, we will go over the services and facilities that are available to you.

I'd like to introduce Mr. William Lawson of the Work Project Administration, a federal agency. He is the camp manager. He would like to say a few words. Then one of his staff will go over the map with you. When he is done, Major Smith will explain the rules. Then Lieutenant Black will talk about facilities and services."

"Mr. Lawson."

"Thank you, Bob. Ladies and gentlemen, I welcome you to Tanforan. I realize that these are unique circumstances that we all find ourselves in. In truth, none of us wants to be here. The sneak attack on Pearl Harbor and the desire by the government to do all it can to prevent future attacks on the resources of our nation have caused this situation. You never expected to be detained. And I certainly never imagined that I would be responsible for managing the detention of so many citizens and residents of this area.

"I recognize that the swiftness of the government's decision to bring you here gave you very little or in most cases no time to dispose of your property and businesses in an orderly process. I know that has left you angry and confused. However, the harsh reality is that this situation will not be reversed. It will make your life in the time ahead less stressful if you can accept that reality.

"It is my responsibility to see that your time with us, despite the reasons for your being here, is as comfortable and valuable as possible. I promise you that my staff and I will treat you as fairly and respectfully as the situation, including the hasty and incomplete construction of this facility, allows."

"Today, because I want this camp to be as self-governing as possible, I'm asking you informally to select a person from your ranks as a representative for every one hundred and fifty people. They will be your house manager and will be paid $12.00 per week. They will be the primary channel for communication between you and my administration. You will give their names to Mr. Williams. Next Tuesday, I would like to meet with that group for the selection of one representative from each of the five camp precincts. They will form an advisory council that will meet with me each week to discuss issues pertaining to camp life.

"If there are any families here where no one speaks English, let Mr. Williams know, and we will have one of my staff who speaks Japanese go over today's presentation with you. Thank you for your attention."

He sat down, and a young man stood up. He had a three-foot pointer in his hand.

"I will show you where everything is, or will be, using this map. Probably by now, you've found most locations, but let's be sure everyone knows where they are.

"We are here. The stables where you are staying are these buildings. Here are the existing latrines and bathhouses. Currently, the only mess hall is under the grandstand. There are also additional latrine facilities in that structure that you can use.

"These structures, " he indicated those in dotted lines, "are one hundred and eighty barracks, eighteen new buildings that will be either mess halls, or classrooms, eighteen shower buildings, twenty-four latrines, six laundry buildings and three hospital buildings. They will be completed in about a month. Major Smith will now go over the basic rules."

"Thank you. The rules for this facility are, with a couple of simple exceptions, the same as the laws you followed before you came here. Respect each other's property and person.

The new rules for your time here are simple. Stay away from the fence. Do not accept or pass anything through the fence. All packages from outside will be brought to the main gate and will be inspected. Visitors are allowed from ten to twelve in the morning and one to four in the afternoon, except on Monday and only in the grandstand area. Follow these rules and things will go smoothly.

"Lieutenant Black will now go over the planned services and facilities."

A young Army officer in his early twenties, and clearly very uncomfortable, stood.

"On the map, Mr. Williams pointed out a number of buildings that are under construction. They are designed to house those services and activities that you were accustomed to in your community. These will include three medical clinics, classrooms, places for worship, a general store, places for recreation, and a library. The administration regrets that these services are not yet available. Expectations are that all will be operational by the end of May."

Mr. Williams then stood.

"This concludes the presentation. Additional

information will be circulated as necessary. You may now return to your quarters."

They returned to their stalls, overwhelmed by the challenges that they faced.

When they were all inside, Bunta spoke. "Now we have some idea of what life will be like while we are here. I overheard two of the soldiers talking. They said it would be at least three months before they move us to a camp.

"We need to make some plans to make life more bearable until then."

"I noticed yesterday that some people were getting packages through the gate. Let's make a list of things we could use, then see if we can find someone to bring them to us."

"It's most important that we get some of their usual and favorite foods for Obachan and Ojichan. And maybe we could get an electric teapot that we could plug into the light socket. We could have tea."

Sandra said, "I'll need some laundry soap. I can do wash in the sink until the laundry is finished. I noticed the toilet paper supply is dwindling quickly. If we had our own, that would be good."

"I didn't see shampoo in the shower room, Mama, only soap. Maybe we could get some of that."

"Any other requests?" Bunta asked. No one spoke.

"OK, if not, let's figure out who we can ask to bring these things to us," Bunta said.

"Gerald, could you ask your boss or one of your friends from work? I think my boss, Mr. Wilson, would help us. Sandra, do you know anyone from the market you could ask? We can write them notes and find someone who's bringing things to the gate and ask them to deliver them. I'm glad we thought to bring paper and pencils."

That evening, the one hundred and fifty people living in the fifty stalls of their stable selected Gerald to be their house manager.

12

TANFORAN ASSEMBLY CENTER

TUESDAY, MAY 12, 1942. DAY FIFTEEN

Despite their worst fears, their ability to adapt and their support for each other had brought them through the first two weeks in this new hell.

Most importantly, they had made contact with Bunta's boss, Mr. Wilson by sending him a letter. He had agreed to come to visit with him one Saturday.

At 8:00 AM that Saturday, Bunta was told he had a visitor and to go to the grandstand. There he saw Mr. Wilson standing in the room used for visitors. He looked very uncomfortable, shifting from foot to foot and glancing nervously around the room.

Several other people were sitting at picnic tables.

Bunta walked over to him, hand extended and a large grin on his face.

"Mr. Wilson, what a joy it is to see you. But I am so sorry it has to be like this. Come sit a table and we can talk."

"Bunta, please call me George." he interrupted with a smile. "Mr. Wilson was your boss. I'm here as your friend."

As they sat at a table, George continued. "Bunta, let me tell you how sorry I, and your friends from work, are that this has happened to you and your family. We all hope that this injustice is resolved soon. Please know that there are many people in the community that do not agree with the government's actions. Some have even contacted their representative in Congress asking that something be done. Until then, five of your coworkers have formed a team to do whatever we can to make the lives of you and your family as comfortable as possible. This should help with that." He handed Bunta two envelopes.

Bunta recognized one of them. It was a pay envelope from the factory.

"This is your last wages. The management didn't want to give them to you, but a lawyer friend of mine helped them see things differently. It's your full weekly wages of $63.45."

"What's this other one?" Bunta asked.

"I took up a collection from some of your friends. It's not much, but I expect every little bit helps."

Bunta opened the envelope. In it was two hundred dollars. Tears filled his eyes.

"This was a spur-of-the-moment idea. I can't guarantee any more, but if you need more, let me know. Now, what can the team do for your family?"

"Thank you, George. You can't imagine what these funds and your team's willingness to help will mean to my family. I cannot thank you enough.

"As you probably know, conditions are terrible here. And not much can be done about most of them. However, things can be done to make our daily living more tolerable.

"The food is not what we are used to eating. The people who run this place can't seem to be able to keep the bathrooms, they call them latrines, supplied with toilet paper or hand soap." "We have only what we could carry with us, so we have only a few clothes. We've been promised a store to buy household supplies, newspapers, magazines, and snack foods. But, so far, that building has not been completed."

"Right now, boredom is a big problem. Since we are not allowed to have radios, books and card games would help pass the hours. My parents have heard that people are forming a mah-jongg group, so that will keep them occupied. I've heard that the camp administration is going to offer us the opportunity to do odd jobs around the camp. That will help fill the time and bring in a little money, as well.

"I have a list of some items and some money to purchase them. Also, here's a list of clothes we left behind and keys to the houses. I sold the houses and contents before we left, but the guy was buying so many houses he may not have gotten to ours yet. If not, you could pick these things up for us? Here's a note from me and Sandra giving you permission to go into the houses if anybody questions you. If you see anything there you could use, take it as well. The buyer said he wasn't really interested in the contents. He was just doing us a favor."

"Thank you. I or one of the team will be back here on Thursday at 1:00. Goodbye and stay safe."

————

THEY HAD FIGURED OUT THE BEST TIMES TO GO TO THE MESS HALL and the latrines when the lines were shorter. The weather had cooperated, so the mud was not as bad. Rachel had found some kids her age, and they were spending time together. Bunta and Gerald had located some more scrap lumber and had made a small table for Haruto and Aiko and a larger one for their room. Mr. Williams had found some hooks they could screw into the walls to hang clothes. Sandra and Aiko had put some of their photographs on the shelves.

They all felt that, as long as Bunta's friends could bring them the supplies they needed, they could manage until they were transferred to the other camp.

The previous Tuesday, Mr. Lawson had met with the twenty-five house managers.

"I've divided the camp into five districts as shown on this map. Please select one of your residents from each district to form an advisory council. They will meet weekly with me to discuss matters about life in the camp."

————

GERALD WAS SELECTED TO SERVE ON THE COUNCIL. THEIR FIRST meeting was a few days later. Mr. Lawson had set out hot tea and sweet rolls. They were politely refused.

"Thank you for agreeing to serve on this council. It is my hope that, through conversation, most of the issues that concern those you are representing can be resolved.

"Unfortunately, your main complaint, your living

conditions, is beyond my control. The Army did not complete the barracks in time for you and those you represent. You will notice that as they have been completed, they are being filled by new arrivals. You will have to stay where you are until you are transferred to the new barracks being built at Topaz Center in Utah."

"What about the type of food you are serving to us?" one of the members asked. "Many people are having digestive problems and diarrhea because it is too high in calories and fat. There are many people among us who are excellent cooks. Would it be possible to let them do the meal preparation?"

"And what about the long lines for everything? It's very hard on the elderly to stand so long."

"And what about the bathrooms and shower buildings? Not all the toilets and showers have partitions, and none have doors. The toilet paper and soap and hot water frequently run out."

"Gentlemen, let me address each of these.

"I feel sure we can use your cooks. The problem I see is that the ingredients come from the Army's supplies. If you want a different menu, you will need to get a list of ingredients to the soldiers in charge of food supply. It will take a while for those changes. Please bring me a list of people who will offer to cook. They will be paid a wage that will be determined. Also, bring me a list of supplies by tomorrow."

"The long lines will get better as facilities are completed. There will be many new mess halls, latrines, shower buildings, and laundry buildings by the end of the month.

"I will ensure that there are partitions between all toilets and showers. Unfortunately, the Army insists that they will not install doors. I apologize for that.

"I will look into the shortage of toilet paper and soap. That should be easy to resolve. Perhaps we need to set up a monitoring system for those items.

"I do not know what the problem is with the hot water. This is the first I've heard of it. I will get back to you on this shortly."

13

TANFORAN ASSEMBLY CENTER

TUESDAY, JUNE 30, 1942. DAY SIXTY-THREE

The sun rose on the last day of their second month at Tanforan. Life was as normal as it was going to get in this abnormal place for human habitation.

Gerald opened his eyes, pulled the earplugs that muted his father's snoring from his ears, and sat up. Seeing that everyone else was waking up, he reached for the light switch that he had installed next to his bed.

It lit only the light in his family's section of the stall. Gerald's installation of a series of splices and switches left the one in his grandparents' room dark.

That's certainly a practical use of my expensive degree.

It was a technique he'd shown to many of the other residents of the stables.

The switches, wiring, and bulbs had been secured through the efforts of the Council, whose members had been elected in a camp-wide election two weeks before.

Any internee twenty-one and over, regardless of citizenship, was allowed to vote for the council members. Eighty percent of them did.

Gerald had wanted to run and continue his service to the residents, but he was just shy of his twenty-fifth birthday, a requirement to run.

Primarily because of the support of Mr. Lawson and the reluctant agreement of his successor, as well as the length of time the facility operated, the political process at Tanforan was much more active than in other Assembly Centers.

By July 13th, the Council had drafted a constitution that provided for a legislative congress made up of thirty-eight representatives from the residents. Feelings were positive that the congress would be effective in securing improvements to conditions in the camp.

Unfortunately, it soon became clear that The Wartime Civil Control Administration, an agency set up by the Army, considered any form of community-elected government to be illegitimate. The eighty candidates who had been nominated realized the futility of their efforts, and the congress never came into existence. After that there were no additional efforts at self-government.

Nonetheless, these efforts showed the commitment by the internees to the democratic processes in the face of unconstitutional repression. Energies shifted to planning for the pending transfer to Topaz, the camp in Utah, scheduled to begin in mid-September.

Better results had been achieved in other areas. But in each improvement, there was often a "however."

The addition of Japanese cooks and the availability of more acceptable foods, plus shifting to food being served family-style at the tables rather than people having to go through serving lines made meals more enjoyable. Aiko and Haruto found most of the meals acceptable.

However, since the Army allotted an average of thirty-seven cents a day per person for camp supplies, (compared to fifty cents per day for soldiers), there was a continual shortage of dairy products and vitamin-rich foods.

There were now nine laundry facilities, so laundry could be done other than in hand sinks. But with almost 8,000 people in camp, there were always long lines, and hot water usually ran out by 9 a.m. Sandra found that the best time to do laundry was around 3:00 a.m. At first, there was some resistance from the guards about breaking curfew, but that soon disappeared.

By late July, the library housed in a 20' x 100' building had over 5,000 adult and children's books and magazines. It was well used, with over three thousand visits a week. However, there were no Japanese language books or magazines. All six of the Horito family took advantage of this service.

The educational programs, primary, high school, and adult were very active due primarily due to the high percentage of internees with college or graduate degrees.

By the end of May, almost 100 percent of the eligible children, including Rachel, had been enrolled. However, the furniture was picnic tables and benches, which were too big for the children. There were almost no supplies or textbooks.

Rachel had set up regular correspondence with two of her classmates from home. They kept her up on school news. She told them some things about life in the camp.

She made a point of leaving out the most unpleasant parts of it.

By June 15th, over seven hundred high school students were attending classes in the grandstand. However, of the twenty college-educated teachers, only three had any teaching experience.

In late June, most of the seniors who had missed their graduation because of being arrested, received their diplomas from the principals of the schools they had been attending,

The practice of religious worship was encouraged and freedom from administrative influence was enjoyed. Japanese could be freely spoken. However, it was mandated that all printed materials be in English.

All sorts of sports were played, and the equipment was donated by schools and churches. Other recreational activities such as dancing, mah-jongg, and other board games, talent shows, and 16mm popular films filled the time of the internees. Gerald, Bunta, and Rachel all played on several teams. When she was not teaching, Sandra took some origami classes. Aiko and Haruto were part of a mah-jongg group.

The administration had spread the word through the *Tanforan Totalizer*, the weekly mimeographed newspaper, that internees were encouraged to apply for jobs to help maintain operations around the camp.

"Papa," Gerald said, "we should do some of these jobs. With our experience and my electrical knowledge, we can help to keep things working so life will be easier for our neighbors."

"I've been considering that too. Not only will it fill some of the time, but it will bring us a little extra money."

"Little is right! Did you notice the wage scale? As a professional, I will be paid at the rate of sixteen dollars a month. The Anglo working next to me will make almost twenty times that amount! And since you are not working in the job you were doing at the clothing factory, you are considered 'unskilled.' They'll pay you eight dollars a month. It'll cost Mama more in laundry soap to keep our clothes clean than we'll make.

"I'm going to do the work to be helpful, not for the money."

"You're right. But I guess it's better than nothing, and it'll keep us busy."

14

TANFORAN TO TOPAZ

AUGUST AND SEPTEMBER, 1942. A TIME OF TRANSITION

By August, it was clear to everyone in the camp that they were going to be transferred to a new facility fifteen miles northwest of Delta, Utah.

Originally called "The Central Utah Relocation Center," it was discovered that the name was too long to fit on postal forms. So, it was changed to Topaz after a nearby mountain.

Daily life didn't change much. The lines for everything remained, despite continuing promises from the administration that they would get shorter.

There were more restrictions placed on visitors and what could be brought into the camp. Visitors had to endure prolonged screening. The visitor center was divided in half by a row of mess hall tables separating visitors from internees. The number of police in the hall was increased to ensure that no notes or contraband were passed. The types of food that could be brought in were restricted. It was limited to citrus fruit and apples.

On Mr. Wilson's last visit, he sat across the table from Bunta and Sandra.

"This is like in the movies when people in prison get visitors. It seems so unreal," he said.

"It took me almost forty-five minutes to get here from outside. This bag of apples must have been searched five or six times. I think a few got taken along the way."

"George," Sandra said, "you have been such a loyal friend. Your visits and kind words have meant so much to us. We will miss you."

She took the apples and started to lean across the table to give him a kiss on the cheek.

"Stop that! You are not allowed to make contact with the visitors," a nearby police guard shouted.

In a surreal occurrence, the commandant of the Military Intelligence Service Language School, Colonel Rasmussen, visited the camp in early August and interviewed 184 internees as possible interpreters for the Pacific operations. The bizarre image of interviewing people imprisoned as possible enemy spies to be interpreters for the very people who were holding them prisoner did not go unnoticed by the other internees.

The only wedding in camp occurred on August 16th

On August 25th, 500 internees, including Bunta, Sandra, and Gerald, cast ballots by mail in the state primary elections.

On August 28th, the first basic clothing for use at Topaz arrived. It was dispersed from the back of Army trucks to the internees who caught the bundles as they were dropped.

Bunta and Gerald got the bundles allotted to their family. When they got back to their stall, they had a mini fashion show, finding some humor in the styleless, drab garments they were given.

On September 9th, the first group of 215 internees left for Topaz.

The Horito family was in the third group of 485 to leave on September 16th.

The last group departed October 1st. In a final teenage prank or act of defiance, depending on your viewpoint, the large cardboard EXIT sign attached to the main mess hall was torn down and over fifty internees signed it. It hangs today in the Topaz Museum.

They were loaded onto buses, their belongings following them on trucks to the station where they boarded trains for the journey to Topaz.

15

THE JOURNEY TO TOPAZ

SEPTEMBER 16, 1942

The Horitos, along with 476 of their fellow internees, stood on the platform next to the tracks. Armed soldiers stood at all the doors leading into the station. Railroad personnel scurried about, each seeming to have some important task. In the lights from the canopy covering the tracks and the platform, they watched as their possessions were loaded into several boxcars by soldiers. The steam escaping from the engine up into the lights cast an eerie feeling to the surroundings.

Then, at about seven p.m., whistles and shouts of "all aboard" rang out as soldiers began to herd the people toward the train cars.

Gerald, Bunta, and a porter had to help Aiko and Haruto up the steep steps into the car. The porter directed them to the left.

"You can take any seat. And you'll notice that the back

flips back and forth. That way, four of you can sit facing each other. We don't arrive in Utah until day after tomorrow, so you want to be comfortable."

Sandra had to smile. "Little do you know just how comfortable we'll be. We haven't been able to sit in such comfort in almost four months. Plush seats, no dust or smell of horse manure, no mud, and no long lines. And actual cool air! We didn't even have that luxury in our home. Oh, yes, we'll be comfortable! Could we make the trip last a week instead of three days?"

The porter looked at her in disbelief while Rachel laughed.

They settled in: Bunta, Sandra, Aiko, and Haruto facing each other, and Gerald and Rachel sitting across the aisle

The whistle gave out three short blasts, the car lurched, and they were on their way.

None of the family had ever ridden a train, so this was a cause for excitement and wonder. They watched spellbound as the people on the platform, the large luggage carts, and the structures of the station passed by the windows. Then, suddenly, all that was gone and replaced by multiple gleaming tracks, some empty and some with a random assortment of train cars, sitting as if waiting for an adventure and strange-colored lights of red, green, and yellow along with paddle-like arms of red and white.

The click, click of the wheels on the tracks increased, and then they were in the darkness of the open country. Here and there, lights on houses and barns flashed by. For a while, a highway paralleled the tracks, and Rachel became fixed on the white and red lights of cars going in both directions. She often found that the car would match the speed of the train, and it became like a race through the night.

I wonder how fast we are going. I'll ask the porter the next time I see him. I'll bet I've never gone this fast!

Aiko stood up, holding on to the seat back as the car swayed.

"I need to find the bathroom. Will you help me, Sandra?"

"Certainly. Here, take my hand."

They disappeared down the aisle, only to return in about five minutes.

"I can't believe it. There were only three people ahead of us. And the toilet had a door!"

At about nine o'clock, the porter came through announcing that beverages and snacks were available for purchase in the lounge car.

As he passed, Rachel grabbed his arm. "Mister Porter, how fast are we going?"

"Between fifty and sixty, depending on the tracks. When we go through towns, we'll slow to about thirty-five.

"Are you and your family going to the lounge car? We've got some nice treats for kids."

"Mama, can we go, please?"

Sandra looked at Bunta. He nodded and said to Gerald, "Please take your sister and see what they have. Get something and come back with a report on the menu. We'll decide if we or your grandparents want anything, and you can get it for us. Here's some money."

"Let's go, Sis. We'll be back shortly," he said over his shoulder.

The lounge car was at the end of the train. They had to pass through a long series of cars like theirs full of people just like them. Everyone seemed to be enjoying these few hours of luxury despite the apprehension of what lay ahead. Most were sleeping. A few babies were crying.

As they passed by a family, they overheard the mother saying.

"Whatever they have for us to live in, it's got to be better than those drafty, cold barracks we were in. They've had plenty of time to build good housing, as well as better facilities."

"I hope you're right," her husband responded.

As Gerald and Rachel navigated the aisle down the moving, swaying train, it became something of a game for Rachel to try walking without holding on. At first, she couldn't do it, but by the time they got to the dining car, she was an expert.

"Looks like you've gotten your 'sea legs,' Sis."

"Don't you mean 'train-legs? she replied.

As they entered the dining car, the stewards were in the process of cleaning tables. A few passengers were lingering at the tables, enjoying the white tablecloths and elegant table settings.

Gerald asked a steward, "Can we eat here?"

"Yes, sir. The mealtimes are posted on the doors at both ends of the car. The next meal is breakfast. We begin at 6:00 and serve until 10:00. Remember, there are five hundred people on this train, so we'll be crowded. The train is so full, and we're not allowed to stop to resupply, so we may not have everything on the menu.

"Also, we've been told on this run that we have to collect for the meals before they are served."

When they got to the lounge car, they found it full of

people. Most were sitting in armchairs. A few were standing, looking out the large windows into the night. There was a low murmur of Japanese.

Gerald saw a combination food counter and bar at one end. There were two white-jacketed men behind the bar restocking the shelf on the back wall. He and Rachel walked to it.

"Can I get some cheese and crackers and a beer, and a soda and cookies for my sister?" One of the men turned to Gerald.

"Sorry sir, we're not allowed to sell alcohol to any of the passengers. How about a soda for you instead?"

Gerald made the purchases, handed a soda and cookies to Rachel, and they headed back to their car.

When they got there, Aiko and Horito were asleep. Their parents were awake and talking quietly.

Gerald heard his mother saying, "I know, but my main concern is Rachel. I realize at her age she's probably the most adaptable, but she's also at a time when her education is critical. The schools at Tanforan were minimal, at best. The teachers were dedicated but completely inexperienced. And where are they going to find even inexperienced ones in the middle of the desert? Also, the lack of textbooks was a real problem. If Rachel had not brought her math and English ones, she would have had nothing.

"Those won't help her much if we're at Topaz for a long time."

"Honey, they've had almost six months to get ready for us. At Tanforan, they had just over one month. I'm sure they've done a much better job."

"Mama, Papa, Gerald, and I found the lounge car. See?"

she said, holding up the soda and the end of a cookie. "You should go get something. It's a real treat."

"And they have a really nice dining car, with white tablecloths and nice dishes," Gerald continued. "We just need to get there by six.

Now, I'm going to the bathroom and then get some sleep. I see the porter put blankets and pillows in our seats. That's a nice touch."

16

ON THE TRAIN,

SEPTEMBER 17, 1942

When Gerald woke up, it was still dark. It took him a couple of seconds to figure out where he was. The clatter of the wheels on the rails reminded him. He looked at his watch. It was 5:35. He stood up and stretched.

It may be a comfortable seat, but sleeping sitting up, even with a pillow and blanket, is not my first choice.

He reached across the aisle and nudged his father's arm.

"Papa," he whispered, "we probably should head to the dining car. It's nearly six. With a stop at the bathroom, they'll be open by the time we get there."

Everybody was up and moving in a couple of minutes. Unfortunately, the line to the bathroom was longer than last evening. By the time they joined the line for breakfast, it had stretched the length of the car just ahead of the dining car.

"We'll have to wait until those being served are finished," the couple in front of them said. "The porter said it would be about thirty minutes."

"That's no better than Tanforan," Rachel complained.

"That's true, Daughter," her mother replied. "But notice you're not standing in mud, and the food will be much better when we get there."

The meal was worth the wait. Comfortable chairs instead of hard benches, hotel-like tablecloths and settings, and even a fresh flower in a small glass vase on each table made them feel like normal human beings again. The extra treat was something they had not experienced at the camp. Everybody got to choose what they wanted to eat.

Conscious of those in line, they all felt the need to eat quickly, but it was still a delightful experience.

Bunta, who at first was displeased at having to pay the steward ten dollars before they got their food, was satisfied.

By the time they got back to their seats, the sun was fully up. They were watching the open desert and the mountains in the distance slide by.

They watched the passing barren landscape or snoozed for a couple of hours until they could feel the train slowing. The porter and two armed soldiers came through the car.

"We're going to be stopping up here for about twenty minutes while the train takes on water and coal." One of the soldiers spoke up. "Anyone who wants to get off for a few minutes can. There will be soldiers about twenty-five yards away from the train on either side, so don't think about running off. Besides, we're a hundred miles from nowhere in the desert, so you wouldn't get far anyway. The whistle will blow when you need to get back on."

They could see a number of soldiers with their rifles getting off on both sides. Once they were set, the porter said, "OK, you can get off now if you want to. Listen for the whistle and get back on quickly."

Gerald and his father led the family to the end of the car and down the steps onto the platform. With the porter's assistance, they helped Aiko and Haruto down the steps.

"This is nice," Sandra said. Even that comfortable seat can get a little hard after a while."

They walked up and back along the side of the car for a few minutes. The ground under their feet was dusty and there was a fine cloud of it blowing in the light breeze, getting on their clothes and in their faces.

"I wonder if this is what it will be like where we are going?" Rachel said, wiping her eyes.

"I don't want to stay out here any longer," Aiko said. "Can we go back in?"

When they were back on the train, Rachel went to the bathroom and brought back several damp towels so they could wipe their faces.

A lot of the other passengers were coming back as well. A few teenage boys stayed out tossing around a softball. The whistle blew, and the soldiers headed back toward the train. The boys waited until the soldiers were right at them before they turned and ran up the stairs.

"Aw, they wouldn't have shot us," one said to his buddy.

"Don't be too sure," responded one of the older men from his seat as the train jerked and picked up speed.

About an hour later, the train began to slow again. The porter came through. "We'll be passing through this little town. It won't take us long."

Suddenly, there was the noise of people running. Two soldiers burst through the door at the front.

"Pull down your shades quickly! Stay away from the windows!"

At the same time, the train jerked forward and picked up speed quickly.

"What happened?" someone asked loudly.

"There was a crowd of people standing by the tracks as we came into the station," one of the soldiers said. "They started throwing rocks and sticks at the train. A couple broke through windows. A young girl a couple of cars ahead was cut on her arm."

Gerald stooped low in his seat and peeked out through the slit at the bottom of the shade.

It looked like maybe twenty-five people—adults and older kids—standing on the platform, yelling and waving a couple of hand-lettered signs that read JAP, Go home, and Kill all JAPs.

He sat back in his seat, his fists and jaw clenched while tears of rage ran down his cheeks.

Thank God my family didn't see that!

Twice more before supper, they were told to pull down the shades again. They didn't slow down for these towns.

Just before people started settling in for their second night, the porter came through. "The train will be arriving at Delta, Utah, about 6:00 a.m. tomorrow. You should have all your personal belongings collected and ready to get off as soon as the doors are opened. There will be no breakfast served on the train. The soldiers will come through in the morning with instructions."

17

ARRIVING AT TOPAZ

At 5:30 a.m., two armed soldiers came through the car.

"We'll be at the station in Delta in thirty minutes. As soon as the porter says the train has fully stopped, you will exit through that end of the car." He pointed toward the front of the train.

"At the bottom of the steps, you will find soldiers who will direct you through the station to buses waiting on the other side. You may get on any of them. Find seats as far to the rear as you can."

Again, Gerald and Bunta got off first and helped Bunta's parents down the steps. The wind was blowing, and dust filled the air.

"Does the wind never stop?" Aiko asked.

They found their way through the station and headed to

the nearest bus. It was half full. They quickly found seats and sat down.

Once the bus was full, an armed soldier stood at the front as the door closed.

"The drive to Topaz will take about forty minutes. Once we get there, another soldier will board and give you instructions. As you get off the bus, you will give him the number on your tag.

"As in Tanforan, your belongings will be delivered to your quarters."

They sat for about twenty minutes.

"All the buses are full now. Driver, follow the bus in front of you."

Because they were not the first bus, mostly all they saw was dust. They could tell by the rough ride that they were on a dirt road.

As they got close to the camp, they could make out many long rectangular dark-brown buildings in straight rows as far as they could see.

The bus stopped. The wind blew the billows of dust away.

Ahead of them were other detainees forming a line headed into a building with a Welcome to Topaz City sign hanging over the door.

"Get off here," the soldier said. "Be ready to give your tag number to the soldier at the bottom of the steps and go to the line headed into the building."

Gerald and his family were part of the third group to arrive at the camp. The first group of 211 arrived a week earlier and were mostly young men and women specifically selected to work at continuing the construction projects going on all over the camp. On the 17th, the first group of 502 regular people arrived.

When this third group arrived, they were greeted not just by officials of the camp but also by a large group of people from the earlier arrivals. Some of them held handmade signs, WELCOME TO TOPAZ—YOUR CAMP and WELCOME TO TOPAZ: JEWEL OF THE DESERT. They waved and clapped and cheered.

The line moved quickly. Once inside, a civilian read their tag number and then looked at a clipboard.

"Family 20464, you are assigned to Barracks Number 9, Block Number 14.

"Two of you will be in Apartment A, and the other four will be in Apartment B. Your belongings will be delivered to you by the end of the day.

"That group over there will be going to Block 14. Join them. You will find fruit, muffins, and water on the table. The Block Manager will join the group shortly to lead you to the block."

A middle-aged Anglo in a khaki shirt and pants and name tag arrived,

"Good morning, and welcome to Topaz City. I am Mr. Smith, the Block Manager for your neighborhood in the city.

"This is about half of you. The others are arriving on later buses. This booklet will give you a lot of valuable information about life here."

He then handed out an 8 1/2 x 11 thirty-page mimeographed booklet to each family entitled "Welcome to Topaz."

"Once you get to your new home, please take time to read the booklet carefully. There are some Do's and Don'ts on pages 26 and 27 that you should pay close attention to."

"I saw the same five-foot barbed wire fence and sentry towers like at Tanforan. Why have you put those up way out here in the empty desert?" one of the men in the group asked.

"They are here for your protection. But please, do not get too close to the fence."

"Now, if you've finished your breakfast, please follow me, and we will go to your new homes. As we walk, notice that the east/west streets have gemstone names, and the north/south ones are named for plants."

Our neighborhood is bordered by "Pearl," "Opal," "Jasmine," and "Iris." These names will help you locate your homes until things become familiar. The main street bordering our neighborhood is Jasmine. So, if you live in Apartment A of Barracks 11, the address you can share with friends and family will be 1411-A, Jasmine Street, Topaz, Utah." The mail pickup and delivery schedule is in the booklet I just gave you."

"They certainly are going to great lengths to make this all seem normal," Sandra said. "Do they think we're all blind idiots?"

As they walked, they could see that each "neighborhood" was composed of twelve long single-story rectangular buildings in two rows on either side of two larger buildings. Every "neighborhood" appeared identical. However, it was unsettling to see how many of the buildings were still under construction. Many had no roofs, doors, or windows.

"Mama, are we going to have a roof?" Rachel asked.

"I certainly hope so. I think Mr. Smith would have told us if our buildings were not finished."

In an effort to change the subject, Bunta said, "I'm glad the streets have names. Otherwise, I'd get lost quickly."

Mr. Smith led them toward a group of buildings that appeared to be completed.

"This is your neighborhood. I know you are relieved to see that construction on the buildings has been completed. Let's go in."

He led them between two of the rectangular buildings. "This is number 8 on your right and number 9 on your left. Directly across are building numbers 3 and 2. There are twelve in all.

The large building in front of you is the dining hall and the one to your left houses the latrines and laundry. The building at the end of our area, just past building 12, is the recreational building. We call it the Rec Hall. That large pile of coal next to the laundry is for the coal-heating stoves in each apartment. It is my responsibility to keep you supplied with coal."

"Now, you can find your apartments and begin to settle in. Your belongings should be in your apartments. If not, they'll be along shortly. If they have not arrived by supper, let me know.

"Lunch will be at noon in the mess hall. A bell will ring to remind you. Everybody in this neighborhood can be seated at the same time. For a while, there will be a serving line. When more people are available to work in the mess hall, we plan to have food set on the tables." He turned and left.

The sense of anxiety and anticipation was palatable in the group. The dust blew. Everything was strange.

"This is us right here," Gerald pointed to the building on their left. "Looks like we're about halfway between the dining hall and the building with the latrines, bathhouses, and laundry."

For the first time, they paused to take a good look at their new home. The buildings looked simply made but seemed larger than the stables at Tanforan.

They were raised off the ground about twelve inches on what appeared to be wood scraps. There were no footings or foundations, and the space under the building was open.

The structure appeared to be frame-built with a tar paper covering held in place by 2-inch-wide board strips in a large grid pattern. A number of windows were visible. There were three doors on one side. In front of each door were steps leading up to a small landing. The doors opened into a small hallway with two doors to the two adjoining apartments.

Bunta located the door with the letters. "A" and "B" They were on the end nearest the buildings in the center. "C" and "D" were in the middle and "E" and "F" were at the end that faced Jasmine Street.

Bunta said, "Let's go into A."

They went into the hall and opened the door on the left to "A." They entered a room with wooden walls, a bare wooden floor, and exposed wooden rafters. There was a single light bulb in the middle of the room attached to a rafter. A pull cord hung from it to about shoulder height on Aiko.

Two small windows on the far wall let light into the

room. An iron pot-bellied stove was set between them. A small wooden box of coal, some kindling, newspaper, and a box of matches were stacked next to it.

Two single wooden beds were set perpendicular against the wall to the left. On each was a thin mattress, an army blanket, and a pillow. None of their belongings had been delivered. There was no evidence of water or a bathroom.

Gerald paced the room off.

"Looks like about twenty feet long and fourteen feet wide."

Sandra answered, "That means there's room for a small table, some chairs, and some shelves. Bunta, you and Gerald need to locate some building materials."

"We'll do that," Bunta responded. "I also just noticed that there is no insulation on the walls or roof. I'll bet there's none under the floor, either. That means it's going to be very hot or very cold in here."

Sandra spoke. "Ojichan and Obachan, do you want to come see our room, or would you like to rest for a while first?

Aiko replied. "We'll go with you, then we'll come back here to finish arranging our quarters. Look at me, talking like a soldier." She smiled.

As they headed toward the hallway between the rooms, two civilians were bringing suitcases and bags into the room. Aiko examined them. "Everything seems to be here," she said, obviously relieved.

They continued into "B." Haruto, the last one to leave, pulled the door shut.

"There's no lock. I wonder if we can get one? I hope

people in this area, what did Mr. Smith call it, 'our neighborhood?' are honest."

As they turned left toward their room, they heard voices outside. They all looked out. Two families, each with two young children, were going into "C' and "D." Nods were exchanged, but no one spoke.

As they entered the room, they again heard voices and footsteps on the stairs. Three young men came toward the door.

"I think you are in the wrong room," Bunta said. "This is Apartment 'B." What is your assignment?"

Looking at the papers given to him, he replied, "We and one other man are assigned to Apartment "B," building 3," one of them said.

"Right apartment, wrong building," Bunta replied. "This is 9. Building 3 is on the other side, directly across from this one." He pointed to his right.

A look of shock and embarrassment appeared on their faces. "Oh we are sorry," a second one said. They immediately bowed, picked up their bags, and quickly went out and headed across the area.

Now, they could look closely at their room. It was identical to "A" except that it was six feet wider, with three windows and four folded metal army cots stacked by the door. There was a stack of four pillows and one of four blankets but no mattress. There were four empty mattress covers laid on top of the blankets.

"Mama, are we going to have to fill our mattresses again?" Rachel whined.

"It looks like it, honey. We'll ask Mr. Smith at lunch.

"Now, we'll leave the boys here to set up the beds and

wait for our belongings to be delivered while you and I go with Ojichan and Obachan back to their room."

As they left, Gerald and Bunta began to unfold and set up the beds. They set up two, perpendicular from each side wall near the stove. They set a pillow, blanket, and mattress cover on each.

"Your mother can decide if this is where she wants them placed."

They stretched out on two of them to wait for their belongings to arrive.

Rachel and Sandra were mostly through helping Aiko and Haruto with their unpacking and arranging things on the floor when the lunch bell rang.

18

DAY 1, CONTINUED. TOPAZ

SEPTEMBER 18, 1942

Bunta and Gerald joined them at the bottom of the stairs, and they headed to the latrines.

Only a few people gathered on either the men's or women's side.

It was the same as at Tanforan. Several rows of toilets with partitions but no doors and a row of washbowls but no soap or towels.

As soon as they stepped out, they found the two lines into the dining hall and joined the end of one of them. It took twenty minutes to get to the serving counter compared to forty-five to fifty at Tanforan.

The dining hall was spartan. Plain, unpainted wooden walls, floor, and raftered ceiling. Windows lined two walls with the kitchen and serving line at one end. Several rows of wooden tables and benches filled the room.

The food resembled the earlier days at Tanforan. Heavy,

starchy stew, crackers, canned figs, water, and a pack of cookies.

Sandra's request for hot tea was met with the response, "We don't have that yet. Maybe next week."

From their time at Tanforan, they realized that, at least for now, there was no alternative. And here, there would be nothing brought in by friends through the barbed wire. So they knew they would have to eat at least some of what was on their tray.

Just as they found an open spot and sat down, Mr. Smith spoke over the PA system.

"Good afternoon, neighbors. I hope you're getting settled in. After lunch, you may want to walk around the city and locate things outside the neighborhood. Various services and activities are located in the Rec buildings throughout the neighborhoods and in the administration area. For example, located in our Rec building are the Catholic and Seventh Day Adventist churches.

"On page 2 of the booklet you got when we met, you will find a complete list of these. The city is one-mile square. On the north border, near the gate you entered, are the two administration buildings, hospital, post office, and other services. There's a map of that area on page 5 of your booklet.

"You will see on the city map in your booklet that our neighborhood is on the east edge of the residential area. Just east of our buildings is the protective fencing and watchtowers manned by Army personnel.

"As I mentioned earlier, for your own safety, stay back from the fence.

"Most of you found the canvas sacks on your blankets.

Between this building and the one behind us, you will find a large pile of hay on a wooden platform. You will use that to stuff those sacks as your mattresses, like you did at Tanforan. If it starts to run low, tell me, and I'll have more brought in.

"Each of your apartments has a supply of coal and materials to start a fire in the stove. I suggest you get the stove heating just before you come to supper. It will get down to the mid-forties during the night. If you need help with starting and managing your stove, ask some of your neighbors for help.

"Tonight, after supper, which starts at 5:45, we'll talk about some of the jobs you will be doing while you are here, and how you can sign up for them.

"And, most importantly, I'll talk about ways you can leave the city permanently.

"Now, I suggest you go check on your belongings, collect the hay for your mattress, and lay the fire in your stove. I'll see you back here this evening."

Gerald and his family headed back to their building. Sandra and Rachel went with Aiko and Haruto to finish laying out their things on the floor, while Bunta and Gerald went to see if their things had been delivered. They had not.

"Papa, if you'll start laying the fire, I'll take these sacks and start filling them with hay. Then you can help me bring them back." Gerald grabbed the four sacks and headed out the door.

When he arrived at the haystack, there was a large group of people, mostly men, already grouped there. About ten surrounded the pile of stuffing and were shaping their sacks while the others waited for an opening. Gerald joined the group.

"Good afternoon," he said to the men closest to him. "I remember seeing some of you around Tanforan. I was a House Manager and the representative on the Advisory Council from District 5.

"I wonder what sort of government is planned for Topaz. I have a feeling we're going to be here for a long time. I hope it will be something that we form and that it will have some real power, or at least influence, over the policies and decisions that affect the conditions of our daily lives. You remember that the Army stopped our efforts at Tanforan?"

"I do remember you," one of the older men close to him replied. "Your name is Gerald. I am Taiga. I get the feeling that at least some of those in charge are making an effort to treat this like any normal city, so perhaps they will let us set up a normal government."

"But it's certainly not a normal city," another said. "Even if we were not here by force, there's a lot wrong with this place. We're the lucky ones in this block. Our buildings are finished. I walked around some before lunch and a lot of the housing buildings are not finished. Many have only floors and walls. No doors, windows, or even roofs. I heard some people say that the people who came before us are having to sleep in the rec halls and dining halls. The administration has even put some in the hospital. Others said that when the group that came in yesterday all turned on the lights at night, several transformers blew. I hope that doesn't happen again tonight."

Just as it was Gerald's turn at the hay pile, Bunta arrived.

It took them about ten minutes to stuff the sacks and button up the openings. As they walked back, Gerald said, "Papa, I've just learned how bad things are in other parts of the camp. We are really fortunate to have been assigned to barracks that are completed. A lot of people are having to sleep in rec halls and dining halls until theirs are finished.

"I've been thinking about how bad the planning has been at Tanforan and here. If the same people who planned these camps have anything to do with the war effort, the US is in serious danger of losing the war."

"Don't worry about that, Son. The war is a noble cause. Americans will expend any effort and endure any sacrifice to win it. Sadly, we, on the other hand, are simply collateral damage resulting from a history of racism. They won't waste their best minds on us. We'll get the leftovers."

They got back to their room, set the mattresses on the cots, and waited for their sheets and other belongings to arrive. Shortly, Sandra and Rachel returned.

"Papa, we've got Ojichan and Ogachan settled in. They're taking a nap. Mama wants you to lay their fire before supper."

"I'm concerned," Sandra said. "I don't know a lot about coal stoves, but that doesn't look like enough coal for more than a couple of days. And that coal supply that Mr. Smith pointed out doesn't look like a lot divided up among seventy-two stoves plus the hot water boiler in the bathhouse. I hope they've got more coming in."

"I'm sure they do. I'll tell Mr. Smith of your concern at supper. Now, let's walk around a little and see what's here."

They walked east to Jasmine. The barbed wire fence was about ten yards past the edge of the street.

"Let's go left," Bunta suggested. "I want to see the admin and security areas. Gerald tells me that the hospital is being used to house internees whose barracks have not been finished yet, so I want to see if they have room for patients."

As they walked north, they passed a guard tower at the corner. It was empty, but there were a large number of MPs in the Security area.

I wonder if they are going to have soldiers in those towers. Gerald thought.

Once they got to the hospital building, they found a crowd of new arrivals around it.

Bunta spoke to a family of four with two small infants standing near the front entrance. "I am Bunta Horito. This is my wife, Sandra. Why are you here?"

"Good evening. I am Takeshi Amari. We, and most of the people here, were assigned to Block 3. When we got there, none of the barracks had roofs; some didn't even have walls. They put as many as they could in the dining hall. The rest of us are here. They said the construction would be complete in about a week. Until then, we will sleep here and eat in whatever dining hall we can find room. What a mess! We're sleeping in hallways, the lobby, and storage rooms.

"We and another family with two teenage girls are sleeping on the floor of a storage room. There is barely enough room to walk between the blankets. I don't know what we'll do when our baggage arrives."

Bunta turned to Sandra. They spoke quietly for a few minutes.

Then Sandra said to the man, "We could share our space with the other family since it'll be for only a week. They may have to sleep on the floor. We can check on beds. Please introduce them to us."

The man left and returned shortly with the family. "This is John Tanaka and his family. I have told them of your offer."

John spoke to Bunta. "You honor us with your kind offer. Were it just my family, we would graciously decline your offer as being too great a sacrifice on your family's part.

"However, my wife Hana recognizes what a burden we are to Ichiro and Ema with their small children, so we will accept. However, you must let us repay you in some way.

"I am a doctor, so if your family has any medical issues, please let me know. The Army let me keep my medical bag. I think they'll use me in the hospital."

"Thank you for the offer," Bunta replied, "but that is not necessary. I think our daughter, Rachel, would like the company of your daughters."

"Yes," Hana replied. "This is Sakura and Akari. I think they would enjoy that as well."

"It's settled then," Sandra said. "Do you have your belongings yet? We can help you carry them. We are in Block 114, not far from here. I wonder if we have to get permission for you to move."

"I had a friend in medical school whose favorite expression was that it was easier to get forgiveness than permission. With all the confusion, probably no one will notice or care.

"No, we don't have our luggage yet, only my medical bag. Ichiro can let us know when it arrives. Are you ready for us to come now?"

"Yes, let's go," Rachel said, excited about having new roommates. "We'll help you with your bedding."

With everybody carrying something, they arrived back at their room shortly. They did get a questioning stare from a passing WRA staff member, but he did not stop them.

When they arrived at the building, they could see a young woman standing on the porch of "E" and "F."

Sandra spoke. "Good afternoon. I am Sandra Horito. My family just arrived next door this morning. We are in "B," and my husband's parents are in "A." While walking after lunch, we came across this family in very cramped conditions at the hospital. They were crowded into a small room with a family with two small infants. We have invited them to stay with us until their barracks is finished. I hope that won't be a problem."

"I'm sure that won't be a problem. I am Hana Sato. My three friends and I are used to a noisy dorm. The four of us were roommates and third-year nursing students at The University of California-San Francisco. Our student visas were canceled, and we were given the opportunity to return to Japan or come here. We chose this place. I hope that was not a mistake."

"What a coincidence," Sandra replied. The husband of the family we've brought here is a doctor, and his wife's name is Hana."

"It is a pleasure to meet you, Mrs. Horito. We look forward to meeting your family and your guests. Let me introduce my roommates, Rika, Nari, and Miyu. Girls, this is Mrs. Sandra Horito. Her family and some temporary guests are in "B." The girls bowed slightly and extended their hands.

Rika asked, "Have you gotten your belongings? We have not. Also, I am embarrassed to say that none of us has ever started a fire in a coal stove. Can your husband or son teach us, please?"

"Certainly, just a moment. Gerald, these ladies need some assistance with their stove."

Gerald stopped talking with Dr. Tanaka and came over. "Gerald, this is Hana. She and her three roommates, Rika, Nari, and Miyu are from the university. They are nursing students, and they need help with their stove."

Wow, Gerald thought, as he saw the beautiful girls standing in front of him, and just when I thought how miserable I was. How did I get so lucky?

19

THE REST OF DAY 1, TOPAZ

SEPTEMBER 18, 1942

"Good afternoon, ladies. I hear you would like to learn how to get a fire started in your stove. Have any of you ever started a campfire?"

"Yes, I have," Nari replied. "Some of my friends wanted to try the new fad of making s'mores. We built a small fire behind the dorm." We'd just gotten the first ones made when campus security came by and were very angry that we built a fire without permission. He wanted to know what we were doing. We made a s'more for him. He really liked it. He still made us put the fire out, but he said he wouldn't report us to the dean. I think it was because we gave him a s'more."

"Do you remember how you built the fire?"

"Yes. We'd gathered some paper and small sticks and a jar of alcohol from the lab. We crumpled the paper, put the small sticks on top, poured on some alcohol and lit it with a match. I think we put too much alcohol on it 'cause it really flamed up at first. Then we put some larger wood pieces until we had it like we wanted it."

"Good story. You're probably lucky you didn't burn the building down," Gerald said with a big grin.

"It's the same process with the stove, except no alcohol. You use the paper and the kindling by the stove and once the fire is started, you use those tongs to put some coal on the flames.

"Before you do all that, however, you need to open the damper in the flue, or you'll fill the room with smoke. You do this by turning this handle to rotate a flap inside. You can control how hot the fire is by adjusting the damper and the sliding opening on the door. Be very careful, though. Both of those will be very hot when there's a fire burning."

Gerald then opened the flue, got down on one knee in front of the stove, and demonstrated the steps for laying the fire. He began by crumpling the paper and then by breaking some of the kindling into smaller pieces and arranging them and the larger pieces in a teepee-shaped stack on top of the paper. The four girls crowded around him, watching his every move.

An observer might have found it difficult to determine whether they were more interested in the process or the teacher.

Once he was finished, Gerald took the kindling and paper out. He stood up, carefully closing the flue behind his back.

"Now it's your turn. Why don't each of you take turns doing what I did? Once you've all done it, we'll light the fire."

The girls, giggling a bit, all stood back. No one wanted to

be first.

Finally, Gerald reached out and took Hana's hand, smiling at her.

"You seem to be in charge here, Hana. You go first. Don't worry; you'll be fine. I'll be right here."

She knelt on one knee, Gerald standing by her shoulder. She placed the crumpled paper and the kindling pieces in the stove just like Gerald had shown them. Then she stood up.

"Very nice, Hana. Are we ready to light the fire?"

She started to say "Yes" but was interrupted by Rika's loud "No! She didn't open the flapper, or whatever it's called."

Gerald laughed. Hana blushed.

"Don't worry, Hana. An easy mistake to make," Gerald said, touching her shoulder reassuringly. "OK, Rika, since you noticed Hana's mistake, you go next."

Rika walked quickly to the stove, firmly turned the handle, knelt down, and confidently laid a perfect fire.

"Good job, Rika." The other three girls clapped.

Then Nari did all the steps correctly and stepped back. Again, the girls clapped.

Just as Miya was about to start, there was a commotion outside. They went to the porch to see two of the kids from one of the middle rooms scuffling over a ball. Their mother was headed over to separate them.

"Glad it was nothing serious," Hana said. "Let's let Miya have her turn." They just were back at the stove when there was a knock at the door. Their belongings were being delivered. It took two men about ten minutes to get everything into the room.

"Before we sort this all out," Miya said. I'm going to do my turn at the fire. She walked over to the stove. Gerald and the other three were distracted by the pile of belongings and didn't watch her closely.

"I'm done," she announced. "Can I go ahead and light the fire?"

"Yes, it looks good," Gerald replied. "Strike one of those long wooden matches and light the paper."

She did so. The flames quickly filled the fire chamber. The kindling crackled and smoke began to come out through the stove's door!

Gerald quickly ran to the stove and turned the damper handle. The smoke disappeared back into the stove.

"Well, there you have a live demonstration of how the damper works," he said, laughing. "We'll let the fire burn for a minute or two and then put on some of the smaller lumps of coal. You're just going to have to learn by trial and error how quickly this coal burns and how to control the rate of burning and the heat with the damper and the door slot. Once you have a good coal fire started, you shouldn't have to use any more paper or kindling until you need to let the fire go out so you can remove the ashes. I didn't show you how to do that. You should be OK for a day or two unless it gets really cold and you need a hotter fire. I'll check back soon.

"Now, I need to get back to my family and our guests. Once you get your stuff sorted out and your fire regulated, please come over and meet the rest of my family, and the doctor and his family."

As he got to the top of the steps, he felt a hand on his shoulder. "Wait, please," a voice said. He turned. Hana was standing right behind him. There were tears on her cheeks.

"Gerald, I'm so afraid. I don't know if I'll be able to survive this. I'm used to luxury and being pampered. My family is wealthy. My father is a very successful doctor in Hiroshima, and my mother is a nurse. I'm an only child, and they have always wanted me to be a nurse as well. I really appreciated the way you put so much care into teaching us such a simple task as starting a fire. I've only known you for a little while, but I think you are a very good person and the kindest man I've ever met." She reached out tentatively and took his hand in hers. "I feel like we can be friends, and I can count on you to help me get through this ordeal."

Putting his other hand on top of hers, he replied.

"Of course, Hana. We're all going to have to figure out how to adjust our lives to this new situation. Finding new friends is going to be an important part of that. Fortunately, I have my family. We are close and will find our strength in each other. My grandparents, though older and frail, have a code of survival that is the family's rock. I get that having only your classmates must be scary. But don't worry. We'll look after you and your friends. And by the way, don't make light of the stove. I hear it can get very cold and windy here, and with our rooms being uninsulated, that stove will be important to keep you and your friends alive."

When he got back to the family's room, his mom and sister were busy sorting out their belongings that had just been delivered. Gerald noticed that all four of their beds were now against the same wall. The Tanakas had spread their bedding on the floor on the other side of the room. They were now helping Sandra and Rachel as they could. Their belongings were still missing.

"Where's Papa?"

"He's with Ojichan and Obachan, starting a fire for them," Sandra responded. "Then he said he was going to try to find Mr. Smith to see if we can get cots for the Tanakas. We need to get them off the cold floor as soon as possible. How did it go with the girls? They certainly are very pretty," she added with a slight smile.

"Just fine," he answered, ignoring her comment. "They got their belongings, and they all know how to start a fire. Before bedtime, I'll go by and see if they've figured out how to control it.

"And Mama, I think we need to take them under our wings. They're scared and, without any adults, they're going to need our help."

Dr. Tanaka replied, "I agree. I was planning to stop by after supper and talk to them about their studies."

"They would appreciate that," Gerald replied. "Also, I learned that Hana's father is a doctor, and her mother is a nurse. They live in Hiroshima. She's hoping to return for a visit once she's finished her studies."

By the time the supper gong sounded, everybody had their belongings. Mr. Amari had come by to tell Dr. Tanaka that their belongings had been delivered. The four men had gone and brought them back to Gerald's family's room. All rooms had fires going and properly damped, though Gerald was sure he'd have to check on the girl's stove once more before the lights went out. Sandra had checked with the two families next to them, and they both had their belongings and fires going. The Horitos, Tanakas, Hana and her roommates, and the two families in the middle rooms all came down their stairs at the same time and headed together to the mess hall. Apartment "F" was still empty.

20

THE END OF DAY 1, TOPAZ

SEPTEMBER 18, 1942

The eighteen new occupants of Barracks 9, Block 14, Topaz, Utah, joined one of the lines headed into the mess hall.

At 5:45, it was still light. Sunset was not for almost two more hours. So, although the wind had begun to pick up again, raising the annoying dust clouds, it was still comfortably warm. The mess hall staff seemed to be getting better at their jobs. The wait in line was not quite fifteen minutes.

When they got their food, the six Horitos, with Hana and Miyu, sat at one table, and Gerald managed to sit next to Hana. He wanted to talk about her studies, but everything he thought about saying sounded awkward in his mind. Instead, he made small talk about the camp. The two other families filled the next table. Rika, Nari, and the Tanakas took the next table and were quickly joined by two others.

Supper was a fried hamburger with two pieces of bread, a scoop of macaroni and cheese, some canned peaches, two cookies, and a choice of water, milk, or coffee. Still no tea! Ketchup and yellow mustard were on the table.

"I'm certainly going to miss the food that came in from outside at Tanforan," Aiko said quietly.

"Oh, me too," Miyu replied. "Our friends and teachers from the university brought us lots of food. We hardly ever went to the mess hall. I'm afraid I will get fat eating this kind of food all the time. Maybe we'll be given the opportunity to grow some vegetables."

As they were finishing the meal, Mr. Smith turned on the PA system.

"Good evening, neighbors. I hope you are all getting settled into your new homes. A couple of questions. Is there anybody who has not received their belongings? Please raise your hand."

About twenty hands went up.

"Please see me as soon as I'm finished. I think we can get your belongings to you before lights out at 10 o'clock.

"Is there anybody who has not been able to start the fire in your stove?" This time, only three hands went up.

"Please give me your apartment number; a staff member will arrive shortly after we leave here.

"Is there any family who does not have enough cots and bedding?"

Dr. Tanaka raised his hand.

Mr. Smith walked over to him.

"What is your name and apartment number?"

"I am Dr. Tanaka. We're in 9-B with the Horitos. Our building in Block 3 has no roof, so we were put in a very small storage room in the hospital, where I expect I'll be assigned to work with another family with two small children. The Horitos met us when they were walking around camp and invited us to stay with them until our apartment is finished. We have bedding but no cots."

Mr. Smith frowned, clearly displeased with this information.

"Your Block Manager did not tell me about this move. Did you get his permission to move your family?"

"No, sir. Since it was going to be for only a few days, we didn't feel it was necessary. And I'll be at the hospital every day, so the camp administration will know where I am."

By now, everybody at the surrounding tables was focused on the exchange between the two men.

"Just because you are a doctor, don't think that gives you any special privileges!" Mr. Smith said, his voice growing louder.

"I cannot promise you cots. I'll have to report to your Block Manager where you are. He may want you to return to the storage room. I'll ask him about cots but don't expect any.

"And just be glad you're a doctor and that we need you here, or you and your family would be sent to another camp where we're putting problem people!"

He then turned and walked back to the middle of the room and picked up the mic.

"For those of you who did not hear that exchange, the man I was speaking with has taken it upon himself to ignore what might seem like a small rule. But it will cause me a lot of extra work. When everyone arrives, there will be over 8,000 people living in this city. Can you imagine the problems if everybody just broke a small rule? I have been told that Japanese people take pride in following the rules. If our life together is going to work, you must follow the rules!

"That's enough for now. We'll talk about jobs tomorrow at breakfast." He turned off the mic, slammed it down on the table, and stormed out.

Many surprised glances were exchanged.

Dr. Tanaka walked quickly over to Bunta, Sandra, and Gerald.

He bowed.

"I sincerely hope we have not caused your family any trouble. We will move back tomorrow."

"Certainly not," Sandra said. "I'm sure Mr. Smith reacted as he did because he was just caught off guard in front of a crowd and felt he had to assert his authority. Bunta will talk with him tomorrow and show him we were just trying to help the community by resolving a difficult housing situation. I'm sure he'll understand."

As they were walking back to the barracks, Gerald caught up to Hana.

"I'm glad you were able to sit at the table with us. Sometime, I'd like to hear about your studies and your life in Japan. I had always wanted to visit the villages where my grandparents came from. Now, I'm not sure that will ever be possible."

"I'm sure there'll be a chance after the war. I certainly hope it won't be too long before I can return to Hiroshima."

"I hope you are right. The future is so uncertain.

"Anyway, it's time to see what sleeping in our new home will be like. At least it doesn't smell like horse sh – manure," he said with a grin.

"If it's OK, I'll come by just before lights out to check on your stove."

"That would be nice." She lightly touched his shoulder, and he headed back to his apartment.

That evening, the people met a constant reality of desert life.

By 8:30, the wind was blowing about fifteen miles an hour. It had started as a breeze about an hour before and seemed to be getting stronger every minute.

"I'd better go take Ojichan and Obachan to the latrine before this gets any stronger," Sandra said. "Bunta, we really need to find something for chamber pots, so they don't have to go out after supper. Rachel, come with me."

When Gerald went out just before 10:00 to check on the girls' fire, he had to lean into the wind and pull his jacket over his mouth and nose.

He knocked on the door. Hana opened it. "You shouldn't have come out in this wind, but I'm glad you did. I think the fire is fine. Can you show us how to adjust the damper and door vent so it'll burn all night without needing any more coal?"

"Sure, we can do that for now, but when it gets really cold, you'll have to add coal a couple of times a night." He showed them what looked like the proper settings for now. "Every stove is different, so you'll have to figure out the best settings for the temperature."

As he was about to leave, he paused and said, "This is a little awkward, but since you're nurses, I'll just say it. You should get something to use as chamber pots, so you don't have to go out after dark, even if it's not windy. It'll be safer that way."

"Gerald," Hana said as he held the doorknob, "thank you," and kissed his cheek.

By the time he walked up the stairs to his apartment, the wind almost blew him off the porch.

No one slept well that night. The howl of the wind and the banging of loose objects made that impossible. It was not until dawn that the wind subsided.

Gerald recalled the warmth of the unexpected kiss several times during his fretful sleep.

21

SEPTEMBER 19-30, 1942

When they awoke, the first thing they noticed was the grittiness in their mouth, nose, eyes, and hair. Then, it was the film of dust that covered everything. Finally, as they pushed back the covers, the cold enveloped them.

"Sandra," Bunta said, looking at his watch. "It's 6:25. It's lighter outside than it looks. The windows are covered in this dust. Please, you and Rachel go check on Ojichan and Obachan. Gerald and I will stoke up the fire in the stove. Please do that for theirs, too. Then help them make the trip to the latrine.

"We'll need to look for facial tissues or small cloths and something to hold water so we can wash our faces when we wake up.

"I'll talk to Mr. Smith at breakfast about getting

something to seal up the cracks to keep most of this dust out."

By 7:45, they were taking their seats at the tables in the mess hall. Breakfast was a bowl of oatmeal with a pat of butter and a packet of sugar, more canned peach slices, two pieces of dry toast, and water. Still no hot tea.

They took the same seats they'd had at supper. Bunta took Hana's elbow and helped her step across the bench to get seated. "Thank you," she said, smiling.

"My friend from the hospital had told me about the wind," Dr. Tanaka told his tablemates. "He had heard from some of the staff that they occur very frequently year-round. They are particularly difficult to endure in the winter when the temperatures can often go below freezing. You never want to be outside for very long then, and especially not alone. It's too easy to get disoriented by the dust and die from hypothermia."

"One winter when I was a young person, several people in our village died from exposure," Haruto said. "It was a very sad day."

The conversation continued around how to prepare for such harsh conditions. Having spent most of their lives in warmer conditions, nobody had any good solutions.

Shortly, Mr. Smith turned on the mic.

"Good morning. I hope you all managed to stay safe during the winds. Unfortunately, this is a frequent occurrence here in the desert. You will learn how to adapt. I and the other staff will do what we can to assist you.

"I have two things to discuss with you this morning. First, I want to apologize for my tone with Dr. Tanaka yesterday evening. It had been a very difficult day, and I overreacted. The action that the doctor and his family took without prior approval is very serious. If their absence from their assigned quarters had been noticed, it could have initiated a search for them as escapees from Topaz, a very complex and difficult activity. However, I should not have reacted as I did. I want to take this opportunity to apologize to Dr. Tanaka, his family, and to each of you. My responsibility is to be your resource and advocate as we begin our life here together.

"Do not be misled, however. The rules of the community, many of which may seem confusing or unimportant to you, must be followed if our life together is going to be as trouble-free as possible. There will be consequences if you break them.

"Now, let's talk about employment opportunities at Topaz. There are many tasks that need to be done to have life here run smoothly. You will have the opportunity and are encouraged to find one of these jobs that you can do. This will not only help your family and neighbors but will give you a way to occupy yourself during the day. Many of these jobs are within the city limits. However, there are also off-site jobs, mainly in agricultural and livestock management in the surrounding area or in the nearby town of Delta.

"You will be paid for your work. While your wages will not compare to what you may have earned back in California, you need to remember that your need for money is different here. Your housing, utilities, meals, basic clothing, and recreation are provided. There is no need for an automobile or other transportation. You will only need to buy personal items and other small items at the store.

"My staff and I will be available over the next few days to talk with you about jobs that are available and how you can secure them. I urge each of you who is capable of working to do so. Your "Welcome to Topaz" booklet that you were given when you arrived describes many of the available services and recreational opportunities available to you. As you step forward to fill the jobs that support these activities, they will become available."

After breakfast, the family and the Tanakas met together in the large apartment.

Bunta spoke. "I agree with Mr. Smith. It is very important that we find jobs or activities to do. Not only will it provide us with some spending money to add to what little we have left, but more importantly, it will keep away the depression that comes from this terrible situation and boredom.

"I'll go find Mr. Smith and make an appointment for us to find things to do. The quicker we do that, the more choices there will be. Rachel, I see there will be a school. I'll get information on that as well.

"Dr. Tanaka, you said you will probably be working at the hospital. Will your wife work there, too? If not, she can come with us to the meeting with Mr. Smith."

"Thank you for the offer. We have not yet decided. May I join you to see Mr. Smith?"

They found Mr. Smith in the mess hall.

"Good morning, sir. I am Bunta Horito from Apartment B in Barracks 9. I think you remember Doctor Tanaka."

"Ah, yes. Dr. Tanaka. Allow me again to apologize for the way I responded to you yesterday. I have checked and have been told that your quarters will be ready in a week.

In the meantime, I am trying to locate beds for your family."

"I fully accept your apology. But it is I who should apologize to you for bringing up this issue in front of everybody. I certainly had no intention of putting you on the spot."

"I hope we both learned and grew from that experience, Doctor. Now, what can I do for you, gentlemen?"

"We are here to talk about jobs and school. My family is my wife, adult son, teenage daughter, and my parents, who are in Apartment A. Dr. Tanaka has a wife and two young girls."

"Excellent. You are wise to start this process early.

"Doctor, I've already been instructed to ask you to use your skills at the hospital. We will not force you to do that, but I'm sure it's where you will feel most at home. Your daughters will be enrolled in school, as will Mr. Horito's daughter, as soon as they are ready to open. Now, please tell me more about your families' skills and interests."

With the guidance of Mr. Smith, by the end of the first week, everyone got assigned to a job that they enjoyed.

Gerald and Bunta were assigned to the maintenance office. Gerald, with five other men, took care of the city's electrical system. Bunta did general maintenance.

Sandra, although she did not have a teaching certificate, was asked to teach English in the adult school. Rachel was enrolled in junior high school.

Haruto and Aiko spent their days with other elderly residents playing mah-jongg, taking craft classes, and helping out at the canteen.

Dr. Tanaka and his wife, who soon moved into their

permanent apartment in Block 3, worked at the hospital. Their girls were enrolled in school. The doctor acted as a mentor to the four nursing students who were assigned to the hospital as well.

What they all quickly discovered was that none of these areas matched the glowing descriptions of them in the promotional material.

Shortages and inefficiency were the norm. Schoolrooms lacked adequate supplies and were closed on very cold days. Customers at the canteen were constantly told the most popular items were sold out. Gerald and Bunta never had the right tools or supplies to correctly make repairs. The Tanakas too, were frustrated by the lack of supplies, medications, and poor management. Only mah-jongg seemed to go smoothly.

"At least," Bunta said to his family one evening when they were all together in the larger apartment, "the frustration of trying to do our jobs or do our studies without the right stuff does take our minds off these terrible living conditions." They were huddled together around the stove, trying to keep warm with a thirty-degree temperature and twenty-mile-per-hour winds outside.

"How are the girls doing? Have you seen Hana recently?" Sandra asked Gerald.

"They are doing well and finding their work at the hospital interesting and, like the rest of us, frustrating because of the problems caused by the camp administration's poor management.

"Hana and I are finding many things to talk about. It's nice to have a friend. I really haven't had a good friend since

Charlie. His death hurt so much I've been reluctant to make friends.

But the uncertainty of things in this camp has given me the courage to find some people other than my family to share things with. She's said that our time together means a lot to her too."

"And it doesn't hurt that she's real pretty," chimed in Rachel.

"Don't tease your brother, sweetie," Sandra replied. "It won't be too long before you'll find a nice boy in your school."

"Yuck," came the reply.

"She's asked me to go to church with her this Sunday. I told her I would. It's a Presbyterian service at Rec. 22. You all know I've never been much of a churchgoer. Looks like she may be a good influence on me," Gerald said with a slight grin.

22

TWENTY-ONE - LIFE AT TOPAZ

OCTOBER 1, 1942 - NOVEMBER 26, 1943

Other than the continuing influx of new internees—this flow continued until October 15th at about 500 a day, reaching a peak population of about eighty-two hundred—life in the camp slowly began to find its routine.

People were expected to be at their jobs eight hours a day, Monday through Friday, and four hours in the morning on Saturday. There was a forty-five-minute lunch break. Internees were paid $14.00 a month for routine work. Doctors and other skilled people were paid $19.00.

Interestingly, start times for meals and work shifted with the seasons. In summer, breakfast started at seven and work at eight. In autumn it was seven-thirty and eight-thirty, and in the winter and spring, it was eight and nine.

The weather continued to be a source of concern. Killing frosts began in late September. The first snowfall was on

October 13th. Temperatures often did not get above the low teens and the winds rarely stopped.

Matters were made worse because a company contracted to supply 7,200 tons of coal a month beginning October 1st had delivered only forty tons by the 23rd. Schools and many other activities were suspended so that coal could be reserved for the barracks, mess halls, and latrines. A large number of internees were taken from their jobs to help deliver coal from a mine 150 miles away. Coal thefts became a serious problem.

Sandra and Akio stood outside of their barracks one cold morning.

"Have you noticed that all the trees and shrubs are dying?" Aiko asked. The camp planners had planted over 7,000 trees and 10,000 shrubs throughout the camp.

"Not just going dormant but dying. Whoever decided to do the planting should have known that there is too little rain, and the soil is too alkaline. What a waste! They could have used that money on insulation for the buildings."

"When we do some planting in the spring, we'll need to figure out how to overcome those conditions," Sandra replied.

The camp administration set up elections for the Community Council in early September. It consisted of eight members, one from each of the occupied blocks. Almost immediately, friction began between the Council and the administration. The administration's attorney said all they did was appoint committees to investigate weaknesses and abuses in the management of the camp.

By the middle of December, all blocks were occupied, so plans were made to elect a council of thirty-four members.

"I'm going to run for election to this council," Gerald announced to his family. "I found the one at Tanforan made some positive differences in our lives, and I'd like to help this one do the same. Instead of just pointing out problems, I hope we can offer some positive solutions."

On the day elections were held, Gerald defeated one other candidate from his block and became their representative.

The Governor of Utah, Herbert Maw, was invited to preside over the installation on January 14th.

Hana sat in the front row of the audience with Gerald's family as he was sworn in.

In January, President Roosevelt issued an Executive Order allowing Japanese Americans, even those in the internment camps, to volunteer for the Army.

On February 1st, he activated the 442nd Regimental Combat Team, which was to be an all-Japanese unit. Many Topaz internees joined that unit, which was to become the most decorated unit for its size and length of service in US military history. The unit had a strength of about 18,000 men. Awards included seven Presidential Unit Citations, twenty-one Medals of Honor, 560 Silver Stars, 4,000 Bronze Stars, and well over 4,000 Purple Hearts. However, the process of qualifying for enlistment into the Army created one of the most controversial problems in the camps.

The War Relocation Authority, which had overseen the whole internment process and managed the camps, created a document that contained what was known as the "loyalty questionnaire." It contained two questions that created considerable controversy.

Question 27 asked, "If the opportunity presents itself

and you are found qualified, would you be willing to volunteer for the Army?"

Question 28 asked, "Will you swear unqualified allegiance to the United States of America and forswear any form of allegiance to the Japanese Emperor?"

Many of the men at Topaz refused, for many reasons, to answer "Yes" to those questions. They were called "The No-No Boys." The administration labeled them as "disloyal" and many were sent to the Tule Lake camp in Newell, California. That camp, the largest of the camps, was operated as a maximum-security segregation center run by the Army which imposed martial law on the occupants.

The most serious incident occurred on April 11th.

James Wakasa, a 63-year-old internee, was walking his dog near the fence. He was killed by a shot from a guard tower 300 yards away. The Army claimed that he was killed trying to go through the fence. The guard claimed his was meant to be a warning shot. However, the WRA investigation determined that Mr. Wakasa and his dog were several feet from the fence, and he was shot in the chest.

The incident resulted in mass strikes by workers in the camp, and about 3,000 internees attended his funeral. An unauthorized monument was erected on the site by the Topaz landscape crew. When the Secretary of War, John McCloy, heard about the monument, he ordered it removed. He was concerned about "the dangers of memorializing the victim of a 'justifiable military action."

The guard, Pfc. Philpot, was found not guilty in a court-martial.

23

GERALD AND HANA

It was Saturday. Hana was changing the dressing on a leg wound of one of the camp's maintenance crew. His team had been finishing the roof on one of the barracks when one of the men on the roof dropped a board that slid off, hitting him in the leg and opening a four-inch gash in his left thigh.

They were in a hallway off the main lobby since the outpatient clinic spaces were full. He sat in a chair while she knelt at his side.

As she removed the old bandage, she saw that the wound was beginning to show signs of infection.

"Mr. Kobayashi, your wound is beginning to get infected. I need to go to supply to get some cream to put on it. Don't worry. We've caught it early. I'll be right back."

She found Dr. Tanaka. "Good morning, Doctor. I need a prescription for some penicillin ointment. One of my patients has a wound that's getting infected."

"Certainly, Hana. It's good to see you. Here's the

prescription, but we may be out. Our supply of medicines has been running very low. If there's none left, get some oregano oil and have the patient take a few drops three times a day. Have him come back in two days."

"Thank you, sir."

Approaching the supply room attendant, she said, "Here's a prescription for some of that new penicillin ointment. A patient's wound is getting infected."

"Sorry ma'am, we've used up all we were sent. Did the doctor suggest oregano oil as a substitute?"

"Yes, he did. Do you have that?"

The attendant gave her a small bottle. "It's very spicy. Have the patient mix it with a little water to take it."

Returning to the patient, Hana handed him the bottle with the instructions from the doctor and the attendant.

She then put on the new bandage. "Keep this dry, and I'll see you back here on Monday."

As he left, Hana sat in the empty chair.

This is no way to have to practice medicine. It's so frustrating. If it weren't for Dr. Tanaka and Rika, Nari, and Miyu, I think I would go do something else. I'm glad Gerald has the afternoon off. It'll be nice to walk with him around the camp. He's such a good listener.

She and Gerald had been spending most of their free time together for the last several months. They both felt a little awkward much of the time since neither had had many close friends, let alone one of the opposite sex in their lives.

Early in the relationship, Gerald had shared with her. "Hana, I'm having difficulty. I enjoy our time together. It helps me forget for a while where we are. But most of the time, I feel like I don't know what to do or say around you."

"I feel that too. But as I said that day when you helped us with the stove, you are the nicest man I've ever met. You're the perfect person for me to learn not to be awkward around." She lightly touched his cheek.

Today, she was waiting for him outside the maintenance building when he finished his work.

Recently, when they would meet, a hug and a light kiss had become a regular thing. Today was no different, except that Hana held the hug a little longer than usual.

"You okay?" Gerald asked, sensing a different mood.

"Not really. Today was more frustrating than usual at the hospital. The shortages keep getting in the way of good medical practice. I sometimes think I should do something else."

"I get your frustration. It's the same way with my job. We can't get parts or supplies. Most of the repairs we do on the electrical system are like putting that new super-strong, wide adhesive tape the military is using on the problem to hold things together. It'll work for a while, but sooner or later, things are gonna fall apart.

"However, I'm discovering that what I learned in school and working for the Navy is not the only way to fix a problem. Being able to work with what you have, not what you'd like, is a useful skill."

"But when your "patch" fails, we just lose power. When mine does, someone may die."

"You're right. That's not a good comparison. But I hope you'll find a way to stick with nursing. This situation won't last forever, and the things you learn in a difficult situation will make you an even better nurse when you're back in a normal environment. Now, let's just enjoy this afternoon."

She took his arm as they walked. The summer heat had broken, and, for a change, there was no wind or dust blowing. As they got to the northwest side of the camp, they could easily see Topaz Mountain and the others surrounding the high plateau where the camp sat. They all appeared purple in the distance.

"This area certainly has beauty," Gerald said pensively. "If only we weren't in the midst of this horror."

"Gerald, have you thought about what you'll do when they release us? Despite my frustration today, I plan to finish my studies after I go see my family in Hiroshima, then when I graduate, maybe return there to work in a hospital with my mother."

"I'm not sure. It will depend a lot on what my family wants to do. They're not sure they want to go back to San Francisco. They would have to start their lives all over again, surrounded by the memories of what they'd lost. Mama thinks that since they have to start again, maybe a new location might be easier. She's even talked about reaching out to her parents and maybe moving to be with them in Oklahoma. Papa thinks it would be easier to go back to familiar surroundings. I'll probably end up going wherever they decide."

"But that's for later. This is now," he said, sliding his arm around her waist and pulling her closer. I think it's time we got to know each other a little better. If only we could find someplace to be alone."

"Why, Mr. Horito, what are you suggesting?" Pushing back from him, she had a coy smile and a sparkle in her eyes.

"Don't act surprised with me, Ms. Sato. I'm aware of the

changes in your body when we hug. Like now," he added, moving his eyes slightly downward.

Hana reflexively crossed her arms over her breasts and blushed.

Gerald laughed.

"Since you've already made assumptions about my moral character," Hana replied, giving him a punch to his shoulder, "it shouldn't surprise you that I think I've already discovered a place that might be perfect for us.

"You may not have noticed, but Apartment F next to mine has never been occupied. Block management is using it for storage, and the windows have been covered over. Someone's taped up a hand-lettered sign saying NO ENTRY, SSTAFF ONLY to the door, but it's not locked. There's plenty of room on the floor and even a pile of blankets that might be useful."

"I am surprised—and delighted! When can we check it out?"

"Well, how about tonight? Then if we feel the need to do so, we can confess our sins at church tomorrow," she said with a big grin.

"Hana, you are something else. What time?"

"How about 7:45? We'll be done with supper by 7:00. That will give me time to get ready."

"What about your roommates? Won't they be curious?"

"They already suspect something is going on between us. We've been going regularly to the library in the evening recently. I'll just suggest they go without me tonight. We should have a couple of hours."

"Okay, I'll see you at supper." He tried to give her a strong kiss, but she drew back.

"Be patient, lover. It won't be long. Oh, and don't eat too much at supper. We learned in school that strenuous activity is not good on a full stomach," she said with that coy smile again.

They sat across from each other at supper. Gerald's family and the four girls crowded at one table. The conversation was about their day, with its frustrations.

"I guess I'm the only one who had a good day," Sandra said. "My twenty students are really eager to improve their English. It's a real boost to work with them."

Even without Hana's earlier comment, Gerald just picked at his food.

What have I gotten myself into? Hana seems so much more sophisticated than I am. I hope I don't disappoint her.

"Are you feeling okay, Son?" Bunta asked. "You're not eating much, and you seem elsewhere."

"We've got a problem over at the electrical shop that I couldn't correct this morning. I think I'll go back over there for a while after supper.

Hana kicked his leg under the table.

At 7:40, Gerald quietly climbed the stairs between E and F. The hallway light was out.

He slowly opened the door and stepped into the room, closing the door behind him. He slid off his shoes.

At first, he could see nothing. Then, the light from a candle appeared.

"Hello, darling. I hoped you might be a little early."

As his eyes adjusted to the candlelight, he saw her standing there, arms to her side and a smile on her face.

She was wearing a long-sleeved flowered silk blouse with small buttons in front. Her skirt was dark-colored, pleated, and came to just below her knees. She was barefoot.

He could see that she had put her long hair up in a bun. It was held in place by what appeared to be crossed chopsticks. And there was a small white flower stuck in front of the bun. He couldn't breathe.

I've never seen anything so beautiful. And she has a flower in her hair! How could she possibly have found a flower in this Godforsaken place?

After what seemed like forever, she moved toward him. "It's okay, dear. You can breathe." She took his hand in hers and brought it to her lips.

She then led him to what looked like a footlocker on which she had placed a blanket.

"Let's sit for a minute and talk. That will help us both relax."

"First, thank you for being here. I was afraid maybe I was too forward earlier and scared you off.

"I want you to know that I'm just as nervous as you are. This is all new to me. I may act like I know what I'm doing, but that's just from nurse training. Being in anatomy class and around people with all sorts of reproductive problems, you think you've figured things out about sex."

"But I assure you, I'm no expert. If this is going to be the beautiful, memorable evening we both are looking forward to and deserve, we're going to figure it out together."

She gave him a long, deep kiss on the mouth and sat back. A fragrance of jasmine followed her.

"Now, so far, I've done all the talking. It's your turn."

"I'll admit that, at first, I was a little taken aback by your forwardness. Then I remembered some of the stories guys told about how their first time was a disaster, and I decided if you were as comfortable as you appeared, I was damn fortunate that my first time was going to be with you.

"Now I have a question. Where did you get that flower?"

She laughed. "I'm glad you noticed it. The girls and I brought some seeds with us. We planted them in tin cans we got from the kitchen as soon as we got here and have been hovering over them since. One just put out its first bloom this morning. The girls are going to be angry with me for taking it, but I think they'll understand.

"Just one other thing. I've learned in anatomy that males and females have different paces in sex. You guys tend to go faster than us girls. Since this is the first time for both of us, we may not have much control, but I ask that we try to match our pace to each other. But, if it doesn't go perfectly this time, we can keep practicing 'til we get it perfect.

"And these will help us get in lots of practice," she said as she reached into her pocket and brought out a handful of matchbook-sized colorful paper boxes.

"What are those?" Gerald looked confused.

"Sweetie, if you don't know what these are, maybe we need to be doing something else."

"Oh," he said, blushing.

"I swiped these packs from supply. There are three to a pack. The Army gives them to all the troops for disease prevention. You'd be horrified at what we learned in school about what soldiers brought home to their wives and girlfriends from earlier wars. I'm not worried about disease, but we certainly don't want to get pregnant in this place."

She stood up, bringing him with her. They wrapped

their arms around each other and pulled in close. Gerald took her head in his hands and gave her a few gentle kisses. The fragrance of jasmine filled his nostrils. She responded, kissing him deeply, and pushing her tongue into his mouth.

Gerald could feel himself getting larger. His heart raced. He stood back. In the soft light, he could make out the outline of her nipples against her blouse.

"Honey. I'm not sure I can do this slowly, but I'll try."

He reached up and touched the small white flower in her hair.

"May I take your flower?" he asked.

She bent close to his ear.

"Honey, I believe that's what we're here for," she whispered as she nibbled his earlobe.

She moved back a pace, reached up, took the flower, kissed it, and gave it to him. She then pulled the wooden sticks from her hair, allowing it to fall to her shoulders, shimmering in the candlelight. She gave her head a shake and pulled her hair back off her face.

Moving forward, she pulled Gerald's shirt from his pants and began to unbutton it. When she was done, she slipped it from his shoulders.

"I like a man with no hair on his chest," she said and bent forward and gently kissed each of his nipples, feeling their hardness on her lips.

As she stood back, Gerald tentatively reached out, placing his hands on her breasts.

"That feels so good," she said quietly. Then he began to unbutton her blouse, slipping it off her shoulders as she had done with his.

She shivered slightly. Her bra was a simple white

garment with a hook in the front. Her breasts swelled beneath it.

"How do I unhook the clasp?" Reaching forward, he took the edge of each cup and twisted. Nothing happened.

"Here, let me help." She put her hands on his and pushed them together. The bra unhooked. She slipped it from her shoulders, and it dropped to the floor.

He pulled her to him. Her skin felt like silk, and the warmth from her body seemed to flow into his soul.

"Gerald," she whispered.

My God! This is amazing. I could stay just like this forever.

Sliding his arms down her back to her waist, his fingers found the zipper on her skirt.

He pulled the tab down. The skirt puddled at her feet as she stepped out of it, kicking it to the side.

Then she reached out and unfastened his belt and zipper and, kneeling, slid his pants down, exposing the large bulge in his shorts.

"My, but you are big," she said as she pulled his shorts down enough to uncover the tip, which she gently kissed,

Gerald groaned.

He took her elbows and helped her stand.

"You've laid out some blankets? I think I need to sit down before my knees give out."

She picked up the candle and led him past a stack of boxes to a pile of blankets. She set the candle on a low box next to the blankets, slid off her panties, and lay down on her back, her right arm folded behind her head, her left one loose by her side.

"Come to me, my lover. She extended her hand.

Gerald quickly stepped out of his shorts, took her hand,

and lay beside her, placing his hand on her breast and laying his head on her outstretched arm. He kissed her cheek.

"I have to tell you, I have never seen a naked woman before. I'm fortunate to have waited for one as beautiful as you."

"Nor have I seen a naked man. The ones in anatomy don't count. They're cold and grey and certainly don't respond to my touch as you have," she said with that coy grin again as she placed her hand around his penis.

She rolled him onto his back as she sat and straddled him. She gently took his penis, unrolled one of the condoms, and placed it on him, then slowly slid him into her, wincing slightly.

"Am I hurting you?"

"No, just a little discomfort. It's over."

It took all of his concentration not to move his hips.

"I know it's difficult, but can we just lie still here like this for a moment? I want to sense the contours of your body and feel your breath on my cheek. We have the rest of the evening for passion."

Then, shortly, she kissed his lips and slowly began to move her hips. Gerald thought he was going to explode.

Two hours later, after using up one pack of condoms, they were snuggled together, one of the blankets pulled over them.

"You are wonderful, Hana. And a beautiful lover. I have never felt such joy. I'll remember this evening for the rest of my life. Thank you."

"I thank you too, my love. In the hospital, I've seen the

results of men who were rough lovers, and there was mild concern in the back of my mind. You have completely put me at ease tonight.

"I'm looking forward to many times like this."

She gently kissed his cheek and lay her head on his shoulder.

24

THE END OF YEAR ONE

The family—Gerald, his parents, grandparents, and Rachel, were returning, along with Hana and Rika, from their small vegetable plot. It was one of many that the internees had been allowed to set up in a large field outside the security fence. Since early spring, they had tilled, fertilized, planted, and watered their 12x12 garden. Haruto and Aiko had decided which crops to grow. They picked their favorites, none of which were on the menu in the dining hall. They chose azuki, daikon, cabbage, and potatoes. Hana and the girls added strawberries and small melons. Everyone took turns tending and harvesting. It had been a very good year. With the small kitchen that they were allowed to build at the edge of the building, they had enjoyed fresh vegetables and fruit since early spring.

Now the season was over. The harsh winter that had been predicted was upon them. The last few weeks had been much colder than the previous year. It rarely got above 55 in the daytime, and the evenings were already often well below freezing.

"This will probably be our last harvest," said Aiko. "I shall miss these small joys," she murmured softly, as she held up a handful of cabbage.

"We may get a few more potatoes," said Horito. "I'll check back in a few days."

"What concerns me the most," said Gerald, "is the coal situation. At our council meeting last evening, we were told that there's been a problem with delivery for the last two months. If that problem doesn't get fixed soon, there may be very little for the stoves in our rooms. We were asked to find volunteers who could chop wood for the stoves to mix with the coal. That means the fires will have to be tended several times on cold nights. It could be a real problem for people like Obachan and Ojichan."

Little did he know that his prediction would come tragically true.

Sunday night, October 25th, the temperature dropped to zero degrees with a thirty-mile wind. As they were turning out the light, Bunta said to Gerald, "I'll check on my parents in a couple of hours. Please do the same at about 2:00."

On his way back from checking on Hana and the girls just before daylight, Gerald thought, *I'll check on Ojichan and Obachan once more.*

As he entered the room, he immediately knew something was wrong. *It's way too cold in here. What happened to the fire?*

"Ojhichan, Obachan wake up.!" He shook them gently, then roughly. They both moaned but did not open their eyes.

"Papa, Mama," he said, bursting into their room. "It's Ojichan and Obachan. They're in trouble. Bring blankets and come help me. Rachel, dress warmly and go get Hana and the girls. Then go find Mr. Smith and tell him to bring a doctor."

They were piling blankets on and rubbing the elders' arms and legs as Hana, leading the other girls, burst into the room.

Hana reached under the blankets, put her hand on Aiko's chest, and did the same with Haruto.

"It's serious hypothermia. They are alive, but just barely. Your grandfather seems worse," she said, looking at Gerald.

We've got to try to make them warmer until the doctor gets here. Everybody, reach under the blankets and rub their hands and feet vigorously!"

Mr. Smith and the doctor rushed into the room, followed by Rachel.

"Mama, are they gonna be okay?" Rachel cried out in tears. Sandra just hugged her.

"Severe hypothermia, Doctor," Hana reported. We need to get them to the hospital."

Placing his hand on Haruto's chest, he said, "I agree. You know we don't have an ambulance, but I brought my car. The heater's on high.

"Let's get them into it quickly. Hana, you and Miya ride in the back with them. Mr. Horito, come sit in the passenger seat. You'll need to sign some papers."

"Mr. Smith, please see that everybody else follows us as quickly as they can."

Mr. Smith brought his car around, and they all headed to

the hospital. By the time they got there, Gerald and Bunta were standing in the lobby.

Sandra and Rachel went to them, and they all hugged.

"The doctor and the girls have taken them back to the emergency room," Bunta said.

He told me we should sit down. They'll let us know something soon."

"Mrs. Horito, Nari and I will stay here with you," Rika said. "Can we get some water or tea? Nari has gone to get some hot towels."

"Tea would be wonderful. Thank you."

As Rika left, Nari returned with several hot towels. "Wipe your face and neck with these. It will help you to relax a little." She handed them to the family.

No one spoke. Sandra held Bunta's hand. Rachel leaned against Gerald's shoulder. The dimly lit lobby smelled of antiseptic. There was the occasional sound of voices in the distance. Rika returned with cups of tea on a tray.

An hour later, the doctor and Hana came into the lobby and walked to the family. Everybody stood up. Hana walked and stood between Gerald and Bunta, taking their hands.

"I am Dr. Kirby. I am so sorry to tell you that Mr. and Mrs. Horito have died. Sandra sobbed and reached out to Bunta as Rachel hugged her. Gerald put his arm around Hana's waist.

"We tried several different methods to elevate their body temperature, but in both of them, it was too low for them to recover. Ms. Sato can give you the details if you want them."

"If any of you want to see them, we can take you to their room."

"Yes, Doctor, we would," Bunta replied. "Gerald and

Rachel, please let Hana take you to them and go ahead. Your mother and I will be there shortly. We need to ask the doctor and Mr. Smith some questions."

Hana took Gerald's hand and put her arm over Rachel's shoulders, then walked with them from the room.

Bunta looked at Dr. Kirby and Mr. Smith. "What happens now, gentlemen? My parents have gravesites in a cemetery in San Francisco. As you know, we have neither the resources nor the freedom to transport them there or to pay for a funeral."

Mr. Smith spoke up. "The administration will handle burial here if you choose. However, I suspect you would not choose that. You may select any of the pastors who conduct services here to do the funeral."

"I do have another suggestion. We have a contract with a funeral home in Delta. They will cremate your parents and deliver the ashes back to you for a memorial service. You may keep the ashes in your home, or the Roman Catholic priest has built several niches behind the altar. He would be glad to store them there until you return home. There will be no cost to your family for any of these services."

"Doctor, may we leave the bodies here until tomorrow? Our family will discuss this and get back to you."

"Certainly. Mr. Horito. I will see to it that happens. If you like, one of your family may sit with them while they are here."

"Perhaps. Now, Sandra and I would like to go see our parents."

When they got to the room, they found Gerald, Rachel, and Hana sitting in chairs. They all came close to the two beds which had been pushed together.

"They look so peaceful. It's as if they are sleeping," Sandra said. "I do hope they were not aware of what was happening."

"They would not have been aware," Hana said. "Hypothermia is called the painless death."

Bunta spoke. "Hana, as you've probably noticed, we are not a practicing religious family. However, I think we would all agree that, although we don't express it, faith in God is important to us.

"Gerald tells us that you attend church fairly regularly and that you've even dragged him with you a couple of times. Could you offer a prayer? Nothing fancy, of course. I don't want to put you on the spot."

"Of course. Let's all join hands."

"Dear God, we ask you to accept the souls of these dear people into your presence and to bring your gentle healing to those of us who mourn. Amen."

"Thank you. Sandra and I have said how glad you and Gerald found each other. You are a gift to our family and have helped bring light into this terrible place.

"Now, Dr. Kirby says they will keep the bodies here until we figure out what to do next. He also offered for us to have someone sit with them until tomorrow."

"I will do that, Papa. Hana, would you sit with me?"

"Certainly. I just need to let the charge nurse know so she can find a replacement for my next shift. Why don't you walk with your family back to Mr. Smith's car while I do that?" She kissed him on the cheek and left the room.

Bunta spoke. "Gerald, since there is no way we can get Ojichan and Obachan back to San Francisco, Mr. Smith has suggested that we have them cremated and the ashes kept here until we go home.

"Their wishes were to be cremated, so this sounds like a good solution. We can bury them in their plot when we get home."

"I certainly agree with that, Papa. You and Mama go ahead and get those arrangements started. I'll stay here until someone comes to pick them up."

They all went to find Mr. Smith.

As they got to the car, Gerald hugged each of them. "Try to get some sleep. I'll see you soon."

When he got back to the room, Hana was setting some cups of tea and little cakes on the bedside table. They kissed and hugged and held on to each other for a long time.

"I thought we could use a little nourishment," she said. "and I might be able to find some fruit juice later.

"That was certainly nice what your father said to me. I knew they liked me, especially Rachel, but I had no idea their feelings were so strong."

"They think of you as family and want to be here for you since your family is so far away."

She handed him a cup of tea and a cake. They sat silently, eating and watching over his grandparents.

"Gerald, you seem troubled. Is it the death of your grandparents, or is there something more?"

"Honey, it's a little scary how you can read me. Yes, there is, and it's why I so quickly offered to keep watch and asked you to sit with me. There's something I need to talk with you about."

"Hmm, this sounds really serious." She put her hand on his knee.

"Ever since we got here, I've been trying to come up with some way to get my family away from this place. I figured I could get away and head east. With my education, I should be able to get a good job and earn enough money so they could come live with me. I'm sure you noticed that several families have been allowed to leave because they had family or someone who would sponsor them further east. I've even thought about contacting Mama's parents in Oklahoma City, but I have no idea how to do that. And I know she would never ask them for any favors.

"I have talked with some of the other men who say there is a network of people who will help me get away from here if I can get to Delta. I've just never followed through because it always seemed too great a risk. But Ojichan and Obachan's death because of this place makes me see I must take this risk for my family. I'm going to ask one of the men to set things up."

Hana stood up and moved her chair until they were facing, knees touching. She took both his hands in hers.

"Gerald, darling. These past two months have been magical for me. Our times of intimacy, our conversations, and our walks have shown me what an amazing person you are and how we, as a couple, are so much more than just two people in love. I've been rethinking my whole future.

"The thought of not having you in my life frightens me and makes me very sad. But then I try to put myself in your place, and I think I understand what you feel you must do. Tell me more of your plans to get away from here."

Gerald told her what he had learned.

"There is a network of good, loyal Americans who are angered at what their government has done to loyal

Japanese citizens. They have agreed, at great personal risk, to help anybody who wants to escape the camp to do so.

"I'm told that if I can get through the fence, there will be a bicycle hidden in the brush about one hundred yards from the camp. That will help me get to the highway about ten miles from here, where a truck will take me where I want to go. They've done it with two other men in the past six months. It takes about a month to get everything set up."

Hana sat silently, holding his hands. She looked deeply into his eyes as if she were searching his soul.

Finally, she spoke. "I wish there were some other way, but wishing won't change the reality. I know you must do this. How will you tell your family?"

"I'm not going to tell them. If they don't know anything, then there is nothing they can be forced to tell the authorities. You must tell them nothing. I don't want them put in danger.

"Also, I won't tell you exactly when I'm going to leave. That way, your surprise will be as genuine as my family's."

She pulled back, standing up with anger in her eyes.

"No, Gerald! I don't accept that. I won't live with that uncertainty for the next month. You'll just have to trust me that I'll know how to act when you leave."

"I'm just trying to protect you," he said, standing.

"I don't need your protection. I need your trust!"

Oh shit. I've really misjudged her.

"I apologize, dear. Please forgive me. I'm still learning what a strong person you are." He put his arms around her waist. She pressed against him.

"I'm told that the arrangements will happen very quickly at the last minute and that my escape will be in the late evening. I won't know the exact date until that morning. I'll tell you as soon as I know."

"That will work. Now, let's turn our attention back on your grandparents."

In the early afternoon, Bunta came into the room.

"Mr. Smith has made the arrangements. The funeral home is on the way to pick up the bodies. You can leave."

That night, as he lay on his cot, Gerald felt a deep sadness. He'd just lied to the person he loved most in the world.

His reason for escaping the camp had suddenly changed.

The arrangements that he had made were no longer to help him get his parents out. Tomorrow he would tell the network to make plans with a renewed purpose,

They were to start him on the road to Japan where he would become a spy against his own country. A country which, in his mind, had murdered his beloved grandparents.!

25

ESCAPE TO SAN FRANCISCO, CALIFORNIA

NOVEMBER 27 - DECEMBER 4, 1943

The sun had slipped behind Topaz Mountain over his right shoulder as he pulled the bicycle from under the pile of brush. With no moon, it was the perfect night for his escape. It was right where the men told him it would be. He was about one hundred yards south of the main gate to the camp. Now, he just had to follow the dirt road past Delta for the ten miles to where it connected with US 50.

It was a bitterly cold night. His breath seemed to freeze in the air in front of his face as he started riding. Fortunately, there was little wind for a change, so the constant dust did not obscure the ruts in the road.

He followed the dirt road until it dead-ended at US 50.

I figured right about traffic. He had seen only two sets of headlights on roads closer to Delta. With luck, there won't be anybody around when the truck arrives.

Laying his bike in the shallow ditch on the side of the road, he checked his watch. *Great. I'm ten minutes early. Hope the guy's on schedule. It's gonna get really cold quickly in this ditch.*

He saw headlights approaching from the south. He stretched out over the bike, using his dark clothes to conceal it. Two vehicles, a car and a truck with a loud exhaust, sped by without slowing. The driver in the truck flicked a cigarette butt out the window. It showered sparks as it hit the road right in front of him. A few notes of a western song floated down along with the butt.

Good. Nobody will see me unless they're looking for me.

A few minutes later, he heard a truck coming from the north. The lights blinked twice, and it stopped at the intersection of the highway and the dirt road.

The window on the passenger side rolled down.

"Quick, toss your bike in the back and follow it in. Put the tarp and some of that hay over you and the bike. We'll stop down the road a piece after we're well clear of Delta, and you can come up here. I heard they caught a man and his wife from the camp trying to sneak onto a freight in Delta last week, so security might have been stepped up some."

Gerald did as he was told, pulling the tarp over him as the driver engaged the gears, and they were off.

After about thirty minutes, Gerald felt the truck slowing and rocking as it pulled off the road.

He raised the corner of the canvas and looked out. He could see nothing except the stars. The crunch of boots on gravel came toward him.

"You can come on out now. It's okay. Sorry I had to do

that to you. Hope you're not frozen. Come on and get in the cab where it's warm."

They climbed in at the same time, Gerald setting his backpack on the floorboard.

The driver, a man in his sixties, dressed in rough western wear, complete with a weathered, stained ten-gallon hat and a bandanna, reached out his hand.

"Howdy, I'm Casey. They didn't tell me your name."

"I'm Gerald." He grabbed the man's hand. The callouses made it feel like a glove. "Thank you for picking me up."

"There ain't much on this road. And this time of night there won't be hardly no traffic, so you can relax. We'll stay on 50 'til we get into Nevada in about two hours, then we'll cut south on to 93 into Las Vegas. That'll take us another six hours. There's a roadside café and fuel stop right at the border. They don't close 'til ten, so we can stop there for gas and some food. It ain't real good, but it's hot and cheap. Besides, the Injun who owns it doesn't mind if we pull off to the side and catch some shut eye.

"'Scuse me for saying anything, but you don't look Japanese. Were you in the camp 'cause of family?"

"Yes. I'm half-Japanese. My father is full-blooded Japanese, born in this country, and, like me, is an American citizen. We were both working for Navy contractors when our family was picked up. My mother was born in Oklahoma City. Somehow, I got her features, and even during the racism before Pearl Harbor, nobody thought I was Japanese.

"My parents, my father's parents, my sister, and I lived in San Francisco. We got to Topaz in September of last year. My grandparents died from the cruel, cold winter weather a couple of months ago. It was because of that that I decided to escape and try to get my family out. I'm going to Las Vegas to get a job and see if the Army will let them come live with me."

"What about you?" Gerald asked. "Why are you risking arrest to help me?"

"My story's sorta like yours. My younger brother was a medical missionary in Japan for three years between 1935 and '38. He married a young Japanese girl who worked with him caring for the villagers. They came home to Los Angeles at the end of his assignment. They were working at a Catholic hospital in the city when his wife was detained. The Army said he didn't have to go to the camp but, obviously, he did. They work together at the camp hospital. I've offered to help them get out, but they feel like it's important for them to stay there.

"Since I haul goods all over the southwest, he got word to the secret grapevine that's in all the camps, the same one that got us together, that I was available to help people like you get away from the camps. So far, I've hauled more than eighty people in the back or up here. Mostly, I've taken them East. Only a couple have gone to Nevada.

"Now, why don't you just relax and maybe take a nap? I'll wake you when we get to the café."

With the truck's heater putting out more warmth than he'd enjoyed in months, along with the hum of the tires, it didn't take Gerald long to fall asleep. As he dozed off, the faces of Hana and his family in their barren rooms floated before him. Tears rolled down his cheeks.

The rocking of the truck as it pulled off the road into the

parking lot of the café and up to the fuel pumps woke Gerald.

"While you fill the tank, I'll check the oil, antifreeze, and tires. There's nothing between here and the outskirts of Las Vegas. We shor don't want to have a problem out there. He pointed southwest.

While they were working on the truck, the owner came out of the building.

"Hi, Casey. Traveling kinda late, aren't you?"

He was a tall, almost skinny Indian with long grey braids and weathered brown skin. He had on a heavy coat that reminded Gerald of an Indian blanket he'd seen in a store. Jeans, moccasins, and a Seattle Indians ball cap completed his outfit.

"Evenin', Red Horse. Yeah, so I was hoping you'd let us rest awhile over by the edge of your place after we eat."

"Sure. Move your truck when you're finished, and come on in. I just put on the last pot of coffee for tonight, and Songbird will rustle you up something to eat."

"Red Horse, this is Gerald," Casey said as they walked through the front door. "He snuck out of Topaz so he could find a job and try to get his family, so I'm carryin' him to Las Vegas."

Red Horse took Gerald's hand. "You don't look like a Jap. How come you were in the camp?"

Gerald repeated the story he'd told Casey earlier. "In the eyes of the Army, I'm just as Japanese and just as suspect as my grandparents. Prejudice-driven fear is an ugly thing."

"Don't talk to me about prejudice, white man. Me and my ancestors have lived with Army and settler persecution since long before you were born.

"But for tonight, we're just three men trying to survive and stay warm. Come on into the store.

"The squaw behind the counter is Songbird, my wife. She may look small, but don't cross her. She can be mean like a snake," he said with a laugh as he ducked a spoon tossed at his head. "Have a seat at the counter and tell her what you want to eat."

Over hot coffee, eggs, sausage, and some sort of sweet bread Songbird said her grandmother taught her to make, they talked about the war, life on the reservation, and in the internment camp.

Casey paid for the food and the gas, and he and Gerald stood up to head to the truck.

"Thanks for your hospitality, friend," Casey said. " I shor don't see how you stay so skinny eating Songbird's cooking. I'll see you on the next trip."

"I'm just about to close for the night. If y'all want to stretch out on the floor instead of sitting up in your truck, you're welcome to. Remember the privy's out behind the building. I just hung a fresh Sears catalog on the nail," he said, smiling.

It was still dark when Casey poked Gerald.

"Time to get moving if we want to get to Las Vegas before too many people are up. I'll let you out on the edge of town.

I know a cheap motel left over from the building of Boulder Dam. You can stay there while you're looking for work.

Now you can sleep for a little while if you need to. Then, you'll need to stay awake to keep me from nodding off. I'll wake you."

Just as they were pulling out on the road and Gerald was pulling his cap over his eyes, Casey let out a loud "Oh shit!"

"What happened?" Gerald said, startled.

"There's a state trooper coming up fast behind us, lights flashing. We may be screwed."

Then he thought for a second. "Did they take photos of you at the camp?"

"No. Why?"

"Well, if this guy's looking for an escaped Japanese, we're probably okay since you don't look anything like a Jap. Let's just stay calm and see what happens."

The trooper whizzed past them. Lights, but no siren.

"Whew! I almost peed in my pants. Hope whatever he's in a hurry to get to doesn't slow us down.

"Now, get some sleep. I'll wake you in about an hour."

They arrived at the outskirts at about seven o'clock. Casey pulled into a busy truck stop.

"This is where you get off. The motel is about four miles down this road on the left."

He shook Gerald's hand. "Good luck. I hope you can get your folks out."

"Thank you, Casey. I enjoyed our time together. I really admire what you're doing to help people out. Good luck. Don't get caught."

He climbed down from the cab, retrieved his bicycle, waved, and headed into town.

26

ESCAPE TO SAN FRANCISCO

NOVEMBER 27 - DECEMBER 4, 1943

He found the motel and checked in.

"I just got off a ride at the truck stop up the road. I need a room. I want to catch a bus to San Francisco. Do you know the schedule and where the bus station is located?"

"I think there's one leaving tonight. The station's about a mile from here. Go back to the stop sign you came through and take a left. The station's just down that road. You can't miss it."

"Thanks. I'll ride on down there now. Back in a while to get the room."

"No rush. We got plenty of empties."

He found the Greyhound Bus station and bought a one-way ticket with most of his remaining cash. The bus left at eight that night and would get in early afternoon the next day.

He returned to the motel and went into the office, bringing his bike with him.

"The bus leaves at eight tonight, so I'll just need the room for a hot shower and a nap."

"That'll be three dollars. Here's your key."

"Sir, I've got this bike I won't be needing anymore. Would you take it off my hands for the room and seven dollars?"

The clerk came around the counter and took hold of the bike, looking it over carefully.

"I'll give you six," he said, pulling the cash out of the register.

"I'll take it. Thank you."

Leaving the bike in the office, he headed to the room.

Now for that shower and nap!

He woke up about six o'clock, pulled on his boots and jacket, grabbed his pack and cap, and headed out the door.

"Thanks again for buying the bike," he said, sticking his head in the office door. "Have a good evening."

The clerk waved, and Gerald headed to the bus.

He got a pop at the food counter and ate the last of the biscuits he'd taken from the mess hall at Topaz. The taste of the biscuit brought back the sounds, smells, and images of his family eating in the mess hall.

By now, his family would be very concerned about where he was, and the camp staff would be alarmed. He hoped his absence would not bring any harm to his family.

Shortly before eight, he got on the bus, pushed his bag above his head, and settled in for the trip.

The next afternoon, the bus pulled into the station in San Francisco. Gerald got off and went inside to the lunch counter. Sitting down, he motioned to the girl behind the counter. "I'll have a cup of black coffee and a sweet roll, please." He'd almost ordered tea, then remembered that not many Anglos drank tea.

He sipped the coffee. *That's not bad. I could get used to it.*

Now, he had to get to his old neighborhood and look up the address he'd been given at the camp. If the guy at the camp was right, that's where he'd find contacts that could get him to Tokyo.

He finished his coffee and roll and headed into the city. He found the address easily in about forty minutes.

He was standing in front of what had once been a two-story brick warehouse, now abandoned. The doors and windows were boarded up, and weeds grew up through the concrete sidewalk.

Akira's instructions were to go to the north side of the building. There, he'd find a four-foot square metal door, two feet off the ground, that appeared to be padlocked. With a hard object, he was to give three quick knocks, pause, and give two slow knocks and wait. He did this and waited for about two minutes. Then the door, padlock and all, swung open. Gerald stepped over the high sill and entered a dimly lit large room, the only light filtering through the boarded-up windows. He immediately felt a sharp point at his throat.

"Akira sent me," he whispered. The sharp point did not move. Then footsteps approached, and a heavily accented voice said, "What is your name?"

"Gerald Horito."

"Where did you come from?"

"Topaz."

"OK. The sharp point disappeared. An electric lantern was turned on and Gerald saw the two men. The younger one to his right still held his knife pointed at Gerald. The other was older, with short-cropped grey hair.

Bowing slightly, the older one said, "I am Mr. Sasaki. Akira said you want to disrupt the US war effort."

"Yes, I want to go to Tokyo and be trained in sabotage and return here or to Hawaii."

"That would be very difficult and costly. Why would we do that?"

"I believe my knowledge of electrical engineering and the ability to pass as White make me a very valuable asset."

"Wait here." The older man left the room as the man with the knife moved closer.

Within a few minutes, the older man returned.

"My colleagues agree. You are worth the effort. It will take a while to arrange. Can you find a place to stay for a few days?"

"Probably, but I have no money."

"That's not a problem. Here's one hundred dollars for a room and food. Be back here exactly at this time in two days."

Two days later, Gerald again knocked at the door. It opened immediately. This time, they led him to a small room in the center of the second floor. Three men and a woman sat around a table where papers and documents were spread around.

"Mr. Horito, we need to take your photo and put together some papers. We've arranged for you to sign on as a deckhand on a freighter going to New Guinea. From there, you will be smuggled to Osaka and then taken to the Army Special Operations training camp outside Tokyo. Take this money and buy clothes and supplies suitable for the voyage and return here at this time tomorrow."

They stood up, and all four people in the room bowed to Gerald and wished him safe travels. He returned the bow, thanked them, and left.

That afternoon, he went down to shops near the docks where he bought a large canvas duffel bag, work clothes, a black wool knit cap, gloves, waterproof boots, toiletries, a couple of paperback books, a notepad, pencils, and a small camera and film.

He got back to the room he had booked earlier. As he was arranging his purchases in the duffel, a feeling of anticipation and apprehension settled in his chest. Images from his nightmare of his old friend, Charlie, and burning ships materialized before his eyes.

Am I doing the right thing? Am I honoring or dishonoring my family? Would Hana understand?

The next day, he returned to the building. This time, however, he was led not into the building but into a waiting car. In twenty minutes, they arrived at the docks and pulled up near a rusty cargo ship flying the flag of Spain. Gerald could just make out the faded name on the bows: Santa Maria.

Before they got out of the car, Mr. Sasaki handed him a small brown envelope.

"Here is your new identity card and some money. We have only changed your last name. Until you get to your destination, you are Gerald Houser. The Master of this vessel knows only that you have agreed to work for your passage to

New Guinea. They will expect you to do general non-skilled cargo and maintenance labor. You will be given a bunk and meals but no pay. The trip will take about twenty days. There are four officers and about fifteen seamen aboard. Two others are working for passage like you. They are going no farther than New Guinea. You will be met on the docks at Lae."

The grey-haired man then led him up the gangplank. A Spaniard in a rumpled Master's uniform and weathered cap stood at the top. His black beard and mustache were trimmed in a Van Dyke style.

"Buenas Tardes," he said to Gerald's companion.

They shook hands and spoke softly for a moment. The Master then motioned to a nearby seaman, who, in turn, motioned for Gerald to follow him. As Gerald moved away, he saw the grey-haired man returning to the car. He suddenly felt very vulnerable.

Have I willingly allowed myself to be shanghaied?

The ship sailed that evening. Gerald had been assigned a bunk and a supervisor, Butch, who spoke English.

"Supper in the galley is at 1900. I'll give you your work assignment and watch-standing schedule. Do what you're told, stay out of trouble, and we'll all be fine. I know you're here just for this voyage, but I'm expecting you to work as hard as the regular crew. They will find ways to test you. You look like you can handle yourself."

By the end of the first day, Gerald's fears had disappeared. The work was going to be hard, but doable. And none of the regulars looked like they could give him any trouble he couldn't handle. He was excited about being at sea.

27

THE PACIFIC OCEAN

DECEMBER 5-27, 1943

The Cargo Officer assigned Gerald to a group of five other men, all regular seamen. One spoke fluent English. Two switched between Spanish and English, and two spoke to each other in a language he did not recognize. They understood enough English to follow the directions of the crew boss and the Cargo Officer. Their day was divided into three parts—watch-standing, working, and free time when they could sleep, eat, and interact with the other crew members.

"Houser. Wake up!"

Gerald opened his eyes to see Butch's face inches from his.

"We need to report to the Cargo Officer, First Officer Rivera, immediately. He's at the aft cargo hold hatch."

"Yessir, " Gerald replied and grabbed for his clothes and life jacket.

They had been at sea for twelve days. During the night, a fierce storm had tossed them about. Gerald and the other crew had to hold on not to get thrown from their bunks.

He followed his teammates up two ladders and aft on the main deck to the hatch near the stern. The hatch was open, and First Officer Rivera, obviously upset, was standing next to it with another team.

"During the storm, a large piece of dredging equipment broke loose from its tie-downs and slid up against cables from the helm to the rudder. The captain just tried to make a course correction and couldn't. We've got to free those cables right now."

He pointed to a rope ladder that had been hooked to the edge of the hold.

"Butch and Diego, follow me with your teams. Here are headlamps."

When they got to the bottom, Rivera led them aft through the semi-darkness. Shortly, their headlamps illuminated a large object up against a bulkhead.

Shining his hand torch over their heads, Rivera directed it to show where the object had crushed a three-inch metal pipe.

"Men, the piece has slid too far from the hatch opening for the crane to move it back into place. You will have to attach block and tackle and get it closer to the opening so we can use the crane. The Cargo Manifest says it weighs eight thousand kilos. We may not have enough tackle to move it."

Gerald and the others attached six half-inch line and pulley systems to the base of the piece and three stanchions forward. Then, two men on each pulley began to haul on the lines. As the lines stretched, the equipment barely moved.

Suddenly, one hook holding a pulley to the equipment failed, and the large block shot toward Gerald and his teammate near one of the stanchions. Gerald caught the motion from the corner of his eye and shoved his teammate to the side. The block, which would have hit him squarely in the chest, struck his upper arm, breaking it. He fell to the deck, screaming. Immediately, Gerald bent over him, holding his good arm.

Butch had two men place the injured seaman on a stretcher to be hoisted up and taken to sick bay. As he was being carried off, he grabbed Gerald's hand.

"Gracias, amigo."

First Office Rivera said to Gerald, "Quick action, mister. You saved that man's life. Thank you. I'll make sure the captain knows this. Right now, though, we've still got to fix the problem. Anybody got any ideas?"

Gerald thought back to his early general engineering courses.

"If we attach the pulleys to the top of the piece, perhaps we could lean it away from the bulkhead just enough to get one of those six-by-six shoring timbers between it and the bulkhead. Then we could get the damaged pipe off the cables."

"Damn, that might just work. OK, men, let's try it.

An hour later, the timber was in place, the damage to the pipe was clear. The piece of equipment was resecured in its new spot, and the captain had been called down to inspect the repair.

"Excellent job, Mister Rivera," he commented as he saw the work. "A novel solution."

"Thank you, Captain, but it was the new guy, Seaman Houser's idea. He's some sort of engineer."

The captain turned to Houser.

"Engineer? What kind?"

"Electrical, sir. But we all learned basic engineering skills in school."

"I could use someone with your skills on the Santa Maria. Would you consider staying with us when we reach New Guinea?"

"Thank you, sir, but I have an important job there. I could not disappoint my new employer."

"I understand. My loss. Best wishes."

Turning to Mister Rivera, he said, "Perhaps we can use Mister Houser's skills for the rest of the voyage. Tell the Chief Engineer to find a spare bunk for him and to use him where he can."

"Sorry, Butch, but you'll be one man short for the rest of the voyage. With one of Diego's team out with the broken arm, it will be a little rough, but we've got only eight days 'til port."

The remainder of the voyage went smoothly. Gerald enjoyed being in the engineering spaces, working his way around the electrical systems that controlled the two large diesel engines and all the other systems on the ship. Although he'd spent several years working on electrical blueprints for the Navy, he'd never had this kind of real-life, hands-on experience with operating systems. What he learned here would probably be useful in his sabotage assignment.

Whenever he had some free time, he'd go up on deck. He particularly enjoyed the early evening as the sun was sinking below the horizon. Although he'd grown up near the bay and the ocean, he'd never spent much time on the water. As a young teenager, he and his father would occasionally go to the public beaches at the Presidio. They could watch small pleasure boats sailing back and forth as well as commercial and Navy vessels entering and leaving the harbor.

"Papa, sometime I would like to take an ocean voyage," he had told his father.

"Who knows, Son? Someday, you may."

Neither of them could have imagined that it would look like this.

Now, he quietly said, "Papa, if I ever see you again, I hope you and Mama will be able to understand why I did this. I miss you and Hana much more that I thought. That I'll probably never see you again hurts more than I thought it would. With an aching heart, he stared at the red orb sinking into the sea.

28

LAE, NEW GUINEA

DECEMBER 27-28, 1943

The Santa Maria docked in Lae, New Guinea at 1300 local time on Monday, December 27th. By 1400, the dockside cranes were in position, and the gangplank off the main deck was secured.

The Master gave the crew eighteen hours leave, giving them enough time to enjoy their favorite bar and whores and return mostly sober in time for a full day's work. Although the Japanese forces had been driven from the area, he didn't want to risk his ship and cargo here any longer than he had to.

He shook hands with his three passengers and bid them "Buena suerte" as they started down the gangplank.

On the dock, Gerald walked across to a small café that had outside tables. He picked one that gave him a view up and down the dock and sat down. A waiter arrived. "Coffee with cream and sugar and some fresh fruit, please."

Waiting for his food to arrive, Gerald took in his surroundings. He was familiar with docks and ports, as his father often took him down to the wharf area in San Francisco on Sundays to watch the activity.

Here, the area was recovering from the earlier Japanese occupation. The sights and sounds of the cargo moving equipment were familiar. The smells and other sounds were very different. Of course, there was the pervasive smell of diesel fuel and salt water. But beyond that, there was the fragrance in the breeze of the local flora and of spices coming from the kitchen over his shoulder. Coupled with the musical quality of the language surrounding him, he was keenly aware that he was in a very different world.

I'm missing my home even more than when I was in the camp.

He had just about finished the fruit when he saw a young man who appeared Japanese heading his way. The man approached his table and bowed slightly. "Mr. Houser?" Gerald nodded.

"I am Ichiro Sato. I've been watching you and waiting until you finished your meal. It is my job to get you to your training camp in Tokyo. Please follow me."

They walked silently for about twenty minutes before arriving at a small boarding house. Ichiro got a key from the elderly man behind the desk and motioned for Gerald to follow him.

They went down a dimly lit hallway to an end room. Unlocking the door, Ichiro stood aside and motioned Gerald in.

As he walked in, he immediately saw two men sitting at the back of the room. At the same time, he felt the sharp point of a knife at his neck. He heard the door being closed and locked behind him.

"Do not move. Drop your bag and put your hands on your head," Ichiro said. The two men stood and walked to him.

Oh shit! What's happening? I thought these people were going to help me!

"Gerald, these men are members of the Japanese secret police. They are here to make sure you are who you say you are. If you are not, they will kill you. Do you understand?"

"Yes."

"I'm going to check you for weapons while they look through your bag. Please stand still."

Ichiro checked him thoroughly, even feeling into his boots. Satisfied, he told Gerald to sit in a chair. They all sat down.

One of the men opened a folder. Gerald noticed that the photo taken in San Francisco was clipped to it.

"Mr. Tanaka and his team in San Francisco did a thorough look into your history, and they believe you are sincere in what you want to do. We will go over all that information again, as well as ask you more details about your father and his parents."

For the next four hours, the two men took turns asking him question after question, sometimes the same one over and over.

"Where was your father born? What town did his parents come from? Why did they move to Hawaii? Are you willing to kill Americans if we send you back?"

At the end of the interrogation, the two men stood up, spoke briefly to Ichiro, and left.

"They are satisfied. We will stay here tonight and tomorrow. On Wednesday, you will get on a secret cargo flight at a small airfield near 7 Mile Drome airfield headed for Manila. You will arrive that afternoon. The next day you will continue on to Tokyo."

Exhausted from the questions and the fear of being killed, Gerald said, "OK, but now I need to sleep."

Ichiro shook him awake the next morning. "You slept through supper and breakfast. Let's go into town and look around and get you some food."

This time, they took a cab into the main part of the city. Many Allied troops were moving about the streets. Signs of the recent occupation by Japanese troops and the fierce fighting that dislodged them were visible everywhere. They were stopped several times, and their papers were checked.

They found a small café, ate, then took a cab home.

Back in the room, Ichiro turned to Gerald.

"I wanted to go into the city, hoping your papers would be checked. I knew mine would pass 'cause they have checked me several times. I wanted to make sure yours would hold up. They will be the basis of the identity you get in your training."

The rest of the day, Ichiro quizzed Gerald about life in the US and especially what it was like in the internment camps. Then he told him about the flight the next day.

"Although the Japanese forces have retreated from this area, I'm in contact with a small group hidden in the jungle next to a small airfield undiscovered by the Allies. They have managed to conceal a captured DC-3.

"Shortly before dawn, you and three others will take off for Tokyo with a fuel stop in Manila. The plane's markings should prevent the Allies from shooting it down. The pilot has a coded message that should prevent Japanese forces from attacking it on the approach.

"Notice that I said 'should' twice. This will be the riskiest part of your journey."

That night, Gerald lay in his bed, unable to sleep.

Recalling images of the difficult conditions and harsh treatment his family was suffering in the camp helped him answer the questions that kept haunting him.

Am I doing the right thing? Would Mama and Papa and Hana approve? Will the ache get easier as I get busy with my mission?

29

IN TRANSIT TO TOKYO

DECEMBER 29-30, 1943

Ichiro shook him awake. It was pitch dark. Gerald looked at his watch. It said 12:30.

"Wake up. We need to leave now in order to be at the plane by 0500. It's a four-hour drive."

They walked outside and Ichiro told him to put his gear in the trunk of the small car that had not been there the day before. "That heavy jacket, cap, and gloves are for you. You'll need them for the flight."

They headed south toward Port Moresby. About eight miles north of the city, they turned off the paved road onto a small dirt road leading into the forest. After about fifteen minutes, a bright light appeared in the road. Ichiro brought the car to a halt and, immediately, a man with a rifle appeared at the passenger window. They spoke briefly, Ichiro showing him some papers, and they were waved on.

After another few minutes, they arrived at a clearing.

There sat an olive-drab painted DC-3 with US Army markings. Several people were loading what looked like 50-gallon metal drums into the cargo door.

"That's the extra fuel needed for the flight. Over there," Ichiro said, pointing to the right where three men stood, "are the other passengers. They are going to the training camp as well.

"Now it's time to get aboard. The flight to Manila will take about ten hours. There are web slings where you can sit or lie down. There's a toilet in the rear.

"Here is some fruit, biscuits, and water. You'll have a chance to get more when you stop in Manila. Good luck."

They shook hands, and Gerald followed the other three onto the plane. As they entered, the pilot was standing by the door. The co-pilot was in the right seat, going over the checklist.

Speaking first in Japanese and then in a language Gerald recognized as German, the pilot said, "Gentlemen, find a place to sit and buckle in."

Pointing just behind the cockpit, he continued, "Those six drums contain extra fuel. About five hours into the flight, the co-pilot will come aft. One of you will assist him in transferring that fuel into the plane's tanks. There is a set of earphones hanging by the drums. Put them on so you can hear him.

"Other than that, get as comfortable as you can and enjoy the flight. The weather looks good, so it will be a smooth one."

He went forward to his seat, then motioned to the co-pilot, who started the starboard engine. Then the port engine started, and the co-pilot signaled a man on the ground to unhook the starting batteries.

As soon as he was clear, the co-pilot increased the engine speed, and the plane started to roll down the grass runway. At the end, the pilot spun the plane around and gave the engines full throttle.

Gerald sat in the back of the plane where the engine roar was deafening. Having never been on a plane before, he thought for a short time that it would shake itself apart.

The pilot released the brakes, and the plane surged forward down the runway, the tail rising quickly. After what seemed like forever, Gerald felt the bouncing stop as the speed increased and the nose tipped up.

In the predawn light, Gerald could see that they barely cleared the trees. The plane continued to climb as it banked slightly to the left on a course NNW toward Manila. Sitting on the starboard side, Gerald could see the sun just beginning to rise above the horizon. Below was the green and brown forest. After about thirty minutes, they were over the water.

Well, I'm glad nobody shot at us. Yet!

Realizing how tired he was from lack of sleep and tension, he put on the coat, cap, and gloves, stretched out on the webbing, and was quickly lulled to sleep by the loud hum of the engines.

A hand on his shoulder woke him up. He could barely make out a voice over the engines.

"Wake up, please, and come help me with the fuel."

At first, he was disoriented. *Where am I? Who is this man?*

Then reality flooded back to him as he recognized the co-pilot pointing to the fuel drums.

"Hai," Gerald answered, standing up and following the man toward the front. As he walked forward, he could see nothing but blue outside in the bright sun. He saw the headset and put it on.

"We're about halfway to Manila. Let's get this fuel transferred."

Using the hand pump, it took about forty minutes to complete the transfer.

The co-pilot bowed to Gerald. "Arigato." Then he returned to his seat.

Gerald went to the rear of the plane and found the toilet, which was not much more than a hole in the floor. When he finished, he returned to his seat.

Now for a feast, he thought, smiling. He pulled the canteen from inside his coat where he'd put it to keep it from freezing, opened the biscuits, and laid out the fruit. *Thanks, Ichiro.*

Noticing that the other passengers had only water, he offered his limited food to them. They hesitated, and then each took one biscuit and a fig. "Danka," the oldest one said.

They ate in silence, looking out the windows.

In the early afternoon, the co-pilot came back. Shouting above the engine noise, he said, "We are approaching the southern end of the Philippines. Military fighter planes will escort us to the airfield in Manila.

"Do not worry. They are here for our protection since we have US Army markings."

A few hours later, they landed at an airfield. Gerald could see Japanese troops, planes, and vehicles out the window. The plane taxied to a group of buildings, and the pilot killed the engines. Immediately, an officer and a soldier with a rifle came aboard.

Speaking in perfect English, the officer said. "You will get off now and go into that building. There you will find food and restrooms and cots. Talk to no one. The plane will depart tomorrow at 0500. Be on it at 0445. Do not leave the immediate area of the building."

They left, and Gerald and the others followed them into the building. It was a large hangar-like structure. The right half was a gathering area where about thirty soldiers, most very young, relaxed in chairs and around tables. As Gerald and the others entered, all eyes turned to stare at them, and conversation stopped.

The officer leading them pointed to the rear of the building, where there were a few cots and a food counter.

"Go there."

Suddenly, from somewhere, a pistol fired, and one of the young soldiers yelled, "American die!" as the man next to Gerald grabbed his shoulder and fell to the floor. Immediately, the officer ran toward the soldier, pulling out his pistol and shooting him in the head.

"These men are our allies, under my protection, not the enemy. Leave them alone!"

He returned to the men, quickly examining the wounded German.

"It's not serious. Sergeant, go get the medic. And bring that soldier's commanding officer to me."

Taking the men to the back corner, he ordered, 'You men, find a cot. Get some food and stay there until I come get you in the morning. Do not leave this immediate area."

The medic appeared. He removed the wounded man's shirt.

"It's just a flesh wound. I'll clean it and put on a bandage. You'll be good to go in the morning.

"Take these pills for the pain and to stop infection. Change the dressing when you get to your destination."

30

THE TRAINING

DECEMBER 1943 - JANUARY 1944

At 0415, Gerald and the other three were awakened by the same officer.

"Get up quickly. Get something to eat and food and water to carry on the flight. Be on the plane in thirty minutes. If you do not get on the plane in time, you will be shot!"

Motivated by that reality, they quickly ate, stuffed food into their pockets, and ran to the plane. Everybody was aboard by 0435.

At 0450, belching smoke, the engines roared to life, and the plane taxied toward the takeoff point, turning onto the runway. At precisely 0500, the pilot released the brakes. The plane lumbered forward, climbing slowly, banking toward the north and the rising sun.

What's waiting for me in Japan? I'd always dreamed of visiting the land of my parents and ancestors, but not like this.

I wonder if the people who run the training will allow me to visit the villages of my parents' homes.

The Americans don't trust me 'cause I'm Japanese. Will the people here distrust me 'cause I'm American?

Have I got the skills and determination to become a successful spy?

With these thoughts turning in his mind, Gerald slipped into a restless sleep.

A hand on his shoulder shook him awake. It was the co-pilot pointing to the drums. Gerald followed him forward and repeated the refueling.

"We will arrive in Tokyo in about seven hours. It will be 2000. Get as much sleep as you can. From what I hear, you will get very little during the first week of your training."

On the approach to the Tokyo airfield, the plane was met by four Zeros. They followed it until touchdown.

As the plane taxied into a large hangar, Gerald could see two black Nissan staff cars, several Japanese army officers, and two grey-haired men in black suits.

When the plane door was opened, the two civilian men approached and waited for Gerald and the other three men to leave the plane. They bowed as the men approached them.

"Good evening, gentlemen. I am Kioto-san, a representative of His Imperial Majesty, Emperor Showa. You know him as Emperor Hirohito.

"On his behalf, I welcome you to Japan and thank you for your willingness to help us defeat our enemies to the east. You have chosen a very dangerous and honorable path."

Again, the two men bowed.

"You are about to begin a difficult seven-month training. It will demand your highest level of physical and mental effort and focus. If you are not able to complete the training, you will be required to remain in Japan until we are victorious.

"Now, please, two of you get into each of the two cars. The trip to the training site will take about an hour."

Again, the two men bowed.

From what I know about bowing, Gerald thought, *these men really hold us in high esteem. I hope we get the same respect from our trainers.*

That hope appeared to be false as they arrived at some sort of compound set deep in the woods.

As soon as the cars stopped, the doors were jerked open by four angry-looking soldiers, each holding four-foot wooden rods.

"Get out immediately and stand in a line right here," one of the men shouted. "No, leave your belongings in the car. You won't have any use for them here. We will give you whatever you need.

"Now, strip completely, including your shoes, and toss everything in a pile behind you."

When that was completed, the four men stood naked, looking bewildered and afraid.

"You say you want to become spies for the Emperor. We do not believe you. You may actually be spies for our enemy. We will determine that before anything else.

"You see, over to your left, four bamboo huts. Go there. You will find a shirt, pants, and sandals. Put them on and wait in the hut. Someone will come to begin the interrogation."

For the next several hours, Gerald sat in the dark on the dirt floor. The temperature must have been in the mid-fifties. He could not sleep. He was too scared and cold, and his bladder was too full.

Shit! I've really screwed up. What a fool I was to believe that I could make a difference. I'll be lucky to get out of this alive. At best, I'll never be able to go home or see my family again.

A flashlight moved in his direction. He stood, not knowing what to expect, setting himself in a defensive stance.

A soldier entered the hut and flipped a hidden switch, turning on a light on the ceiling.

"Good evening, Mr. Houser."

The calm voice and warm smile completely threw Gerald off balance.

"Relax. We know you are who you say you are. The men who interrogated you in Lae passed on their report of you to us. Take a minute, go relieve yourself behind the hut, then return."

When Gerald returned, he continued. "Your three traveling companions did not get the same level of scrutiny you did. In fact, we have good reason to believe that one of them is actually a double agent. We just don't know which one yet. So, for a while, we will keep up the act that you are all suspect. It shouldn't take us long to determine if our information is correct. In the meantime, it will appear that you are being subjected to the same rough treatment and interrogations that they are enduring. Right now, they are getting the same thorough questioning you endured in Lae —without the opportunity to take a piss," he added with a smile. "You will be confined to your huts except to use the slit trench ten yards behind the huts. You will be kept separate from each other. Your meals will be brought to you."

In two days, the four men were reassembled in a large classroom-like structure. They all still wore the same identical grey shirts and pants and black sandals.

The older man was gone, replaced by someone close to Gerald's age. At the front of the room, the four soldiers who had met their car were seated at a large table. Gerald and the others were given chairs on the other side of the table. No one mentioned the personnel change.

"Gentlemen, today your training begins. My colleagues and I will be mentors and guides. Over the next seven months, we and our trainers will turn you into the best covert operations team in the world.

"In front of you is a thick folder. This contains your new identity and the Legend that will keep you alive and above suspicion in the US. You will learn the information in your folder so thoroughly that if we wake you in the middle of the night, you will answer any question about your Legend correctly, without hesitation. Use every opportunity to quiz each other. You have one month to commit it to memory. Beginning in month two, we will ask you questions about your Legend anytime, anywhere. If you fail to answer correctly three times, you will be dropped from the program and placed in detention for the duration of the war.

"Please open your folder.

"The first thing you will see is a US Passport. It will pass the most intense scrutiny. This is you. Beginning now, you will only use, and be addressed by, the name you find there."

Gerald opened his passport.

"David NMN West" and his photo stared back at him.

That'll be easy to remember. I hope the rest of the stuff is as simple.

"David West, stand up." Gerald did.

"William Davis, stand up. You will go by Bill.

Jackson Ball, stand up. You will go by Jack.

Samuel Hurst, stand up. You will go by Sam.

"As you go out the front door, you will see a building to your right. That will be your quarters for the training. There, you will find beds and footlockers with clothes and other gear you'll use in your training.

"Before you leave, you will choose one of you to be the team leader for a month. That job will rotate among you for the next six months. In the final month, we will pick the individual we determine to be the best leader during your mission.

"You are dismissed as soon as you pick your leader until 1700 for supper in the mess hall next to your barracks."

They stood up. Gerald said, "Let's place our passports face down on the table, move them around, and turn one over. He will be our first leader."

The flipped passport belonged to Bill Davis.

31

THE TRAINING CONTINUES.

The next morning, the lights were turned on in their quarters at 0400. One of the four trainers stood by the door.

"This morning, we are going to determine your physical condition. We will start with calisthenics and lifting weights. There is no target number of repetitions for each activity, but you will be timed. You will do as many repetitions as you can in the time period. After the exercises, it will be light enough for a five-kilometer run. Again, you will be timed. Once the run is completed, you will shower, get breakfast, and report to the building you were in yesterday at 0610. This will be your primary classroom. Be in front of this building in five minutes in sweatsuits and running shoes.

"Bill, there is a list of exercises posted on a board outside this building, with a time after each. You will call each exercise, then call 'Start.' Each of you will have your reps counted. I will call 'Halt' at the end of the time.

"Once all exercises have been completed, you will start the run. A staff member will lead you through the first course. There are three different ones. They are all convoluted, with switchbacks, intersections, and forks. You will be led through each one twice. After that, you will figure out the correct way to go on your own. Then, you will run the courses in the dark using hand torches. Then you will run them only by moonlight. At some point, random obstacles will be introduced."

When they were all in front of the building, the instructor said, "Bill, call the first exercise."

For the next hour, they went through jumping jacks, push-ups, sit-ups, pull-ups, squats, lifting weights, and weighted sled pulls. No one quit or passed out.

Damn, I sure am thankful for all the hard work we had to do back at Topaz. Without that, I'd be in trouble.

"Take a bathroom break, get some water, and be back here in three minutes for the run."

The trainer set a pace that would get them through the course in fifty minutes.

"This is a good, easy pace," Bill said. The others agreed. It gave them time to pay attention to the turns and directional choices of the course.

When the run was done, the instructor said, "You have twenty-five minutes to be in the training room. If you can shower and eat breakfast in that time, good. Otherwise, it's up to you what you cut short. Do not be late!"

Sam was the last through the door of the training room, with less than a minute to spare.

"Gentlemen," the man who seemed to be the senior

trainer said, "the number of reps that you did today and your time on the run are your baseline numbers. Over the next seven months, you will improve your rep numbers by 50 percent. You will never drop below your run time today, no matter how difficult the course becomes. You will begin each day with the exercises and run.

"My associate will tell you what areas of training you will complete during your time here."

The youngest man stood up.

"There are eight areas in which you will become proficient."

He went to a large board and removed the covering. On the board, the areas were listed.

- Small arms use
- Martial arts self-defense
- Silent killing
- Support network and other contacts
- Communication and codes
- Blending in
- Information on Oak Ridge, Tennessee
- Suicide

"Except for the first and last one, we will introduce you to each of the areas for a day or two. Then, we will combine all of them throughout each day for the rest of your time here.

"We'll go now to the armory, where you will be given a handgun. Never let this weapon out of your sight. You will carry it with you everywhere. It will be strapped to you in your shoulder holster at all times, including in the shower. The only exception is when you are asleep. Then it will be under your pillow."

32

THE TRAINING

JANUARY 1944

For the next seven months, they were intensely trained in the eight areas they were shown earlier.

"Gentlemen," the senior instructor spoke, "this is the final week of your training. Your performance has far exceeded our expectations.

"We have every expectation that you will be successful in your mission. His Majesty will be very proud.

"In consultation, the staff has determined that Mr. West will be your team leader. You each have performed so well that it was a difficult choice.

"In the end, we chose Mr. West because, having been born and raised in America, he has the best understanding of the way Americans think and act.

"You may find yourselves in a situation where that instinctual knowledge could be the difference between success and failure, or even life and death."

His three colleagues stood and applauded. David stood and bowed to the instructors and then to his teammates.

During the past months, David had quickly mastered the skills.

However, he found the training on silent killing the most difficult to get his mind around.

I knew I was going to have to do things I'd never done before if I was to complete my part of the mission. I just never thought I'd have to kill somebody. I hope I'm never in a situation where I have to.

He found the information on Oak Ridge the most interesting. They were all amazed at how detailed it was and how good the photos were.

"If the Americans are not any better at protecting their secrets than this, we should have an easy job disrupting the process," Bill said.

"Even from these photos, I can see several ways to mess up their electrical systems," David replied.

"And now, gentlemen, I want to introduce you to two other people who will further prepare you for your mission."

Turning to a side door, he spoke a few words in Japanese.

Immediately, the door opened, and two people came in. One was a middle-aged man in a white lab coat, and the other a young female in a white nurse's dress, pushing a small metal wheeled cart with some objects on it.

"Gentlemen, this is Dr. Abe. He is a dentist. Today, he and his nurse will put you to sleep and remove a molar from your mouth, which he will then replace with a hollow tooth. You will learn how to remove that false tooth with your tongue.

"On your last day, we will provide you with a cyanide capsule to put in that hollow tooth. Its purpose needs no explanation. You should hope you never have to use it. That will mean you have failed the Emperor.

"Okay. Who wants to be first?"

On July 14th, they were awakened by a fierce thunderstorm. The rain was coming down hard, and the flashes of lightning were constant. There was a smell of ozone in the air.

"I certainly hope this is not a sign," Bill said to his teammates. Today they would be "graduated" and taken to Tokyo. From there, they would be transported to the US.

"Well, we're up early. We might as well finish packing and head over to the classroom. We're not due there for another hour, but I'd rather wait there than here. I'm anxious to get this mission underway."

When they got there, all of their instructors were standing around drinking tea and smoking cigarettes.

"Looks like the storm got you up early, as well," David said.

The senior instructor replied, "Yes, but we have to wait to get started. Your ride is not here yet, nor is the Emperor's representative.

"We can go ahead and give you these. Please be very careful putting them in your tooth. We'd hate to waste any of the training you've received," he said, smiling.

One of the other instructors passed around a small tray. It contained four pea-sized white capsules resting on a silk napkin.

"You may want to drink your tea before you put these in.

You don't want to risk swallowing your tooth before it has the opportunity to seat fully," he said.

As they were standing around, there was a knock at the door. An Army captain in full dress uniform opened the door and stood to one side, saluting.

An elderly gentleman dressed in a black suit, wearing a sash over his left shoulder fastened at his waist with a large medallion and carrying an ivory-handled walking stick, strode into the room.

Immediately, all of the instructors came to attention and bowed deeply.

They held the bow until the gentleman said something in Japanese. Then they stood erect.

The gentleman then walked to David.

In perfect English, he said, "Mr. West, I am the honorable Kinji Tachibana, representative of His Imperial Majesty Emperor Hirohito.

"I am here on his behalf to thank you for your service to our nation and to wish you every success on your mission."

"His Majesty has ordered this mission personally, so it has the highest priority among all our armed forces. You and your team are honored to have been chosen.

"I am told by your instructors that you are the most qualified team we have ever put into the field. We know that you will not fail."

He took one step backward and bowed deeply. The team hesitated and then bowed in return.

Mr. Tachibana then turned to their senior instructor.

"Colonel, please take these fine men to Tokyo."

He turned and left. The instructors bowed.

As soon as he and the captain had departed, the senior instructor, who the team now realized was a colonel, said to David, "Your cars are waiting. Best wishes."

He bowed. David and the team headed through the downpour to the waiting cars.

33

THE MISSION BEGINS

JULY 3, 1944

It was a stormy morning when David and his team were driven through the gate of the Yokosuka Naval Base at 0600. The rain was falling in sheets, and the wind gusts rocked the vehicles. Visibility was so limited that they were almost on top of the grey silhouette moored to the pier before they saw it.

The newly commissioned I-202-class sat low in the water, the gangplank angling down from the pier to the ship's deck.

The team, dressed in Western-style civilian clothes and rain gear and carrying large backpacks, approached the two armed sailors at the top of the gangplank. They turned and silently bowed to the senior trainer who had fashioned their lives for the past seven months. They presented their papers to the Petty Officer, who looked at them briefly and waved them down the gangplank. Despite the storm, the boat was stable, and they had no trouble getting to the open hatch just forward of the looming conning tower. They were just able to make out three figures clad in foul-weather gear staring at them from the top of the tower.

At the hatch, another Petty Officer spoke.

"Go down this ladder. An officer will take you to the captain."

They dropped their backpacks into the hands of a sailor below and climbed down the ladder.

"Welcome aboard, gentlemen. Follow me to the captain."

He went aft a few steps and descended another ladder to what seemed to be the control room.

"Captain, these are the men we are to take to Baja. They have been in training for their mission for seven months. Our boat has the honor of being selected by the Admiralty for this part of their mission."

He bowed slightly and stood back.

"Gentlemen," the captain began, "I am told that none of you have ever been aboard a submarine. You will find life here very different. There are thirty-one of us crammed into a space that is 194 feet by 19 feet. We can get you the 5,600 miles to just off the beach at Baja in eleven days if there are no problems. We will run submerged as we are designed to travel faster underwater. You will sleep on the deck in the torpedo room forward and remain there while you are awake. You will leave only to eat in the crew mess and to use the head. Your major problem will be boredom since your only job will be to stay out of the way of the crew. If you have any questions or problems, you will speak to the senior Petty Officer, who will relay your message to the XO, who will bring it to me, if needed. If conditions allow, one of my officers will give each of you, in turn, a tour of this boat. She is the pride of the Navy, the newest addition to the fleet, and an amazing machine of war. With weapons like this, we will not be defeated.

"We have been ordered to avoid any action on the voyage over, so things should go smoothly. But you never know. Unexpected trouble can come out of nowhere. Mr. West, do you have any questions?"

"No, Captain. Not at this moment. However, it surely is not lost on you and your crew just how important our team and our mission are to the Emperor. To take this incredible vessel out of the fight for eleven days to transport us across the Pacific is a strategically risky decision by your leaders. I know we can count on you to employ all of your skills, knowledge, and experience to get us to our destination safely. Let nothing distract you from those orders.

"Now, please have someone take us forward. We will be out of your way so that you can do your job."

The officer led them forward down a narrow passageway and through several compartments connected by watertight hatches with shin-high thresholds. Jack, fourth in line and distracted by the radio shack, struck his shin hard against one of them.

"Damn, that hurt. I hope we don't have to move around in the dark."

His teammates, as well as the young officer, all laughed.

Passing through the last door, they found themselves in the torpedo room. It appeared to be about forty feet long. On racks on both sides were ten Type 95 torpedoes.

Placing his hand on one of them, the officer said, "Each

of these fish is 23.5 feet long, 20 inches in diameter, and weighs 3,648 pounds. They are fed into the tubes using chains and sliding racks."

There was a narrow walkway between them leading to the forward bulkhead that housed the loading doors for the four torpedo firing tubes. There were hammocks for six people hung from the overhead around the torpedoes. Each one held a seaman. The officer pointed to the space between the nose of the torpedoes and the forward bulkhead.

"A seaman is bringing bedding. You'll put it on the deck here. It's a quiet place unless we're firing these fish or doing a drill. Neither of those should occur on this trip. If they do, you will grab your bedding and gear and get up against the rear bulkhead. The hatch will be sealed.

"We passed through the crew's mess and a head on the port side. You'll eat when these seamen do. Settle in and make yourselves as comfortable as possible. We get underway in thirty minutes."

Once the bedding had been delivered, they spread it out. As they were laying out the bedding, the deck began to vibrate beneath them.

"Those are the engines," one of the seamen said. "We'll be underway as soon as the mooring lines are released. We'll stay on the surface until we've cleared the harbor. That will take about twenty minutes. Then, we'll dive to our cruising depth of fifty meters. You'll feel the pressure change in your ears. We can go much deeper, but that's the most efficient depth, balancing speed and safety. The captain will keep us at that depth, except every two days when we come to the surface to recharge the batteries or if there is some emergency. The dive alarm will sound just before we start our dive. I suggest you either sit on the deck or grab hold of something as soon as you hear it."

They sat down on their mats. There was just barely enough space to walk between them.

"Let's assess our situation," David said. "We're essentially confined to this twelve by fifteen-foot space for eleven days. We can do regular exercises to stay ready, but I'm not sure that will be enough. Perhaps I can convince the captain that, in order to maintain our physical readiness, he allows us, one at a time, to walk the length of the boat several times a day."

"After the way you spoke to him, I doubt he'll be inclined to grant us any favors," Bill responded.

"I just wanted him to be very clear about how important our mission is to the Emperor. I think I can get him to see that we need a lot of exercise to be ready when we're put ashore. Let's give it twenty-four hours and see how we feel. Now, let's test how easy it is to get some sleep. After lunch, we will go over our plans for getting from Baja to Oak Ridge. Bring your notes with you to lunch. I'll ask the XO if we can use one of the tables in the mess between meals to go over our plans."

The dive alarm sounded. The deck tilted sharply down. They were on their way. Once the deck leveled out, they slept 'til lunch.

After lunch had been cleared and the crew had gone, they opened their notes on one of the tables. The cook came over with a pot of coffee and four mugs. They quickly covered their notes.

"I'm sorry, guys. I'll check before I come close again. I

just wanted to bring you some coffee." He set it on the table and turned back to the galley.

"Thank you, Cookie. We just wouldn't want to have to kill you," David said with a smile. The cook laughed.

"OK, the captain said he plans to put us ashore around midnight Friday the 14th, about five miles west of Tijuana. We'll make our way to the town, where we'll locate our contact, who will take our packs across the border under a load of watermelons. They'll be at our check-in point in San Diego. Then we'll blend in with the other tourists until evening. There will be the usual large crowd of tourists returning to the US after an evening of partying. Most will be drunk and rowdy, so the Border Patrol will be busy. We have entry stamps on our passports into Mexico on the 13th. There should be no problem getting into the US. Taxis are always waiting to take people into San Diego. Once we get there, we'll check in with our contact and decide whether to get to Oak Ridge by bus, train, or buy a car."

"What happens if we get detained?" Jack asked.

"We've got three options. We can talk our way out, escape, or swallow our pills."

34

ABOARD THE SUB

By the third day, they were into a routine. They'd sleep as late as they could and still get breakfast, then exercise until lunch. Then they'd work on their plans and quiz each other on their Legends until supper. Exercise again, visit with the crew in the torpedo spaces, and sleep.

They became friends with the six sailors who lived with them in the small space. Because these sailors had nothing to do except the routine tasks of checking the valves, switches, and gauges that controlled the launch of a torpedo, they and the four visitors had plenty of time to get to know each other.

Because this was one of the primary naval vessels in the Japanese Navy, these six torpedomen were seasoned veterans. Each had served a number of tours on smaller boats. The most junior, a young man in his early twenties, had been on submarines for three years, and the senior, a Chief Petty Officer, was in his twentieth year and due to retire the following October.

After lunch, the Chief spoke. "Would you like to learn how we fire the torpedoes?"

"Of course," David replied.

So, for the next two hours, they learned what every part of the systems did. There were four firing tubes, two on the port side and two on the starboard side. Since the outer doors were closed, the inner doors could be opened to inspect the interior of the tube. Each man was invited to stick his head and shoulders into the tube.

"You know, instead of surfacing and putting you in a rubber boat to go ashore, we could just give you breathing gear and let you swim out through the tubes," the young sailor said with a smile.

"A lot safer for us; just a little more exciting for you!"

"Thanks, but I think we'll pass on your offer," David replied. "Your captain will just have to take the risk of surfacing and casting us adrift in that small rubber boat. That'll be enough excitement for us, thank you."

"Now, tell me about those decals," he said, pointing to a spot near the top of the forward bulkhead.

"Those are our kills," one of the other sailors said, "one for each vessel sunk.

"The six black ones represent merchant ships; the four red ones are warships. They are destroyers who were guarding convoys. We have a very skilled captain. We have been on three patrols and never missed a target. We are the newest boat in the fleet and have the best kills per patrol record," he said with obvious pride

"Now you understand what we do," said the Chief. "What can you tell us about your job? It must be very important to turn this killer boat into a taxi."

It was obvious that he was not pleased with the ship's orders.

David replied. "I certainly understand your frustration, Chief. Unfortunately, our mission is top secret, so I can't tell you much. Our team has just completed seven months of very intense training for a job that, if successful, will be far more destructive to the enemy's war effort than even your boat's impressive kill record. The Emperor and the senior Navy staff have decided what we will accomplish is worth pulling you out of action for a few days.

"What I can tell you is our target is the most important and most highly classified program of the entire Allied effort. It's so secret that what we accomplish will only become known when Japan wins the war and chooses to reveal to the world what we have done.

"This is what I shared with your Captin yesterday. He told me that this explanation was very helpful, and he is honored that the Emperor has selected this boat for this critical mission. I think he plans to make a statement about us, our mission, and how important a role your boat is playing in assisting us with reaching our goal to the entire crew later today."

The demeanor of the crew, and especially the Chief, changed noticeably once David finished. It's as though they realized they were part of something important and unique and they were taking ownership of it.

David and the team excused themselves. "We now need to go to the mess and continue working on our plans."

While they were working, a voice came over the 1MC.

"Attention, this is the captain. By now, you are all aware that this is not our usual mission. You are also aware that we are hosting a team of four men who we are delivering secretly to the US.

"I know that many of you, including me, have been concerned, even angry, that we have been taken away from our primary duty of destroying enemy ships.

"Let me assure you that what we are doing is of supreme importance to the Emperor and the war effort. I am sure that each of you shares with me the honor this mission brings to each of us. One day, you may be able to tell your children and grandchildren about this important role you played in our ultimate victory.

"Our visitors know that they need to stay out of the way of us doing our jobs, so they will confine themselves to the forward torpedo room and the crew's mess. However, in order to maintain their fitness, today I have given permission for them, individually, to walk with an escort the length of the boat a couple of times a day. If you see them, you may greet them but do not engage them in conversation.

"We will put them ashore in one of our rubber boats off the coast of Baja, Mexico in eleven days.

"We have been instructed by the admiralty to avoid any enemy contact while on this mission. If we are detected, we will take evasive maneuvers. That is all."

35

ABOARD THE SUB

For the next seven days, everything followed the normal routine. When the sub surfaced to charge the batteries, the team was invited to go out on the deck and enjoy the fresh air and night sky.

On one such night, instead of remaining on the bridge atop the conning tower, the captain came out on the deck with the team. They stood silently as the deck rocked gently in the long swells. There was only a quarter moon, and the stars were so bright it was as if you could reach up and touch them. The hum of the diesel generators and the quiet splash of the sea against the hull were the only sounds.

The voice of the captain broke the silence.

"This is one of my most favorite times on a mission. The smell of the salt air, the beauty and stillness of the sky. So peaceful.

"Sometime, after this evolution, I will return to my cabin

once we are underway and write a haiku. Tonight, it will speak to your safety on your mission.

"One could almost imagine this peace is everywhere. I imagine that my wife and children are looking at the same sky outside our home in Nagasaki right now. It helps soothe the ache of their absence. I know the emperor is correct in prosecuting this war against the West. I wish it could be over soon so I can return to them. I have spent too many months away from them, missing important milestones in their lives. At least, next August, I will be granted one month's leave to be with them.

"I know your mission is secret, but can you tell me a little about yourselves? You are not Japanese. Respectfully, I'm curious why you are here."

David began.

"I am one-half Japanese. My father is an American-born Japanese; my mother is American. Our family was forced into an internment camp by the American Army. Although they did not treat us badly, we had to leave everything behind and were put in a very primitive living situation where the weather was extremely harsh. When the weather killed my grandparents, I made up my mind to hurt the Americans in some way. I escaped the camp and was assisted by a secret network to go to Tokyo. That is why I am here."

Then Bill spoke. "Sam and I are German. We were recruited by the Abwehr to assist the Japanese effort. We traveled from Germany to South America and then to Tokyo. We met David at the training camp."

Jack spoke last.

"I am French. After Germany conquered my country in

1940, many of my countrymen cooperated with the Nazis. My sister's husband was one of them. But she was not. She opposed his actions and secretly supported the Resistance. One night, some Resistance fighters, guided by an American spy, broke into their home and shot them both in front of their two young children. At that moment, I wanted to hurt not only the Nazis but also the Resistance and the Americans. Like David, I felt supporting the Japanese was the best avenue for my anger. So here I am."

"You are certainly a diverse group. The emperor is fortunate to have such broad appeal. My crew and I salute you."

One of the ship's crew approached the captain. He saluted and bowed.

"The chief engineer reports the batteries are fully charged. He bowed and left.

"Gentlemen, it's time to return to below decks. We'll be diving shortly. The water's a little too cold for a swim."

———

It was 0300 the morning of June 13 in the radio shack of the Navy Bombing Squadron, VB2, at NAS San Diego.

CPO Sandy O'Brian stormed through the door, still wiping sleep from his eyes. A knock on the door from the duty PO thirty minutes earlier had rudely awakened him from a sound sleep.

"Sorry, Chief," the Petty Officer said, entering the room, "but Chief Evans is sick, and you need to take his watch at the listening shack."

"Sick, hell, that slacker is hung over or still drunk," he

growled as he threw off the covers. "How he ever made Chief is a goddamn mystery. Alright, tell the guys I'll be there in thirty minutes."

The two Petty Officers hunched over the radios, listening into their headphones. They looked up at O'Brian as he came into the room. Despite the unexpected call to duty, his uniform and grooming could have withstood a close inspection.

"Mornin', Chief," the one nearest the door said. "You couda stayed in bed. It's mind-numbing quiet here tonight. Either those sonar buoys the PV-1s have been dropping off Baha ain't worth a shit, or there's nothing moving out there."

"Don't worry about the buoys, Martino. They work just fine. If there's anything out there, they'll find it. Just keep your focus on your receivers."

He turned his attention to the readings from the buoys for the last six hours. Nothing.

I get the guys' frustrations. Listening to nothing for six hours would drive me crazy. I hope the brass who thought up this idea know what they're doing.

He started filling out the pile of duty reports on his desk. He'd been at this mundane task for almost an hour when Martino shouted.

"Hey, Chief, I got something!" He flipped the switch, sending the signal to the speaker.

A stream of Morse dots and dashes filled the room.

"Which buoy or buoys is it?" O'Brian asked.

Martino checked the sheet listing the unique signal sent from each buoy when it was activated.

"It looks like one that was dropped yesterday about two hundred miles due west of Tijuana."

They all listened in silence as the noise filled the room. Suddenly, there was silence.

"What happened?" the other petty officer asked.

"If it's a valid target, it's moved out of range. If it's a target, it'll be acquired by another buoy in the area. Just listen."

They sat in the silent room, watching the secondhand on the clock sweep off the seconds.

At fourteen minutes and thirty seconds, another Morse signal filled the room. This one had a different pattern.

"Martino, is this in the same area?"

"Yes, Chief. It's one of the same batch dropped in that area."

"We may well have found us a Jap sub, gentlemen. I'm calling OPS."

Hi hand trembled so much that it took him twice to dial the number correctly. "Lieutenant, I think we've caught a fish. We've gotten several returns from that batch of buoys that were deployed yesterday west of Baja."

A pause.

"Yessir, we will."

Hanging up the phone, he stood up, rubbed his face with his hands, and took a few slow, deep breaths.

"OK boys, the boss wants us to report any new signals from different buoys. He's requesting a PBY Catalina with those new Mark 9 depth charges be launched. It'll be over the area in a few minutes."

At the same time, the I-202 was completing her last battery charging evolution before they reached the coast off

Baja. The captain had ordered a standard dive as the port lookout suddenly shouted.

"Aircraft off the port beam several miles out. It appears to be closing."

"Crash dive," the captain shouted into the voice tube. "Clear the bridge."

The alarm claxon blared as he practically pushed the two lookouts down the ladder, grabbing the hatch closed behind him. The sea rapidly rose up the conning tower.

Every man in the well-trained crew carried out the emergency duties they had practiced innumerable times. The angle of the dive approached thirty degrees very quickly. Anything not secured fell forward. The crew clung to anything they could.

David and the team were alone at a table in the crew's mess. Their chairs started sliding forward as their papers slid from the table. Their coffee cups and the half-empty pot shattered on the deck, the pieces sliding rapidly to the bulkhead. They luckily grabbed the legs of the table which was secured to the deck as the clatter from objects in the kitchen filled the space.

"What the shit's happening?" Sam yelled. "Are we sinking? I didn't hear any explosions. Where's the cook? Somebody needs to tell us what's happening."

At that precise moment, one hundred feet above them, the PBY's pilot gave the command, "Drop one fish!"

"Fish away," replied the crew chief.

Three seconds later, the tear-shaped object encasing 200 pounds of super-explosive Torpex dove into the sea just forward of the sub's bow, missing the port side of the hull by two feet. It sank quickly as the sub continued its crash dive.

Its violent explosion occurred thirty feet behind and sixty feet below the diving sub.

While the actual damage to the boat's hull was minor—the rudder and twin props were not damaged—the force of the explosion drove the stern upward violently, so that the angle of the dive increased from thirty degrees to sixty degrees instantly.

The condition in the sub went from difficult to impossible. Members of the crew flew forward, crashing into the first solid, fixed object or crew member that got in their way. Even some heavy equipment broke from fastening and hurled forward. The lights flickered, then went out. Emergency red lighting came on.

In the control room, the two helmsmen who controlled the rudder and the dive planes and the captain were strapped in their seats.

"Blow forward ballast! Full up on the planes! Full astern!" shouted the captain.

"Blow forward ballast. Full up on the planes. Full astern, aye," came the immediate reply.

Seeming to take forever, the angle of the dive slowly lessened.

"Ahead one-third. Maintain this heading. Hold at thirty degrees. Level off at three hundred feet."

"Ahead one-third. Maintain this heading. Hold at thirty degrees. Level off at three hundred feet, aye."

"Chief, get me a damage and casualty report and find out the condition of our passengers."

"Aye, Captain"

"Three hundred and twenty-five feet," the lead helmsman called out.

"Engines full stop. We'll coast into three hundred."

"Engines full stop. Aye."

"Sonar. Any more depth charges?"

"Negative, Captain."

"Three hundred feet, no forward movement," the helmsman called out.

"We'll hold this position until we assess the status of the boat, crew, and passengers. What's your report, Chief?"

The chief spoke up.

"Captain, the hull is sound. The engines and all navigational surfaces are operational. There is no serious internal damage. Most of the crew have some cuts and bruises. One member has a broken arm, and one is unconscious. The medic is checking him out now.

"The passengers are a little shaken and banged up, but nothing serious. They were working on plans alone in the mess. There was no crew member to give them any information, so they thought we were sinking."

"Alright. Thank you. Let me know about the unconscious man as soon as the medic reports and when everybody else is patched up."

"XO, give me your assessment of what happened and what do we do next."

"Yes, sir."

"I think we must have set off some sonar buoys. That's the only explanation for that one PBY homing in on our position. I have no idea why they only sent one plane or dropped just the one charge. Maybe they weren't sure we were here. Then, the way that one explosion increased our dive so radically, we got under the thermocline really quickly, and the buoys lost us."

"Do you think we are able to continue our mission?" replied the captain.

"Yes, sir. We are only fifty miles off the coast. We can wait here until dark. If we stay at this depth until we surface at the coast, we should remain undetected."

"My conclusion, exactly, XO. Thank you. You will find yourself in command of one of these boats before you know it.

"Now, let's go check on the crew and our guests," he said, giving his officer a strong pat on his shoulder.

36

ABOARD THE SUB. JUST OFF THE COAST
OF BAJA, MEXICO

0400, JULY 13, 1944

"Blow all ballast. Rise to periscope depth." The captain's voice broke the silence and waiting of the past several hours.

"Blow all ballast. Rise to periscope depth, aye," came the reply.

David and his team, with all their gear, had been brought forward to the space just below the control room. They looked at each other with a mixture of relief and concern as they heard that command and felt the gentle rise of the deck beneath their feet.

"OK, guys," said David. "This is what we have been waiting for. In just a few hours, we'll be across the border into California."

"As soon as the captain searches the area and decides it's safe, we'll surface and get into a rubber boat."

"Periscope depth, Captain."

"Up scope," he ordered.

There was complete silence as he slowly rotated the scope 360 degrees twice.

"All clear. Surface. Chief, get the team ready to break out the dingy." The captain climbed down the ladder to the space below.

"Mister West, get your team ready. As soon as the dingy is inflated, you will get into it through that hatch." He pointed forward. "We will submerge as soon as you clear the deck."

"We're twenty-five hundred yards off the coast. It appears deserted. There is no moon. The seas are calm, and there's a slight onshore breeze. You should be able to make land in about forty minutes.

"When you reach land, I suggest you unload your gear, then take the boat offshore about twenty yards and sink it."

He saluted and extended his hand.

"It has been my and the crew's honor to have this part in your mission. Best wishes, and may your efforts be successful and bring honor to the emperor."

"Thank you, Captain. You and your crew have been most gracious. I know you are now anxious to get back to the mission you have been doing so well.

"Perhaps we will meet again to celebrate our great victory."

He bowed. The captain did the same.

"Dingy's ready," came the call from the bridge.

"Alright, men, let's go," David said.

The fresh air enveloped them as they climbed through the hatch onto the wet deck. The black dingy glistened even in the moonless night.

They quickly loaded their gear into the dingy. David and Jack each took an oar as several crew members pushed them to the side of the deck.

As soon as they cleared the deck, they heard the command to dive and the sound of the horn as the sub slipped silently below the surface. In just over a minute, they were alone on the black water.

For a while, all they could hear was the noise of the oars as they pushed them toward the coast. Their destination was a spot about two miles south of the US border. From there, it was about nine miles through very sparsely populated areas into Tijuana. They planned to take about four hours to make the trip. They would get rid of their packs and wander about the city, watching the tourists and timing their border crossing when there was a large number crossing at one time late in the evening.

"I'm beginning to see some lights, boss," Sam said to David, "but nothing close to the shore. If we continue due east, we should be fine."

"Good. It's just five o'clock. By the time we offload our gear and sink the boat, it'll be about six. If we stay on schedule, we will get to the city about ten.

"Let's get started. We'll split into two groups to avoid being noticed as much as possible. Sam, you will be with me. Jack and Bill follow when we're about one hundred yards off. We'll stay on the roads unless there are too many houses, then we'll move to the fields and woods. We don't want to be noticed by the local police."

It was just after ten when they reached the outskirts of Tijuana. The locals were busy setting up their market shops and businesses for the day. A few tourists were visible, most looking hung over. A few had whores hanging on their arms. There was a strong fragrance of vomit and stale beer in the air.

"We're supposed to meet our contact at five o'clock at a cantina just off the main square," David said. "Split up, find something to eat. Meet back here at four-thirty. Stay out of trouble. No liquor or women!" he said, smiling.

At five, they were at the cantina. The guitars were loud, and the conversations around them were louder. David had rejected the offers of several rough-looking females. There were beers and nachos on the table. David had ordered them so they'd blend in. "Drink that one slowly," David said. "That'll be it 'til we get some to drink as we cross the border."

At five-thirty, a Mexican approached the table.

"Senior, I am Juan. Are you the importers from Asia?"

Finally! thought David. I was forgetting that the locals operate at a different speed.

"Yes," David replied. Our company brings in fine dresses for the ladies."

"Bueno. Follow me, por favor."

He led them down a narrow side street. They were the only foreigners in sight.

"Boss," whispered Bill. "Are you sure about this guy? I'm feeling pretty vulnerable right now."

"He knew the password. We're gonna be doing risky things like this from now on. Just stay on the alert."

"No worry. I'm about to jump out of my skin!"

Juan paused in front of what looked like a large garage door and pulled it open. Inside was an ancient, faded red

Ford truck with a large stake bed. The floor of the bed was covered with large green and white watermelons.

"Put your packs on the melons in the middle. The rest of the load is coming shortly to fill the bed. I'll leave as soon as it arrives and head to San Diego. Your packs will be at your check-in spot when you arrive." He led them out to the street, closing the door behind them. "Via con Dios."

Returning to the main square, David said. "We'll wander again until about midnight, then meet back here and head to the border crossing. Buy a beer to carry with you. We'll separate and blend in with the crowd to cross. You have your US passports with entry stamps from two days ago. Once we're through, we'll get two taxis to get to San Diego.

"If you have any problems with the US officials, you're on your own. If there is a problem, those who get through will wait at the check-in location for twenty-four hours."

There was no problem at the border. By twelve-thirty, they were standing together on US soil near a bunch of taxis.

"OK," David said. "That's another hurdle behind us. Let's get some taxis and head to San Diego."

37

THE MISSION CONTINUES. SAN DIEGO

JULY 14, 1944

The trip to their check-in location in San Diego took about an hour and a half. They were dropped off at a nondescript two-story building about two-thirty in the morning.

David stood at the battered front door and gave the password, "Red."

After a short pause, he heard, "Sky."

He responded, "Morning," and the door opened.

"Come in quickly," said a voice from behind the door.

The room was very dimly lit. David could make out three shadows in the middle of the room.

A muffled voice said, "Please sit."

As they did, the lights were brightened, and the team saw that the three shadows were men wearing hoods with eyeholes.

They were handed their packs by another person from behind.

"Please forgive the drama," said the man in the center. "It is better for us and for you that you not see our faces."

"We are going to provide you with US dollars, bus tickets to Knoxville, Tennessee, which is twenty-five miles from Oak Ridge, and some places to stop along the twenty-two-hundred-mile trip.

"We have papers supporting your Legends showing that you are civilian employees of the Army Corps of Engineers with specialized skills that will be useful at the facility. It will be up to you to figure out how best to become involved in the activity there and to figure out how to slow down or derail the process.

"Finally! Here is the latest contact list for friends in the area around Oak Ridge. The information is as of last week. As you know, it is subject to change without notice.

"One final caution. Your mission is taking you to the most secure location in this country. We told our Tokyo contacts that this mission was impossible. They chose to conduct it anyway. It is our opinion that yours is a suicide mission.

"You will stay here tonight. There are some cots, Army C-rations, and a toilet. Tomorrow, we will take you to the Greyhound Bus station.

"Your cots and food are through that door. The toilet is further down the hall. Be ready to leave at 0700.

"Good luck and good night."

"What have we gotten ourselves into?" Sam asked the group as they sat on the cots.

"If these people, who probably have better intel than

those who trained us, don't think we can succeed, what are we going to do?"

"We're going to do what we were trained to do," David replied sharply.

"We all knew this was going to be very difficult, so shut up, get some food and sleep, and be ready to go by 0645."

As they rode to the bus station, David said, "We will travel as individuals. You've probably noticed that our packs are not alike, so we won't look like a group. We'll stay well apart in public. No conversations. We'll have separate rooms. We can get together at night only if necessary, but we must take care not to be observed. It will take us three days to get to Knoxville. There, I'll contact one of our support team to learn the best way to get through security at the site."

Three days later, they arrived without incident at the bus station in Knoxville. Their destination: the huge facility at Oak Ridge, which was twenty-seven miles away.

David called the phone number he'd been given in San Diego. The person who answered said he'd meet David at the bus station in thirty minutes.

A middle-aged Negro approached the bench where David sat.

"Mr. West?"

"Yes," David replied. The man sat down next to him on the bench.

Two men sitting on the bench across the aisle from them stared as he sat down. It was unusual to see a White man and a Negro sitting together in a public place in Knoxville in 1944.

David, too, looked a little surprised.

"Don't be surprised, Mr. West," the man said softly. "You have your reasons for what you are doing. I have mine, and they go back over one hundred years.

"Besides, it's good cover. Nobody around here would think a 'nigger' could be smart enough to engage in espionage," he said, smiling.

"Your team has been given a tough assignment. Security around that operation is very tight. I work there as a janitor, so I'm in and out daily, and I go pretty much anywhere around the facility.

"Nobody pays any attention to me. My ID gets me into even the most secure areas. It's like I'm invisible, so I can get close and listen in on conversations as I pick up trash and sweep. There are ten of us who work our shift. I'm the only one who does this.

"The best time to get into the facility will be in the morning. A lot of people live outside the gate, so there's a crowd going through security at that time.

"Your team will go through security separately. As new hires, they will send you to In-processing to get your work assignments. As single men, you will also be assigned to barracks on the campus, so you won't have to go through security daily.

"From what I overhear, the process is plagued with problems. I'm not sure you can do anything to make it worse. This whole scientific field of foolin' with atoms is so new, it seems solving one problem creates two more.

"Their goal is to produce enough stuff to make a bomb. They'll ship that stuff to a new facility they've set up in New Mexico, where they'll build some bombs and blow them up.

"If you want my advice, your best course is to keep your

heads down here and do your jobs so well that you get selected as part of the group that goes to New Mexico.

"Seems like having a specific target, like a bomb, would be easier than finding a place to disrupt all the theoretical processes going on here."

Without giving Gerald an opportunity to respond, he stood up and, in a slightly louder voice, said, "Yasser, Mr. Jones, me and my wife can shore help you in your new home. We's pleased fo' the offer. Thank you."

DAVID FOUND THE OTHER TEAM MEMBERS SITTING IN THE BUS station with the other passengers. He motioned for them to come to him.

"There's a park around the corner that has a small café and a pond with ducks. A lot of people go there to feed the ducks. Put your packs in lockers, and we'll meet there in fifteen minutes."

When they got there, David said, "Let's go to the café and get some lunch."

When they were seated at a table, he told them what the contact had said.

"I think he's probably right about waiting 'til New Mexico. But let's go to work for a day or two and see if we can discover any vulnerable spots now.

"We'll get back here after work in three days and do an assessment. Now, go wander around town 'til tonight. Then get your packs and find a room. We'll be at the front security gate at 0630 tomorrow."

By 0700, they had all been passed through security and were waiting at In-processing with about twenty other newcomers. By 1100, they were on the way to their assignments, each in a different part of the operation.

Three days later, they were back at the café,

"Your contact is right," Jack said. "This place is so confusing; I wouldn't know what to try and break. Nothing around here looks like anything I've ever read or heard about. I don't even understand most of the words the technicians are using."

"Okay," David said. "I heard yesterday that work at the facility in New Mexico is well underway. So, as soon as the scientists here complete their work, the operation will move there."

"So let's focus on being noticed for the quality of our work, not as troublemakers. We'll certainly gain important information that we can send back to Japan."

That opportunity came more quickly than the team expected. In mid-September, just sixty days after arriving at Oak Ridge, they were offered the opportunity to move to the site referred to as "Project Y" in Los Alamos, New Mexico.

38

THE END OF THE MISSION, LOS ALAMOS, NM

SEPTEMBER 16, 1944 - JULY 15, 1945

They arrived in the desert with thirty other technicians. Already, about 5,500 people, scientists, engineers, technicians, and Army military security, many with families, were at the site.

Once through security, they went to their assigned quarters. David and Bill were in one building. Jack and Sam were in the one next to it.

Once they'd stored their gear, they were back outside. Standing next to Jack and looking at the facility map, David said quietly, "Let's take a day or two to get the feel of the place. We'll sit together in the mess hall day after tomorrow. Pass that on to Sam." He then walked to find the small general store.

He noticed several small motorcycles with Sale signs on them near the front entrance.

He asked one of the women coming out of the store with

a bag of groceries. "'S'cuse me, ma'am. I just arrived. Please tell me about these." She paused briefly, looking him over. Seeing his badge, she decided to answer him.

"People mostly use them to go into Santa Fe when they have time off. They buy them when they come and sell them when they leave. There's a dealer who's set up a shop in White Rock near here.

"These are from people who couldn't sell theirs before they left. Most people are able to sell them before they leave. There's a couple of them for sale on that notice board."

A few days later, David bought a '41 Indian from one of his coworkers. He encouraged his team to do the same.

"We'll probably need to make a quick exit after we foul up the process. Motorcycles would be a good way to do that." Within the first month, they all had purchased bikes.

The team met in the mess hall on the third day.

"We need to find a place we can meet," David said.

Bill offered, "There's a vehicle maintenance building not far from the barracks. It backs up to a fence. There's no activity in the evening, and it has a back door away from any security lights. I think that would work."

"Let's meet there tomorrow just as it gets dark," said David.

The team assembled at 2000.

"What have we learned about the process and how to stop it?" David asked.

Bill spoke up. "The goal is to build an explosive device; I think they're calling it 'The Gadget.' It's going to be detonated from a tall tower a number of miles out in the desert from here. I understand they're building observation buildings and control rooms about five and a half miles from the tower."

"Okay," replied David. "This gives us a much more traditional mechanical operation to work with. It's wires, generators, normal buildings, and a tower. We should be able to figure out several vulnerable points at which we can interrupt the operation.

"We need to do the same thing here we did in Oak Ridge. Do our assigned tasks so well that we become familiar, trusted faces to those around us. Then when the big day approaches, we'll be more likely to be able to set up a disruption unnoticed. I think the scientists are planning on a test sometime in the summer, so we've time to make that happen.

"We'll meet here on this same date for the next three months to see how things are going. Now, let's get our plans moving."

Two weeks later, David stood behind Bill in the lunch line.

"Bill, how is it going, setting up a way to send reports to Tokyo?"

"Not good, boss. We're too isolated out here. I need to figure a way to get into Santa Fe and make contact with someone on our support team."

"Keep working on that. It's very important that we get information out."

The team members continued what they had done at Oak Ridge. By early 1945, their skills had made them invaluable members of the team.

They spent as many off-hours as possible cultivating the friendships of key personnel. David was even able to develop a professional friendship with Robert Oppenheimer, who was impressed with his ability to "think outside the box" on complicated electrical problems.

With the help of a contact he located in Santa Fe, Bill was able to develop a system for getting copies of secret materials back to Tokyo.

By February, the team had worked out three possible ways to stop the process.

The most audacious was to rig the hoist, which was to take the bomb to the top of the tower so that it would fail at the top, causing The Gadget to fall to earth.

"I'm pretty sure it won't explode," Bill said. "It takes a strong electrical charge to set off the explosive shell."

Another was to cut the wires from the control room to the bomb.

"That will work unless they test the circuits before firing," said Jack. "The trick will be to do the cut as close to the time of explosion as possible. One of us will have to work our way onto the group that's in the blast observation building nearby."

The last, and perhaps the most realistic, was to blow up the generators supplying power to the control room so completely that it would take a long time to replace them.

"There are several places where explosive charges can be set unnoticed. We'll have to figure out how to build an explosive." Sam said.

"Alright, let's meet back here in a month for a status update," David said.

By mid-June, the talk was that the test of The Gadget would take place in about a month.

Bill's Santa Fe contact had been able to have a number of sticks of dynamite smuggled inside a crate of vehicle parts.

Because of his connection with Oppenheimer, David had been assigned to do the final assembly of the electrical control panels in the forward observation buildings.

The idea of causing the cable on the hoist to break had been abandoned. They had been unable to figure out how to get one of the team close to the tower.

Now, they were just continuing to do their jobs. ...and wait.

David had not slept well for several nights. Thoughts whirled in his brain. The doubts about what he was doing that had been in the back of his mind since he escaped the camp had only grown stronger as he realized the futility of their plans.

Why don't I feel good about what I'm doing? Was I too impulsive in setting out on this path?

The more I learn about this project, the more I realize that, at best, we can only delay it briefly. The people putting this together are too smart and have too many resources to be stopped.

Also, many of those I've met and worked with over these months don't look like monsters.

I've only heard racist language from some of the soldiers.

I certainly learned during the training that the Japanese can be just as racist as those who interred my family.

I didn't realize how much I'd miss my family and, especially, Hana.

If we succeed in the sabotage, there's a good chance we'll be caught and probably executed.

By the morning of the 14th, he had made the difficult decision.

If I can, I'm going to stop this plot. How do I do that?

He decided his best possibility was, somehow, to alert those in charge about the sabotage attempt.

The only part of their plan that was ready was the dynamite charges under the two massive generators.

I'll write a note telling them about the explosives under the generators and that they should question Bill Davis, Jack Ball, and Sam Hurst about it.

I'll slip it in the doorway of the MP's guard shack when they're changing shifts this evening.

Then, I'll simply take my motorcycle out and head north to that shack I found earlier.

39

JEMEZ MOUNTAINS, NEW MEXICO.

JULY 14, 1945

The sun was sinking behind the mountains ahead of him, its rays turning the few wispy clouds varying shades of red and orange. The lengthening shadows around him quickly fading into darkness. He'd been riding west for almost two hours. The red '41 Indian Sport Scout with its 750-cc flathead v-twin he'd bought from one of his coworkers purred flawlessly, performing as if it felt at home in the sand and dust of the place.

I'm sure glad I grabbed these gloves from Bill's locker. It's a lot colder out here than I expected.

Since escaping the assembly compound at the Los Alamos site, he'd been riding in the desert, staying off the roads in case the MPs were looking for him.

His heart rate was finally returning to normal as the last effects of the adrenalin drained from his system. Since he hadn't seen signs of any pursuers since he left Los Alamos, he was breathing a little easier. Then, as he paused to drink from his canteen, he saw moving lights a few miles back. His fear immediately returned.

He jammed his canteen back into the case, kicked the bike into gear, and sped off, going faster in the darkness than he should have.

As he attempted a sharp turn into the narrow canyon, he felt the motorcycle's back wheel skid from under him in the thick dust. It went down hard on his left leg. "Damn," he cried as a sharp pain shot up the side of his left leg and body. His helmet and the noise of the engine muffled his cry. Stars flashed in his eyes, mingling with the starlit sky of the coal-black desert night.

Killing the engine, he lay still for a few moments, collecting his thoughts and mentally checking out his body. Then he carefully pulled himself from under the machine and slowly got to his feet, gingerly testing his leg. *No breaks*, he thought, thankful for the soft ground, as he uprighted the bike.

He pulled a small flashlight from his jacket pocket. That's when he saw the front fender stuck out sharply from the wheel. Wincing as he balanced on his left leg, he kicked the fender back with his right foot, making sure it didn't touch the tire. He remounted and kick-started the engine, relieved that it started with the first try.

"Thank you, friend. You're as tough as they said you were."

He gently released pressure on the clutch lever and slowly continued into the canyon. He stopped about ten yards in, walking back to the canyon's entrance. Using his foot and jacket, he erased his tire and skid marks that showed his turning into the canyon.

Returning to the bike, scratching over his footprints behind him with a stick he found, he headed deeper into the darkness. The narrow beam of the mostly blacked-out headlight barely illuminated the narrow trail between the rocks.

Up ahead, he could just make out the aging, weathered shack in the narrow beam. It backed up almost against the canyon wall under a low outcropping of rock, which protected the back half of the structure from the elements.

He pulled to the back. There was just enough space for him to push the bike out of sight, hiding it mostly with a piece of rotten tarp and a fallen branch. He limped to the front, letting himself into the shack through the door hanging by one hinge.

He discovered the structure in early June. While supposedly on a liberty pass from Los Alamos to Taos, he drove his bike into the desert to work out an escape route. He'd heard the locals working construction at the site say the hills were full of old squatter or prospector camps.

"Yeah, them guys from back east would come out here lookin' for a piece of land or a vein of gold. Nobody's out there anymore. Just a lot of busted dreams."

In the light from his flashlight, the shack was as he remembered.

There was a chair with a broken back, a rickety table, a makeshift shelf with an empty Folgers coffee can, a frame that once held some sort of crude mattress, a flue that had been attached to a small iron stove, probably, taken by scavengers, and thick dust and cobwebs everywhere.

Feeling dizzy, he sat in the chair and realized his pants leg felt cold. Aiming the light at his leg, he saw that the inside of his pants had a large tear. From just above his knee, running down into his boot, was a dark, shiny red stain.

"Damn!" he shouted. "It must have been that fender."

With the light, he followed the trail of dark red splotches in the dust to the door.

I've got to stop the bleeding or die here, probably never to be found.

He swept the light around the cabin and saw the pieces of rope webbing hanging from the bed frame. He started to stand to get a piece and fell backward into the chair, almost passing out.

Whoa, this is really bad. I've gotta fix this now.

Sliding to the floor, he dragged his body to the bed and, using his knife, cut a length of rope. With his waning energy, he broke a leg from the chair. Then, using the technique he'd learned in training, he fashioned a tourniquet that he placed just above the wound and tightened it until the bleeding stopped.

Exhausted by the effort, he propped himself against the bed frame, took a long drink from his canteen, and allowed himself to doze. As he lost consciousness, the events in San Francisco from three years ago that had brought him to this place flooded back into his mind.

"Gerald," he heard his mother's voice say, "go help your father with that luggage. The Army trucks will be here soon."

40

JEMEZ MOUNTAINS, NEW MEXICO

JULY 15, 1945

David slowly awoke to a bright sun warming his face through the window and the roar of wind down the canyon.

A crushing headache, a cotton-dry mouth and a numbness in his leg snapped him back to reality.

How long have I been out? he wondered.

Looking at his watch, he realized it had been about five hours, and he knew he had to do something before he got any weaker. He slowly loosened the tourniquet and, seeing that the bleeding had stopped, replaced it with a wide strip of cloth torn from his pants leg.

His original plan, when he thought he could leave the assembly area without being noticed, was at first light, to fire up the Scout, head southwest to Phoenix, west to Lancaster, California, and then northwest to San Francisco.

At 55 mph eight hours a day, he felt he could make the 1,222-mile trip in just under three days.

Unfortunately, in his weakened condition, that idea was trash. Not only that, but he didn't know where his trackers were or if they'd given up.

As an alternative, he felt he could make the eighty-mile run to Albuquerque. There, he could find a drugstore to get painkillers, antibiotics, and bandages, and then a room with a bath and some food.

I can sell the Scout or, at worst, ditch it, he figured and, tomorrow, take a bus to San Francisco.

As for my trackers, since they haven't found me yet, I can probably be OK heading to Albuquerque.

That decision made, he slowly stood up, using the remains of the chair and bed for help, took a drink from the almost empty canteen, and limped slowly to the door.

"Alright, you bastards," he yelled, "if you're out there waiting, here I come."

He stepped into the bright sunlight and stopped. Hearing nothing except the wind and seeing no movement, he headed, limping, to the rear of the shack, pausing on the way to pee. The hard ground caused the liquid to splatter onto his boots.

"Damn, I must be weaker than I thought. Can't even piss straight."

With effort, he uncovered the Scout and pulled it from behind the shack. Carefully, so as not to reopen the wound, he mounted it and pushed down on the kickstarter. The muffled roar of the engine, reverberating off the canyon walls, seemed to bring strength into his body. With the rays of the sun reaching the canyon floor, he put the Scout in gear, determined to make the tough trip to first aid and rest.

Weighing the risk of discovery versus the ease of the ride, he opted to head for paved highways instead of the rougher ride through the desert.

I certainly don't want to reopen my wound before I can give it some proper first aid. He was confident that he could patch himself up adequately because of the survival techniques he received from the medics during the training at the Covert Ops school in Tokyo.

The traffic on the road was very light at this early hour. Since he wasn't encountering any other vehicles, he felt he could make a quick stop at a roadside café to get a cup of coffee and a piece of pie. When he entered, he saw he was the only one in the place, and there was only one person, probably the owner, busy in the kitchen. He was able to sit at the counter without the blood and torn pants being noticed.

"What'll it be, friend?" he heard from the kitchen.

"Coffee and a piece of your apple pie, please," he replied.

"Good choice. It just came out of the oven about thirty minutes ago. Cream and sugar?"

"No, just black, please."

Setting the coffee and pie and a fork in front of him, he asked, "Where are you headed so early in the morning?"

"Back home to Albuquerque," David replied. "I drove into the mountains yesterday to an old cabin I found. I was thinking about maybe doing some prospecting. But then this morning, I took a spill and hurt my leg, so I need to go home to take care of it. Getting rich will just have to wait," he said with a smile.

"You're wasting your time," the owner said. "Over the years, I've seen a number of guys come here to try their luck. None found anything worth coming back for. The only activity around here is at that hush-hush site south of Albuquerque. Army trucks and cars are coming and going. Folks say the activity has really picked up in the last week. I hear a group of kids tried to sneak in through a back gate. They got a couple of hundred yards in when a couple of Jeeps and guys with rifles stopped them and took them to the local sheriff's office."

"Yeah, I've heard the gossip," said David. "Don't put much stock in it. Just war jitters, I'm guessing."

David finished the pie and coffee, paid the check, thanked the owner who had returned to the kitchen and headed for the Scout, feeling a little stronger. He headed south again toward town.

The shops were just beginning to open as he rode into downtown. He quickly located a pharmacy.

"Good morning," the clerk behind the counter said, alerted by the small bell attached to the door. "What can I do...," pausing abruptly as he saw David's torn and bloody trousers and general disheveled appearance. "Are you okay? What happened?"

"I was riding my motorcycle out in the desert and took a spill. Fortunately, I only cut my leg. I patched it up with a piece of my pants leg enough to get back to town. Now I just need some first aid supplies—antiseptic cleaner, cotton balls, and bandages; then I'll head home to fix it properly." David made sure to smile politely while relating his tale.

Filling the brown paper bag with those items, the clerk

took David's cash, gave him back some change, and said, "Good luck, sir. You really should go to the hospital."

As he turned to go, David caught a view of himself in a mirror behind the counter.

Damn, I do look pretty rough. I'd better clean up a little before I attract the attention of a suspicious policeman.

Driving to a nearby filling station, he pulled to the side and went into the restroom. There, he cut the other leg off his pants so they looked like shorts, rinsed the shorts in the sink, got out most of the blood, and, using the pants leg as a cloth, washed his face and slicked down his hair. Satisfied that he looked unremarkable, he went out to the Scout.

"OK, friend," he muttered to himself, "you've made it this far. Now you need to find food, some fresh clothes, and a bed."

Finding a phone booth, he looked for a boarding house in the dangling phone book. There was one five blocks away and close to the bus station. He headed that way, taking a slight detour to stop at a grocery store to pick up a box of salt, a bag of lemons, and a jar of local honey. Using a survival trick the medics had taught him, he'd put the salt, juice from the lemons, and the honey into water to make a basic electrolyte drink to ease some effects of the blood loss.

He saw a general store down the block where he stopped to buy a pair of jeans and a shirt. He arrived at the boarding house and parked the Scout next to the large porch which surrounded the house on three sides. The three-story wood shingled house looked like it dated from the 1880s, with the large influx of population due to the arrival of the railroad. As he walked toward the steps, a boney, brown bloodhound cautiously greeted him.

"Hi, gal. Are you the official greeter?" he said, reaching down to scratch her head.

Walking up the steps, he saw several of the guests sitting in some of the many rocking chairs on the porch. Two were engaged in a game of checkers. None appeared to pay him any attention. Inside the large entry hall, he found the registration desk with a stooped, elderly, gray-haired lady in a bright yellow-and-red dress behind it. To the left, he saw the dining room, and the smell of the aromas from the midday meal reminded him how hungry he was. Approaching the desk, he put his packages on the floor.

"Good afternoon, ma'am. I'd like a room and meals for two nights," he said, "and a bath. And do you have a room that faces south?"

"Yes, sir. The room is eight dollars for a single. A double is nine. Meals are a dollar fifty for breakfast, two fifty for midday, and four dollars for supper. The bath is seventy-five cents, including towel and soap. Hot water is one dollar extra."

"I'll take the single room, hot bath, and five meals." The lady made some additions on a scratch pad.

"That'll be thirty-seventy-five, payable in advance," she replied with a warm smile. "You'll put four quarters in the meter to get your hot water."

As he counted out the cash and signed the register, she handed him a key.

"This is for your room, number 203. It's on the second floor at the end of the stairs," pointing to the curving staircase to his right. "The bathroom is at the end of the hallway and locks from the inside. Here's your towel. Leave it in your room when you leave."

"Thank you, ma'am. When's supper?"
"Six o'clock, and please be prompt."
"I certainly will," he replied.

41

ALBUQUERQUE, NEW MEXICO

JULY 15, 1945

David slowly climbed the winding staircase, each of the sixteen steps more difficult than the last. The adrenaline that had kept him going was gone. He was now running solely on the drive to get home to his family.

He unlocked the door to his room, dropped his shopping bags on the floor, and saw that he had a clear view to the north toward Los Alamos, then collapsed onto the bed.

I've got four hours 'til supper. *I'll just lie here for a few minutes, then mix the electrolyte. That'll give me time for a bath and a couple of hours sleep before supper.*

Later, he looked at his watch and saw he'd been asleep for an hour. That's when he noticed the pitcher of water, washbowl, hand towel, and a glass on the small chest of drawers by the curtained window. He poured salt into the glass, squeezed in the juice from two lemons, half the jar of honey, and water from the pitcher, using his knife to stir it 'til everything was dissolved. That made about two glasses of the basic electrolyte he needed. He drank it slowly, feeling the strong liquid seeming to spread from his stomach throughout his body. Within a few minutes, he felt some of his strength returning.

"Now for that bath" he said to himself as he picked up his new pants and shirt, the towel, and four quarters, heading for the bathroom.

Relieved to find it unoccupied, he went in, switching on the light and locking the door behind him. He put his new clothes on the bench, holding a large bar of lye soap in a flat dish. Then, after lowering the hinged pipe from the water heater to the lip of the tub and putting the plug in the drain, he put his four quarters into the meter and turned on the gas. Hearing the whoosh of the flames under the boiler, he stripped down and waited. At eight minutes by his watch, he heard the flames stop. Steaming water flowed into the tub after he turned the valve on the lowered pipe. He turned the cold-water faucet on the tub, cooling the water down just enough for him to get in. He grabbed the soap, laid his towel next to the tub, and lowered himself gently into the welcoming warmth, being careful to keep his right knee and wound out of the water. Then he put his head back and thought of home and the joy of seeing his family and Hana again and hearing his name, Gerald, spoken after more than three years.

After about twenty minutes, the water had lost most of its warmth. He quickly rinsed off and got out of the tub. After drying off, he washed his undershorts and socks in the warm water, rinsed them under the cold faucet, and squeezed most of the water out. He'd hang them by the window in his room, and they'd be dry in the morning. Getting into his clothes, he drained and rinsed out the tub and headed back to his room. He hung his shorts and socks on the chair by the window, pulled off his clothes, and picked up the first aid stuff. Cleaning the wound, he saw that a scab was forming. He then applied a proper dressing.

Seeing that he had just under two hours 'til supper, he slid between the sheets. Setting his internal alarm clock— another skill he'd learned from the Tokyo training—for 5:50, he went to sleep.

At precisely 5:50, he woke up, put on his shirt, jeans, and boots, and headed downstairs. As he got to the top of the stairs, he could hear voices and smell food, so he quickly went down, feeling much more refreshed than on his earlier trip up.

As he walked toward the dining room, he saw that there were about twelve to fourteen people standing around the two large tables. All were men except for the two well-dressed younger women who appeared to be the wives of the two similarly dressed young men. The other ten, ranging in age from late twenties to late sixties, were dressed like him in jeans, work shirts, and boots. They all turned to look at him as he arrived, making him definitely feel like a newcomer.

"Good evening," he said with a smile. "Hope I'm not late." He headed to one of the four vacant chairs next to one of the couples. "I just got in from Tucumcari, headed to California for a job. I'm glad to find such a fine place to stop along the way."

Two young girls started bringing steaming bowls and

platters of food from the kitchen and setting them on the tables. David's stomach growled noticeably, to the obvious displeasure of the lady on his left.

"Sorry, ma'am, it's been a long time and a hard day since breakfast."

During dinner, the chatter was mostly about the war, the weather, and all the rationing that was so inconvenient. A newspaper reporter seated at the table said that he'd heard rumors about some secret project the government was conducting south from there out in the desert. David breathed a sigh of relief when nobody picked up on the comment.

"What job are you going to in California?" asked the lady on his left.

"I'm an electrical engineer. I'll be going to work with the Navy on some technical projects they're developing."

"I'm so tired of all this war stuff," she pouted, slamming her fork on the table. "It's ended in Europe. Why not in the Pacific?"

Her husband placed his hand over hers.

"Now honey, I've told you, the Marines and Navy are doing a good job, but the Japs are really tough. It's not going to be over anytime soon. We just have to be patient."

I think we all will be surprised very soon, David thought, lightly touching his wound under the table.

After supper, David returned to his room. Looking out the window to the north, he wondered,

Was I successful? Will it happen soon?

42

ALBUQUERQUE, NEW MEXICO

JULY 16, 1945

It was a sultry night. David slept with the window open. At 5:29 a.m., a brilliant flash of light low in the sky that seemed to go on for several seconds startled him and the other guests with rooms facing south. That was followed by what sounded like faraway thunder. Several came out into the hall.

"What was that?"

"It was too bright to be lightning. It sounded more like an explosion."

Shortly, when nothing else happened, people went back to bed.

Lying wide awake in his bed, David felt the nagging concern that had been in his chest for several days fade away. He knew now he'd been successful in his efforts to thwart the work of his colleagues.

I hope I've lost them for good. If they ever find me, I'm sure they'll kill me.

Now, he was aware that a mixed feeling of success and sadness had replaced the concern.

I've probably helped bring the war to an end, but I've also helped bring great trouble to the land of my grandparents and ancestors.

At breakfast, there was some conversation about the early morning event. Since only the few guests on the south side had seen it, the topic quickly changed to the news that the Philippines had finally been liberated earlier in the month. David excused himself early and went outside.

It's probably my imagination, but I think I can smell smoke.

He headed to his bike. It started on the first crank, and he headed out to find the bus station. He found it, went in, and headed to the ticket booth, noticing a small group of soldiers who looked like they'd just arrived.

"What's the schedule for the bus to San Francisco?"

"It leaves at 11:00, in three hours," was the response. "Want a ticket?"

That'll give me time to go back, get my stuff, find a car dealer where I can sell the Scout, and get back here.

"Yes, a one-way ticket, please. When does it get there?"

"About 7:00 tomorrow morning. That'll be thirty-three dollars."

David counted out the money, noting that he had only seventy-five left.

With what I get for the Scout, I should have enough to find my family and Hana when I get there.

As he turned to leave, he saw that soldiers had blocked

the three doors to the building. Each stood with his M-1 at port arms. Clearly, they meant business, and no one was going out or coming in. The other six passengers, an elderly couple and a young couple with two small children spread out on the benches, had looks of confusion or fear on their faces.

"Attention, please," said the one with sergeant stripes on his sleeves. "I'm Sergeant O'Riley. I need you to get your identification papers out. Corporal Watkins and I will come to each of you to check them. Remain in your seats. You, sir," he turned to David, "take a seat over there," pointing to his left, away from the others.

David had a moment of panic, although he was sure not to reveal it.

Are they looking for me, or is this for something else? Do I use the forged papers from my training? They've gotten me cleared into several top-secret atomic bomb operations but link me to the Los Alamos project. Or my real ones from three years ago in San Francisco, which may be on a Watch List somewhere?

Deciding that they were more likely looking for people related to Los Alamos than for someone who had escaped from an internment camp three years ago, he chose his real ones.

By the time the two men approached him, he had slowed his breathing to normal and had his papers out.

"I see your name is Gerald Horito and your address is San Francisco. Are you Japanese?" he asked harshly, placing his hand on the butt of the .45 on his hip.

The image of the soldier in his office three years ago, paper in hand and gun on his hip, flashed in David's mind.

David replied, "I am one-half Japanese, born in this

country, as was my father. My mother is American, born in Oklahoma City. The soldiers moved our family to the internment camps in 1942, where we lived until they were closed. My father's parents died in the camp. My parents and sister went back to San Francisco. I went to Oklahoma City to visit my mother's parents. Now I'm going home to join my family and try to get my old job with the Navy back."

The sergeant relaxed a little and gave the papers back.

"Ok, you're free to go. But be careful; a lot of people still hate Japs."

He and Corporal Watkins then moved on to the other passengers.

David headed back to the boarding house, packed up his belongings, and went down to the desk.

"I'm leaving now," he said, turning in his key.

"It's before nine, so I can give you a refund for meals and one night," the elderly clerk replied.

"Thank you," he said and held out his hand for the cash. "I enjoyed the visit. Perhaps I'll return." The clerk smiled and nodded.

Back on the Scout, he headed to the bus station, put his stuff in a locker, and went to look for a car dealership that would buy his bike. About three blocks down Main Street, he spotted "Bob's Western Motors" with strings of colorful small triangle pennants strung from the light poles. A 5'x5' yellow-and-black sign attached to the fence announced loudly !!CASH FOR YOUR CAR!!.

Pulling in next to the small, weathered, white clapboard office raised up on concrete pillars, he hit the kill switch and got off. A balding, pot-bellied man in a white shirt and loosened tie appeared in the door.

"Mornin' sir, are you Bob?" David said. "I want to sell my Scout."

Coming down the stairs, he replied, "Yessir, I am, and good morning to you."

He came over and sat on the bike.

"She's a beaut and well cared for, except for that dent in the fender. Not much call for bikes right now, though. What you want for her?"

"I paid four-twenty-five for her. I'm askin' four hundred."

"I can go as high as three-twenty-five, but no more."

"How about three-seventy-five?"

"Three-forty" Bob replied.

Smiling on the inside but poker-faced on the outside, David said, "Done!"

Cash in his pocket, he started walking back to the bus station, each man sure he'd gotten the better of the other. Approaching the station, he saw the soldiers were still there. The sergeant saw him and nodded but said nothing. David got a cup of coffee at the lunch counter and sat down to wait for his bus to arrive.

In just twenty-two hours and two meal stops, I can start looking for my family and Hana. There've been times over the past years when I feared this time would never come.

The bus left on time, and in the early morning of the next day, July 17th, he arrived in San Francisco.

43

SAN FRANCISCO AND TULE LAKE,
CALIFORNIA

JULY 17. 1945 - JANUARY 15, 1946

Stepping off the bus, the familiar sounds and smells of the city enveloped him.

How strange. After three years and all that's happened, it's still home.

He headed into the station to get some breakfast and take some time to think through his next moves. As soon as he sat at the counter, the waitress set a steaming cup of coffee in front of him.

"Cream and sugar? What can I get you?"

"I take it black. I'll have pancakes and sausage, please."

Savoring the familiar, strong flavor of San Francisco's Imperial coffee, he wondered,

Are my family's two homes still there? Were they able to go back to them after they were released from the camp? If not, how can I find them?

How do I start looking for Hana? Maybe she and her friends are back at the nursing school. I'll go check there first.

The pancakes and sausage arrived, and he focused on eating.

David finished his breakfast, paid the check, and asked the waitress if he could get a city bus to the UCSF Nursing School.

"Certainly. You walk one block southwest to 2nd Street, and catch the Botanical Gardens bus. It runs about every twenty minutes and takes about forty minutes. There's one due at that stop in about ten minutes."

"Thank you," he said as he headed to the door and turned left.

Getting off the bus, and walking around the campus, he looked for any building with 'Nursing' on it.

"Ah, there you are," he said, crossing the street, and walking up the broad flight of stairs through large glass doors.

He walked to a reception desk and spoke to the young woman behind it.

"Good morning. I'm trying to locate a third-year nursing student who was studying here in 1942. Her studies were interrupted until this past October. I was hoping that she may have returned to continue her studies."

"The Registrar's office would have those records. That's the door to their offices across the lobby." Gerald nodded in thanks and headed for that office.

When he came to the desk inside, there was an older woman, he guessed about his mother's age, behind a counter.

He repeated his request to her.

She paused for a moment, slowly wiping her glasses as if she were reflecting on his question.

"You're talking about one of our Japanese students who was interred, I'm guessing. What a tragedy for them and this institution."

"Some returned. Many did not. Do you have a name?"

"Hana Sato," he replied.

She picked up the phone on her desk, dialed two numbers, and waited.

"Mr. Ito, there is a young man here asking about one of our Japanese internee students. May I send him back? Thank you.

"Go down this hallway. His office is the first door on the left. I hope you find who you are looking for. I remember Hana. She was one of our brightest students."

Gerald did not miss the past tense. It was a punch in the gut.

She's not here. Now, what do I do?

He found Mr. Ito in a small, cluttered office. There were several flowering plants on the windowsill. One reminded him of the small white flower Hana wore in her hair that first evening.

Mr. Ito had a full head of silver-white hair. He appeared to be in his early seventies. He stood as Gerald entered. He bowed. Gerald returned the bow.

"I am Jonathan Ito. Tell me more about who you are looking for."

"Sir, I am Gerald Horito. Hana Sato and I were at Topaz. We became close friends. If things had been different, we probably would have married. But a tragedy occurred with some of my family, and I escaped in order to find a way to get my family and Hana out. I was unsuccessful. I have not seen my family or Hana since. I am back now, hoping to find them."

"Please sit, Gerald. Let me check my records. You say she was one of the internees taken in 1942?"

He pulled out a card file drawer and flipped through the cards. "Here she is." He pulled one out and set it on the desk in front of him.

"Yes, I thought this is who we are discussing. I wanted to be sure. My memory is not what it used to be.

"This is such a sad case. She probably told you that her family lived in Hiroshima. He was a doctor, and she a nurse.

"They were killed in the bomb blast. Their bodies were never found.

"When the internees were released last October, a family, yours, I expect, brought her back to us.

"She came out of courtesy to tell us that not only had her family's death made it impossible to pay the costs of schooling, but that tragedy has crushed her desire to continue in nursing.

"She left, and we've lost track of her. What a loss. She was a bright light and an inspiration to the entire class. I think she had what it takes to become a physician. What a loss."

Gerald interjected. "She was with three of her roommates. Are any of them here?"

"No. A request was made through us from a school back East, offering them scholarships to leave Topaz and join one of their classes. Those three took the offer. I think I understand now why Hana didn't. I suspect it had something to do with you."

He stood up and offered his hand.

"I'm so sorry, my boy. I offer you my best wishes in finding her. I hope these events have not broken her spirit."

Gerald had no recollection of leaving the building. The bright sun startled him back to the present.

He sat down on the steps, put his head in his hands, and wept.

Finally, he stood.

Now I must find my family. I can't face the thought of losing everyone.

God, what a thoughtless fool I was to leave the camp!

I can catch a bus back to near our old homes. I'll start looking there.

As he got close to his old neighborhood, images from four years ago of Army trucks, men with guns, and families treated like cattle flashed in his mind.

When he arrived in front of the two houses where his family and grandparents had lived, he could see that they were occupied. There were two strange cars parked in the common drive, and lawn furniture and potted plants were in front of both houses. The grass had been recently cut. The vegetable garden that they had all so faithfully cared for was gone. Grass was in its place. Walking up to the front door of his parent's home, he knocked on the door. A Negro teenage girl appeared.

"Good morning, I'm Gerald Horito. My family lived in this house three years ago."

The girl took a couple of steps back from the screen.

"Daddy, there's a man here to see you," she said, looking over her shoulder. Gerald heard approaching steps, and a tall, middle-aged man came into view.

"May I help you?" he asked.

"Good morning, sir. As I told your daughter, I used to live here with my family. I hoped I would find them here."

"I don't know nothin' about your family. We bought this house and the one next door from a representative of the city in November 1942 when my family and my sister's family moved here from Mississippi. Many of the abandoned houses in this area had been vandalized. Some had been burned down. The city made efforts to stop the destruction. The houses on these two streets were taken over by the housing bureau, secured, and put up for auction."

"But this was our family home! We didn't abandon it! They forced us out! Surely, you've heard the stories!"

"I did. But that's not my concern. We bought these houses, fair and square, from the city. We have the deeds. Now, get off my property, or I'll have to call the police."

With that, he slammed the door.

Gerald, stunned, stood silent for a moment, turned, and walked back to the street. He'd gone only a half block when a police car came up behind him. There was a short blast on the siren, and one of the officers got out and came toward him, his hand on his gun.

"Sir, let me see some identification."

Gerald pulled his California driver's license from his wallet and handed it to the officer.

"Mr. Horito, this has an address just down the block. Was it you who threatened the people who live there now?"

"I didn't threaten anybody. I was just looking for my family. We used to live there."

"That's not what he said. He said you scared his

daughter and threatened him. You had better come down to the station with us."

Gerald reluctantly got into the back seat of the patrol car. He noticed there were no handles on the inside of the door.

When they got to the station, the officer led him by the arm to a room off to the side and pushed him through the door.

"I'll be back." He left, shutting the door behind him. As Gerald sat in one of the two chairs, he noticed that this door too, had no handles on the inside.

Now what? He waited.

After about thirty minutes, another officer and an Army sergeant came into the room.

"Mr. Horito, your name is on a list of escapees from the Topaz camp. We're turning you over to the Army's control." He left the room.

The sergeant spoke. "Mr. Horito, I've been instructed to take you to Tule Lake camp, where you will stay until released. You won't escape that place!"

Gerald had heard of Tule Lake. It was the largest internment camp. A place with high security and martial law, run by the Army, not the WRA. It's where internees considered disloyal or troublemakers were sent.

"Can't I be sent back to Topaz? My family is there." The man did not respond. He pulled Gerald from the chair and cuffed him.

"Let's go"

Six hours later, they arrived at the gates to Tule Lake. It was dark.

"I have prisoner Gerald Horito for delivery."

The gate opened, and Gerald was led through. The gate closed.

"Follow me," said the guard with a carbine in his hand.

He led him to a large square building with bars on the windows. Inside, the walls were lined with cells with bars on all sides.

The guard led him to one, removed his cuffs, and pushed him in.

"You'll be processed tomorrow morning." There's bread and water on the bed and a pot in the corner."

The next day, an officer with a briefcase, accompanied by a soldier with a pistol on his belt and carrying a small table and chair, came into the cell.

"Mr. Horito, you are assigned to Tule Lake for the remainder of the war. Once we complete this paperwork, this man will escort you to your barracks."

"There, you will be assigned team and work assignments. Schedules for meals, work, and shower schedules are posted on the bulletin board in the barracks.

"You will be issued clothes and boots. Laundry will be done weekly according to the posted schedule.

"Sign here."

For the next six months, Gerald lived in hell. It was worse than anything he had experienced in the last three and a half years.

44

TULE LAKE AND SAN FRANCISCO, CALIFORNIA

JANUARY 15-17, 1946

At 7:00 a.m., a guard came into the barracks.

"On your feet. You have thirty minutes to gather your belongings and report to the front gate. You are being released. You will be processed out, given two hundred dollars, and put on a bus to San Francisco." He turned and walked out.

Gerald scrambled, along with the forty-nine other men in the barracks, to collect their things and head to the gate. Six hours later, he stood on the sidewalk in front of the same bus station where he'd been six months ago.

First, I'll put this bag in a locker, get something to eat, and start where I left off in July.

He deposited his bag and ate the first good food he'd tasted in months.

Now what? Where do I look from here? Perhaps the

factory where Papa worked, if it's still there, may know something about him.

Walking to the bus stop where he and his father always caught the bus to work, Gerald saw that the next bus to the factory would arrive in about ten minutes. He waited with several other riders, feeling fortunate that he passed for White.

When he got off at the factory where his father had worked, he went to the guard shack at the gate entrance.

"Good morning." The guard looked up from his newspaper.

"I'm Gerald Horito. My father used to work at this plant. His foreman was Mr. Wilson. Do you know if he still works here?"

The guard looked at a list on a clipboard hanging from the wall.

"Yes, he does."

"Would it be possible for me to speak with him?"

Picking up a phone, the guard spoke briefly to someone on the other end.

"Mr. Wilson will see you at that door. Here, clip this tag to your shirt."

Gerald walked to the door, noticing the stacks of fifty-gallon drums around the yard.

Those must be the dyes Papa's team used for the cloth.

He waited only a few minutes by the door before it opened, and a gray-haired man appeared.

With a big smile and an outstretched hand, he walked toward Gerald.

"Gerald, what a nice surprise. What can I do for you?"

"I'm looking for my father. I just got here from

Oklahoma. I heard everybody had been released from the camps. I went to our old home. Unhelpful strangers were living there. So, I came here hoping to find you and see if you knew anything about my father and family."

"When your family found out that your home had been auctioned off and there was nothing they could do to get it back, they had to find someplace to stay. All they could afford was a rooming house in a trashy part of town. Your father came to me looking for work. I couldn't give him his old job in the dye shop back, but I was able to take him on loading and unloading trucks in shipping. It was hard work and didn't pay as well as his other job. He took it 'cause he needed to have money for the family. He said you'd gone to Oklahoma City, where you got a job so you could look after your mom's parents. He worked here 'til mid-February, then told me he'd found a better-paying job down at the wharf. That's the last I've seen or heard from him. I hope he did okay. He was the best worker we had at the plant."

"Do you know where they were living? Maybe they're still there."

Mr. Wilson scratched an address on a scrap of paper.

Gerald looked at it and said, "Thanks," and turned to leave.

"Good luck," he heard Mr. Wilson say as he headed to the gate.

Arriving at the address Mr. Wilson had given him, he paused before going in. In front of him was what had once been a nice hotel. Now, it looked derelict. There were weeds growing next to the building. Several of the windows had been boarded up. The neon sign was not working and was hanging at an angle. The glass in the front door was cracked and had been taped.

I can't believe my family had to live in this dump.

Sadness and anger brought tears to his eyes.

Gerald entered the dirty lobby and asked the half-asleep clerk if the Horito family lived there.

"There ain't no Japs living here now and ain't been since June when I started workin' here," was the curt reply.

Feeling totally drained and defeated, Gerald got out of the slums as quickly as he could, found a small hotel, and crashed.

He woke up shortly after three a.m. to the sound of a passing fire truck.

My last hope is to contact my mother's family.

They, like his father's family, had disowned her when she got married. They had never reconciled as his Papa's family had, but his mother had written and received a few letters from her mother over the years. Gerald knew only that their last name was Bryan, that they lived in Oklahoma City, that his grandfather was some type of minister, and that his grandmother was a pediatrician. His mother had two younger brothers. He did not know anyone's first name.

"Not much to go on," he said to the pigeon roosting on the windowsill.

The next morning, he returned to the bus station and bought a ticket to Oklahoma City, noting that it was a twenty-six-hour trip. He had a two-hour wait. He'd get there early the next afternoon.

Damn long trip.

He boarded, located a seat with no one near, and sat down. He noticed the bus had only eight other passengers.

Wonder how they stay in business?

He looked at his ticket and saw that the route took them through Albuquerque. He walked forward to the driver.

"Can I do an overnight layover in Albuquerque on this ticket?" he asked.

"Yes. One night only."

Good. I can break up the trip if I need to. I already know a good place to stay.

He settled back in his seat and opened the newspaper he'd bought at the station. There were stories of the final return of troops from the Pacific Theater. Others featured General MacArthur's efforts to stabilize and rebuild Japan and its people. On the back page was a photo of the surrender ceremony on the USS Missouri the previous September. Also, some chilling photos of Hiroshima and Nagasaki after the bombing.

As he dozed off, relaxed by the hum of the tires and the gentle swaying of the bus, Gerald wondered, *What would the world be like if our team had been successful in delaying the completion of the bomb at the Trinity site?*

45

ALBUQUERQUE, NEW MEXICO

JANUARY 18. 1946

David awoke as the bus stopped for a break at a crossroads café and hotel at the intersection of the road headed north to Las Vegas in Kingman, Arizona. It was the halfway point to Albuquerque. The night sky flickered with stars as he and most of the other passengers got off and headed to the café.

"I love the night sky in the desert. Everything seems so crisp and peaceful," he said to the man next to him.

"It sure weren't peaceful on Guadalcanal," was the reply. "We hated the night. That's when the Nips would try to sneak into our lines. I've never liked the night since."

"You were in the Marines, huh?"

"Yeah, still am. I was with the 1/7 with 'Chesty' Puller on 'The Canal.' I was there almost a month when I got this," he said, holding up what remained of his right hand. "They sent me stateside to recover and tried to muster me out. I knew it'd be rough trying to find work with my injury, so I got them to let me stay in 'til the end of my contract. Now, I'm trying to get a disability discharge. Right now, I'm headed home to see my family. Where'd you serve?"

"I never did. I was rejected because of a bad back. I have an engineering degree, so I work in a plant making electrical systems for the Navy," he lied.

"You're lucky. I never had a choice. The draft got me."

They continued inside, got their coffee and pie, and talked about life in the "City by the Bay." Returning to the bus, they went back to their separate seats and spent the rest of the trip in silence.

When they arrived in Albuquerque, the driver said, "If you're planning to stay over, you'll need to go inside and get your ticket revalidated. The bus tomorrow leaves at nine in the morning."

I think I will.

Finishing that task, he started on the five-block walk to the boarding house where he'd stayed earlier. He saw a bar ahead that appeared to be open, so he stopped in for a beer. The place was mostly empty at that time of day. The bartender was stacking up glasses for the evening crowd. Jimmie Davis's "There's a New Moon Over My Shoulder" could be heard from the jukebox. A couple were holding hands at a table in the back, and two guys were sitting at the other end of the bar.

"I'll have a Shiner Bock, please," Gerald said to the barkeep, "and some peanuts."

The bartender placed them in front of him. Gerald took a long drink, ate a handful of peanuts, and wondered what he'd find in Oklahoma City.

Can I find my grandparents? Will my family be there? Will they know anything about Hana?

Brought on by the sad words of the song, a sense of hopelessness overcame him. He closed his eyes and put his head in his hands, oblivious to everything around him.

He didn't hear the bathroom door slam or the approach of someone behind him.

He was startled by a hand on his shoulder and the press of something hard in the small of his back.

"Well, hello, David," a familiar voice whispered in his ear. "I'll bet you thought you'd never hear my voice again. No, don't try anything. I don't want to shoot you in here, but I will."

O, God! Of all the terrible luck. How could Bill Davis and I end up in the same bar almost seven months and a hundred miles from the last place I saw him?

"What you're gonna do now is finish your beer, pay your tab, stand up slowly, and walk toward the door. I'll be right beside you."

Gerald did as he was told. He didn't want to put anybody in the bar at risk. Nobody in the room seemed to notice the two men leaving.

"Now, you're gonna walk to the corner of the building, turn left down that alley, and head toward those woods across that field.

You know, your betrayal not only ruined the plot, but sticking that note in the MP's guard shack as you were running almost got Jack, Sam, and me caught. At first light, we saw six MPs armed with rifles headed toward our barracks. Escaping out the back door, we hid in a storage building. Just as they got close, an alarm sounded, and they turned and ran to the main building. In the confusion, we were able to get away. We separated, and I worked my way here to get my emergency stash. I've been here since, working for a car dealership. Now I get to settle up with a guy I thought was my friend. Good luck for me, bad luck for you."

They were just getting to the edge of the woods. Gerald appeared to trip on a root and, as he was falling, pivoted and drove his foot deep into Bill's groin. Bill staggered, and before he could recover, Gerald grabbed his long, thin-bladed killing knife from his boot, drove it deep between Bill's ribs into his heart, and twisted it. Bill died in seconds.

Wiping the few drops of blood remaining on the knife on Bill's shirt, he returned it to his boot. He grabbed Bill's arms and dragged him deeper into the woods, pushing his body up next to a fallen tree. He checked Bill's pockets for any identity papers and removed them. Then he covered his body with leaves and used a small branch to brush over the drag marks.

Then he turned aside, fell to his knees and vomited!

I didn't need to kill him! They trained us too well. I should have just knocked him out and tied him up. I could have hidden out 'til the bus left tomorrow. Now, what do I do?

As the effects of the adrenalin drained from his body, he assessed his situation.

I'll probably be OK. There's a good chance he won't be found before I leave tomorrow. Now, I need to get to the boarding house.

As he approached the building, the bloodhound ran to him, tail wagging.

"Hello again, gal. You're still here. Glad you remember me. Good to see you, too."

This time, the dog followed him up the stairs onto the porch, sniffing at his boots.

"Looks like you've made a friend," a guest in one of the rocking chairs said. "She doesn't usually pay that much attention to people."

I'll bet she's smelling my knife. I'd better clean it and my boot more thoroughly when I get to the room.

When he entered the lobby, the same desk clerk looked up.

"Hello! You're back."

"Yep, I said I might be back."

"Your old room's available. Want it?"

"That would be nice, thanks. Just for one night, however, and I don't need a bath. I'll eat supper and breakfast."

He paid the bill, signed the register, got his key, and headed up to his room. The light smell of cigar smoke remained from the last roomer, despite the Air Wick.

Whew! I'd better open that window for a while.

He sat on the bed and pulled off his boots. He pulled the knife out, scrubbed it thoroughly with soap and water in the basin, and, using the hem of his shirt to get some of the liquid off the Air Wick room freshener bottle, wiped it on his knife and boot.

"That should fool you, my furry friend."

At supper, the crowd hadn't changed much since the last time he was here. Several nodded to him as he entered the room. As they were sitting down, he heard one of the men behind him say, "Wonder where Mr. Davis is. It's not like him to miss a meal."

"I heard him say he was going into town for a beer," another guest replied. "Maybe he decided to eat at the bar."

"Yeah, that's probably it. I guess we'll see him at breakfast."

Damn, thought Gerald, now I'd better get out of here before breakfast. When Bill's not here then, people may begin to get curious.

Early the next morning, Gerald dropped his key on the counter and headed toward the bus station. The dog, lying on the porch, raised her eyebrows as he passed but showed no other interest.

He arrived at the station at seven, got a paper, coffee, and toast, and waited for his bus.

46

OKLAHOMA CITY, OKLAHOMA

JANUARY 19-21, 1946

When the bus arrived at the station in Oklahoma City, it was late afternoon. Gerald bought a map of the city and a cup of coffee and sat in a phone booth. He opened the large directory hanging from a chain from the wall. With the directory balanced on one knee, a notepad on the other, and his coffee perched on top of the phone, he turned to the "Bs." There were six pages of three columns of names, addresses, and phone numbers. Fortunately, there were only twenty-seven "Bryans," and only two of these had "Rev." with the name.

It looks like it's gonna be a simple task to locate Mama's parents.

He wrote the information for the two in the pad, then took the pad, map, and coffee to a booth in the small café. He spread out the map, almost knocking over his coffee.

He searched for and found the names of the two streets he'd written on the pad, circling them with a pencil. One looked like it was only a few blocks from the bus station, while the other was about three miles to the northwest.

Finishing his coffee, he folded the map showing the area of the first street, East California Avenue, and headed out. He figured he had a couple of hours before dark, and he hoped to find his grandparents before then.

As he approached the street number he'd written down, he saw what appeared to be a dilapidated stone church that must have been impressive in its day. Some of the windows had been boarded up, one of the gutters was hanging down, and there was a hand-lettered sign over the door SOUTHSIDE COMMUNITY MISSION-A Ministry of First Pentecostal Church. Next to it, within the sagging wrought iron fence, was an equally dilapidated two-story brick home.

Gerald walked up the crumbling concrete steps onto the porch and knocked on the weathered but imposing, heavy oak door with leaded glass inserts.

A young Negro man opened the door.

"Hello," he said. "How can I help you?"

"I'm looking for Rev. Bryan."

"That's me. What can I do for you?"

Oops. Wrong guess, thought Gerald.

"I'm looking for my grandfather, Rev. Bryan. There were two Rev. Bryans in the phone book, and this address was the closest to the bus station. It looks like I picked the wrong one."

The young Rev. Bryan gave a large smile and a laugh.

"Your grandfather and I know of each other 'cause of mistakes like the one you've made, but we live in very different worlds. We've met only once. It's when I first moved to town, saw his name in the directory, and decided to pay a courtesy, curiosity visit to his church. We had a courteous but short visit. I invited him to come see my work anytime. He never has.

"You're looking for St. Swithin's Episcopal Church up near the country club." Pausing, he added, "You'll probably want to call ahead rather than just showing up."

Gerald thanked the young pastor and headed back toward the bus station.

Given the pastor's veiled warning about what sort of welcome I might receive if I just show up, I think I'll find a place to stay tonight and show up tomorrow when it's fully light.

He found a decent hotel and rented a room. When he got to the room, he dropped his knapsack on the bed and looked at himself in the mirror.

"You are looking a little rough," he said to the image before him. "Before I go knock on their door, I think I'll go get a haircut, get my beard shaved off, and get my boots shined. That and a new shirt should do the trick."

After getting a shower in the free-standing, footed iron tub, he put on his last pair of clean shorts and socks. Then he dressed and went down to the lobby.

"Is there a barbershop nearby and a place to get a shine?" he asked the young clerk at the desk.

"There's one attached to the hotel. Just go through that side door. They open at ten, and I hear that Uncle Willy gives the best shine in town."

"Tomorrow, I want to visit some family who live out near the country club. Can I get a bus or trolley out near that area?"

"Yessir, go one block north and catch the Northside Line. That'll get you to about one-half mile of their main entrance. The trolley runs every hour on the half-hour from nine-thirty 'til five-thirty. It'll cost you a dollar fifty each way."

After getting a sandwich across the street, Gerald returned to his room.

He kicked off his boots and stretched out on the bed, and his thoughts turned to tomorrow.

Will my family be there? Or will my grandparents know where they are?

Gerald had never met or spoken to his mother's parents. He'd only seen a photo of them in their thirties that his mother had kept in her bedroom in San Francisco and on a shelf in their one-room "prison" in the internment camp. He figured they'd be in their late seventies now.

Would they have blamed my father for how their daughter was treated, being forced to live in the terrible conditions of the camp? Would they have taken them in if they came here?

As the questions and images swirled in his mind, Gerald fell into a troubled sleep.

In the morning, he was waiting at the barbershop door when it opened. Thirty minutes later, with a shave, haircut, and freshly shined boots, he felt like a new man. With a fresh shirt from the store around the corner, he returned to his room, put on the new shirt, and again stood in front of the mirror.

"Now that's more like it," he exclaimed to his reflection. "I certainly look presentable enough not to frighten my grandparents.

I still have time to get something to eat."

The trolley was right on time. He boarded, bought his ticket, and settled back to enjoy the sights, sounds, and smells of the city.

"The next stop is yours, mister."

Moving up to stand beside the driver, Gerald asked,

"Do you know this part of town? I'm looking for St. Swithin's Episcopal Church."

The driver frowned as he looked him over from head to toe.

"That's in the ritziest part of town. Are you maybe looking for St. John's? It's a newer church west of here."

Maybe I'm not as presentable as I thought.

"No, sir. It's St. Swithin's. My grandfather is the minister there."

"Harrumph. I guess I made a wrong assumption. We stop at the Five Points intersection of North, Country Club, and Church. Church runs northeast from here. St. Swithin's is three blocks out Church. You can't miss it. You'll see the steeple after you've gone a block."

The trolley pulled to a stop. The driver opened the doors.

"Good luck," he said.

As he stepped to the curb, Gerald recalled, *That's what Mr. Wilson said back in San Francisco when he gave me an address for my family. I sure hope this time my luck is better.*

As he walked up the sidewalk of the tree-lined street, the size and beauty of the houses, set back from the street behind manicured lawns, intimidated him. He'd seen such obvious displays of wealth only in pictures. Most of the houses had gated driveways.

Now I understand the driver asking me if I was in the wrong section of town. Maybe I should have called ahead. Oh well, it's too late to turn back now.

Soon, he could see the tall green, copper-clad spire rising above the trees. The street took a slight curve to the left, and as he rounded the bend, St. Swithin's came into view.

The church certainly fit the tone of the neighborhood. A massive structure with flying buttresses and tall clerestory windows sat in the midst of a century-old graveyard and towering shade trees. The rose window over the main doorway must have been at least twelve feet in diameter. A beautiful black four-foot-high wrought iron fence circled the entire block, enclosing the church, attached buildings, and a home, not unlike the one he'd visited earlier, except in pristine condition.

A sign next to the front gate had SAINT SWITHIN's in four-inch gold lettering across the curved top. Two-inch letters below read; EST. 1840 The service times were listed below that. Across the bottom, GERALD READ, THE REV. DR. WILLIAM R. BRYAN, D.MIN. RECTOR.

Walking down the sidewalk to the gate in front of the house, he paused, took a few deep breaths, and walked in. As he reached the top step, he heard what sounded like jazz coming from inside. That felt somehow welcoming, so he felt more relaxed as he pressed the doorbell and took a step back. A series of eight chimed notes came through the door. After what seemed like an eternity, he heard the click of a lock, and a Negro woman in a crisp maid's uniform opened the door.

Her expression changed from pleasant to neutral as she saw Gerald. She moved slightly behind the edge of the door.

"May I help you, sir?"

47

OKLAHOMA CITY, OKLAHOMA

JANUARY 21, 1946

"Good afternoon, ma'am," he said as he stepped back a step so as not to frighten her. "I am Reverend and Doctor Bryan's grandson. My mother is their daughter, Sandra. I..."

Her wide-eyed, open-mouthed, silent surprise caused him to pause.

Catching her breath, she replied, "Just a minute, please," and quickly shut the door, leaving him standing on the porch.

Now what? He moved closer to the door, hoping to hear anything from inside. There was only silence.

After what seemed like forever, though it was only two minutes, the door swung open fully. There stood a large grey-haired man, fully four inches taller than Gerald. He was in a dark grey suit with a black vest and white collar. He did not look happy and certainly not welcoming. Gerald took a step back. This time it was he who was frightened.

"Sir, what's the meaning of this? My daughter told me her son was dead."

Emotions swirled in his head. *My mother's alive. This man has talked to her. She thinks I'm dead.* He was speechless.

Recovering his voice, his heart racing, he blurted out, "Sir, I am Gerald. I can understand her believing I'm dead. My family has not seen or heard from me since I escaped the internment camp almost three years ago. Are they here? I have identification."

"Sandra, her husband, and their daughter live in the city but not here. I've called a friend of mine from the police department who's on his way over here now. You sit on that swing, pointing past Gerald's right shoulder, "'til he gets here, and don't leave. Do you want some water?"

"Yes, please."

"Sarah will bring it to you."

With that, he quickly turned and went back into the house, closing the door. As Gerald was sitting on the swing, the door reopened, and the maid who had answered the door earlier came out with a glass of water.

"Is you really Mr. Gerald?" There was wonder in her voice.

"Yes, ma'am, I am. Do you know my family?"

"Mr. Bryan said I weren't to talk to you." She gave him the glass and turned back toward the door. Pausing mid-step and looking back over her shoulder, she whispered, "Yes."

Gerald sat on the swing, willing himself to calm down.

In all his months of training and working with the sabotage team, nothing was as unsettling as waiting for what was going to happen next.

Sitting there, he saw the curtains in the glass next to the door move slightly, and a female face appeared in the crack.

The police car with two men arrived about fifteen minutes later. One was in uniform, and one in a suit. They came quickly up the steps, the uniformed man moving to stand in front of Gerald, his hand on his gun. He said nothing. The other one raised his hand to knock as the door opened. Reverend Bryan took him in, leaving the door open. Gerald could hear conversation but not words.

His grandfather and the plainclothes policeman came over and stood in front of Gerald.

"Stand up, please," his grandfather said firmly. "You say you have identification. Give it to the detective."

Gerald, very slowly, his eyes on the gun, pulled his electrical plant ID from his pocket and handed it to him. The detective examined it closely, looking at both sides several times. He held the photo up to Gerald's face.

"Mister Bryan, this is the man in the photo, and the address matches the one you have from your daughter's home in San Francisco. I believe this is your grandson." Gerald took a deep breath and relaxed a little.

"However, this ID has expired. It's almost four years out of date."

"I can explain," Gerald said, looking at his grandfather. "When I escaped from the camp, my goal was to find some way to get my family released. I couldn't go back to my old job. I was afraid they'd turn me in. Instead, I heard there was a lot of construction in Las Vegas. I figured with my electrical skills, I could easily get a job as an electrician. The job bosses didn't care that I had no ID. They really needed skilled workers. After a couple of months, I located a guy who would make me some high-quality false papers. I stayed in Vegas for about six months. Then I heard that the government needed electricians for a big operation they were setting up in Tennessee, some town called Oak Ridge. I figured if I could get in on a government operation, I might find somebody who'd know how to help my family."

It never failed to amaze Gerald how his experiences over the last three years had made it so easy for him to lie without thinking.

"I worked in Oak Ridge in what was called 'The Manhattan Project' for a little over a year. In October '44, the government moved a group of us to Los Alamos. I worked there until three weeks ago.

"That's when I headed to San Francisco. I heard from some of the soldiers at the site that the camps had closed in October. I wanted to find my family. My search led me here."

There was a long silence while the three men took in his story.

Finally, his grandfather broke the silence.

Turning to the detective, he said, "Bill, you and the officer can go. This is my grandson, and I can take it from here. Thank you for your quick response. I'll see you at Rotary on Monday."

The detective and Mr. Bryan shook hands. He and the policeman left.

"Well, Gerald, you and I and your grandmother need to

figure out how to prepare your parents and sister for a big surprise."

"And I think we have one for you, too," he said mysteriously.

Placing his arm around his shoulders, he led Gerald into the house.

48

REUNION, OKLAHOMA CITY

JANUARY 21, 1946

Gerald's grandfather led him down a hall into his study. It was a paneled room with bookcases to the ceiling on one wall. The opposite wall was filled with framed certificates and photos of his grandfather with groups or individuals. There was a large desk set into a bay window at the other end of the room. In the center was a couch and two chairs grouped around a coffee table. A large Oriental carpet covered almost the entire floor. To one side of the desk was a small prayer desk with a Bible and prayer book set on it.

The smell of books and leather was pleasantly calming to Gerald.

"Please sit, Gerald. I'll be right back." He returned a few minutes later with a beautiful lady with short grey hair. She was almost as tall as his grandfather.

"Gerald, this is your grandmother, Vera. Vera, this is Gerald."

As Gerald stood up, she walked over to the couch and embraced him. Gerald could feel the wetness of her tears as she hugged him tightly.

Stepping back, she put a hand on each of his shoulders.

"You were lost, and now you are found. Thanks be to God!

"Please, sit, and let's talk. Your Grandfather and I are so eager to hear all about you."

They each took a seat around the coffee table. William put his hand on Vera's arm.

"Please, dear, before we get started, I have something I need to say to our grandson.

"Gerald, I owe you a sincere and long overdue apology. It's one I've already shared with your parents and sister. Now, I'm so thankful that God has given me the opportunity to offer it to you.

"When our daughter married your father, I let my disappointment, anger and prejudice overwhelm my responsibility as a father and a Christian. Despite appeals from your grandmother, I banished Sandra from our family. I never spoke to her again.

"Fortunately, Vera made the effort to keep some connection through letters. Yes, Vera," patting her hand and smiling, "I knew about your little secret.

"So, in the difficulty your family was having to overcome with the terrible injustice of being put into the internment camp in Utah, Sandra had the courage to reach out to us.

"We immediately sent them plane tickets and invited

them to come home to us. When they got here, I asked for their forgiveness, and now I ask for yours."

He reached for Gerald's hand. "Please forgive my blindness."

Gerald stood up. His cheeks were now the ones wet with tears. "Grandfather, I forgive you completely, and I am so very grateful to both of you for bringing my family here. When can I see Mama and Papa and Rachel?"

"That you are alive is a great shock to me and your grandmother. It's going to be a much bigger one for your family. Do we tell them you're alive before they see you, or let the reunion be a surprise?"

"I think the reunion should be a surprise. They will have so many questions for me. The quicker they get answers, the better."

"I agree, " his grandfather said. "I will call them and invite them for supper. We often do that, so they'll think nothing about it."

He excused himself and went out.

"You are certainly looking well, Gerald," his grandmother said. "I heard you telling the men on the porch about your work in Las Vegas and with the government project. It must have agreed with you. And I imagine working for the government must have been very exciting. Tell me more about it."

Gerald paused before answering his grandmother.

Do I maintain the lie I've created? Can I be dishonest with these people who seem to love me? If I tell them the truth, will they feel an obligation to turn me over to the authorities?

Deciding to hide the truth, at least for a while, he responded.

"Yes, Grandmother, it was hard but good work. Las Vegas was a boomtown. Construction was everywhere, and the people were from all over the country. It was very exciting. I learned a lot working with my hands. The government job was very 'hush-hush.' We could only talk about what we were doing with those who worked next to us. Because of my experience with electrical design, I was often called on by others to consult on a problem. I learned a lot there, too."

His grandfather came back into the study.

"I've spoken to your mother. They'll be here about five-thirty for cocktails. I told them I had some interesting news to share with them." His wide smile caused Vera to laugh.

"From what you've told me, you've had a long trip here from San Francisco, so I imagine you could use a little rest before supper. Do you have any luggage back at the hotel? I can send the chauffeur to get it, close out your bill, and bring it here."

"Thank you, Grandfather. That's very kind. Yes, I would like to rest. Are these clothes okay to meet my parents?"

"I think we can find you a couple of pairs of pants left by your uncles. I'll have Sarah bring them to you in the guest room. There's a bathroom with fresh towels next to the room. Feel free to use it. Sarah will knock on your door at five. The room's at the top of the stairs, first door on the left."

The bedroom was like nothing he'd ever seen: a thick rug, a couch, two upholstered chairs, a chest of drawers made from a dark inlaid wood that was as tall as he was, and a large, canopied bed covered in a brilliant blue-and-white spread that sat in an alcove. Wooden lattice shutters were used to cover the windows. A late afternoon sun shining through cast bright ribbons of light on the bed and rug, dust motes dancing in them. A large fan hung from the twelve-foot ceiling, its revolutions bathing the room in a gentle breeze. There were beautiful paintings and lithographs on the walls.

He went to the door of the bathroom and flipped on the light. Pale yellow tiles with white moldings covered the walls, floor, and ceiling. A marble vanity with double sinks, a six-foot marble tub, and a toilet behind an oak door were set against the walls. The fragrance of a floral cleanser hung in the air. Another fan hung at the ready. It was larger than his room at home. Turning back into the bedroom, he noticed several family photographs grouped on a side table that matched the chest of drawers. He walked over to them. There were four of them: a family grouping of his grandparents and three teenage children, one of his grandfather in his robes, and one of his grandmother in her white coat holding a stethoscope in one hand. Then there was one, almost hidden behind the others, of his mother holding a young baby in a white dress and light blue cap.

That's me! as his eyes filled with tears.

There was a knock on the door, and Sarah was there with three pairs of pants on hangers. Her eyes sparkled, and she had a broad smile on her face.

"These was your Uncle Frank's. I believe they'll fit. I'll be back later to check." She paused. "Mr. Gerald, you 'shore have made us all happy by comin' home. I jes' know your parents and sister will be delighted. All these yeas' they thought you was dead!"

"Thank you, Sarah. I'm so thankful to be here. I just hope my family can forgive me for leaving them the way I did."

"Mr. Gerald, I jes' knows they will. They never spoke of you in anger, only sadness, wishin' they could get you back."

Laying the pants on the chair, he took her hands in his.

"Sarah, you have lifted a heavy burden from me. Thank you."

"I gots to go fix supper, Mr. Gerald. I'll see you downstairs in a while."

49

REUNION, OKLAHOMA CITY

JANUARY 22, 1946

Unable to wait any longer, Gerald went downstairs shortly after five. He heard voices in the study and headed there.

"Hello, Grandson," his grandmother said as he entered. "What a special joy it is to say that word. Your two uncles, Frank and Charles, each have two daughters. So, you are our only grandson!

"You look refreshed. Frank's trousers look like they were made for you. I'm glad you're down a little early. We need to think about how to handle the logistics of this reunion.

"Your family will arrive about five-thirty. We thought it might be best to bring everybody in here and get them seated with a cocktail. Then William will go out and bring you in. That way, if anyone gets overwhelmed at your appearance, they'll at least be sitting."

"That sounds like a good idea. Where can I wait?"

William answered. "You can wait in the kitchen with Sarah and Lucas, our chauffeur." Would you like to take something to drink with you?" gesturing toward the bar that had been set up.

"That sounds nice. A bourbon on ice, please. Maybe that'll help me relax."

"May I bring you something, dear?" he asked as he and Gerald moved to the bar.

"A sherry would be nice, thank you."

William brought her a glass of sherry and returned to pour a short drink for Gerald.

"Don't want you to get too relaxed," as he smiled and handed the glass to Gerald.

"Turn left out of the study door and go to the end of the hall, just past the dining room. That's where the kitchen is. I'll come get you when the time seems right."

Gerald walked down the hall, noticing the dining room to his right and the table set for six. He opened the door to the kitchen and walked in.

Immediately, Sarah and Lucas, who had been sitting at a table drinking coffee, stood.

Various pots were simmering on the stove. The aroma of fresh-baked bread filled the space.

"Mr. Gerald, this is my husband, Lucas Knighton. Lucas, this is Ms. Sandra's son, Gerald. You fetched his stuff from the hotel earlier."

Walking over, Gerald extended his hand. "Pleased to meet you, Mr. Knighton, I'm Gerald Horito." Lucas hesitated a minute and then reached out and shook Gerald's hand warmly.

"We sho' is pleased you're here, Mr. Gerald. I 'spect you're gonna put ten years' life, at least, back into Ms. Sandra. And your daddy and Ms. Rachel will be so excited."

"Can we sit? Ms. Knighton, I don't want to interrupt your getting supper ready. It sure does smell good."

"You're no trouble, Mr. Gerald, and please, just call us Sarah and Lucas."

Gerald and Lucas sat at the table while Sarah went around the kitchen, busy with getting supper ready.

The drink, the warmth, and the buzz of preparation in the kitchen made it all seem like a dream.

Is this really happening? First, I meet my mother's parents. And now I'm about to see my family after two years. It's almost too much.

A few minutes later, his grandfather came into the kitchen.

"Your family is very curious about my 'interesting news.' Let's not keep them waiting any longer."

He took Gerald by the elbow and led him down the hall. They paused just outside the door. His grandfather coughed to announce their presence and led him in.

The conversation ceased immediately. All eyes focused on Gerald. There was a momentary silence. Then his mother screamed "Gerald" and rushed to him, smothering him in an embrace, her whole body shaking.

"We thought you were dead!"

His father and Rachel reached him, each adding to the hug, everybody crying and talking at once.

Then William's voice broke in. "Sandra, Bunta, Rachel, let him breathe. Come, everybody. Sit down and give him a chance to speak. Then you can ask your questions as we go to supper."

Gerald began. "Mother, Father, Sis, I am so sorry that I left you like I did. I was having an increasingly difficult time accepting life in the camp. Then, when Ojichan and Obachan died from the cold, I knew I had to get out and find a way to get you out of that terrible place. I didn't want to tell you I was leaving. I was afraid you'd stop me."

"You should have left us a note.," Rachel said. "You just disappeared. We didn't know what happened."

"I figured that if you knew nothing, you wouldn't have to lie to the guards when they discovered I was missing. Then, maybe they wouldn't punish you. Remember how they treated Ito's family when the Block Manager discovered they had helped him get through the wire?"

"Once you got away from the camp, where did you go?" asked his father. "What did you do?"

At that moment, Lucas appeared at the door. "Excuse me. Sarah has supper on the table."

William stood. "Let's continue this over the delicious meal Sarah has prepared for us as a celebration of Gerald's return."

Gerald, relieved for the moment not to have to answer his father's questions, thought,

How long can I keep up this lie? Doesn't my family deserve to know the truth? Can I really ever be comfortable with them, keeping this truth from them? I wish there was someone I could talk to.

William gestured toward the door. They all followed Lucas toward the dining room. Sandra touched her father's arm, slowing him down.

She whispered into his ear. "Let's not mention Hana. I need to tell her this news and let her decide if she wants to reunite with Gerald."

He squeezed her hand.

They gathered around the table. William extended his hands to Sandra and Rachel. The others completed the circle with theirs.

"Let us give thanks and ask God's Blessings," William intoned in his church voice.

"Almighty God, we give you thanks for all the blessings of this life. For this world, this great nation and for this community in which we live.

We give you thanks for our friends and family, and most especially for the wonderful gift of the return of Gerald, who was lost to us.

Give us the grace and wisdom to help him as he rejoins our family and as he seeks to find his place in this community.

We ask now that You bless this food and those who prepared it, that it may nourish our bodies as this family nourishes our spirits.

Give us grateful hearts and keep us always mindful of the needs of others.

Amen."

"Vera, please start the potatoes around."

For a few moments, there was an awkward silence. Everybody had so many questions but didn't seem to know where to begin.

Gerald broke the ice. "Though I'm sure it is painful to recall, I want to hear about the rest of your time at Topaz.

Was it easier or harder? Did they ever build the high school? Were there a lot of people able to find places to go so they could leave? Did the government do anything to help you get your lives started again? Did they give you any money to help offset your losses?

He couldn't bring himself to ask about Hana. He was afraid of what he would hear.

"There's so much I've wondered and worried about."

"We'll have plenty of time to talk about those things," his mother said. "Now I want to hear how you found us."

"As soon as I got to San Francisco, I went to find our home. It and Obichan and Ojichan's home are now occupied by families from Mississippi who, according to one of the neighborhood shopkeepers, were escaping something he called the 'Jim Crow South.'

"As much as it hurt that we had lost these homes because of people's fear and prejudice, at least other victims of racial hatred found refuge in them. I guess even terrible events can have some good consequences.

"And Papa, I found your former boss, Mr. Wilson. He said several times you were the best worker he ever had and that he was glad he was able to help you while you were at Tanforan. But he didn't know where to find you. Are you working now?"

"Yes, I am. Your mother is too. With your grandfather's help, I got hired at a men's clothing manufacturing company. I work in the cutting/assembly department. With my experience from the plant in San Francisco, they made me a shift foreman after six months. Sandra, tell Gerald what you're doing."

Sandra replied, "You know I dropped out of Oklahoma

City University after three years to go to San Francisco. I planned to work for a few years and return to college. Then I met your father, and my life changed. Now, with Father's encouragement, I've re-enrolled and completed my degree in criminology. I've just graduated from the city Police Academy. My special training is in foreign national monitoring and apprehension. I'll be working closely with the FBI."

Damn! I'm sure glad I didn't tell anybody what I've really been doing! Now, I'll probably never be able to.

"Gerald," his grandfather asked, "now that you've found your family, what are your plans? Do you want to stay here in Oklahoma City? Certainly, with your education and experience, there are a number of jobs you're qualified to do. I helped your parents and would do the same for you."

"That would be wonderful, Grandfather. Thank you. But perhaps we can discuss that tomorrow?"

"Of course. Our joy at seeing you has made me overlook how tired you must be from the journey here. And I'm sure the excitement of the evening has taken its toll on all of us."

Vera spoke up. "Sandra, I know you had not planned on houseguests, so Gerald can stay with us over the weekend.

"Now, let's go to the study for coffee and some of the delicious dessert Sarah has made for us."

Conversation continued, pausing only as everybody dug into Sarah's famous crème brûlée, as they all caught up with each other's lives. At about eight-thirty, Sandra stood up.

"I think we'll leave now. Father, I know it has saddened you and Mother that our family has not attended services at St. Swithin's. There are several reasons for our absence.

"But now, I think Gerald's appearance is some kind of

sign. So, at least for next Sunday, we will be there. I hope that we, Gerald, and Mother, can be in a pew together."

"Sandra, nothing could make your father and me happier," Vera said as she hugged her. "Thank you. Please plan to stay for dinner afterward."

William, too surprised and overcome by emotion, could only grasp Bunta's hand and hug his daughter and granddaughter.

After seeing their family off, Vera, William, and Gerald stood in the hall.

Vera spoke. "I think your grandfather and I will retire for the night. You are welcome to relax in the study. There is today's newspaper and several current magazines. Or you may visit with Sarah and Lucas in the kitchen. I'm sure they are very curious about you.

"I've asked them to delay breakfast until nine to give you time to get a good rest. We'll see you in the morning." She gave him a hug and kissed his cheek. "Welcome home, Grandson."

"Thank you, Grandmother. It's a joy for me to be here. Grandfather, before you go, may I speak to you in your study?"

"Certainly. Come with me."

Following him into the study, Gerald asked, "Sir, may I close the door?"

With a quizzical look, he responded, "Yes. Would you like a nightcap?"

"No, I'm fine. I have an important and difficult matter to discuss with you. Please, let's sit.

"I have something that's troubling me greatly, but I'm afraid to discuss it."

"I remember that one of my high school friends who was Catholic said he could tell the Father anything, and it would have to remain secret. Is it the same in the Episcopal Church?"

"Yes, it's called Confession. It's one of our Sacraments. We're not as strict about it as the Roman church is, but we do use it. People make their confession when they seek God's forgiveness for sins they have committed. The Church gives me the power to offer that forgiveness if the person is truly remorseful. Anything you tell me in confession cannot and will not be made public. It's called the Seal of the Confessional."

"I would like to confess some things. I am remorseful, and I think hearing I'm forgiven would give me some peace, but what I really need is advice about what to do next. Can you do both?"

"Well, that's a bit unusual, but let's try. If I can give advice that you find helpful, I will."

"Do we have to go to the church to do this?

"No, right here is fine. Let me get my purple stole and Prayer Book. I suggest you kneel at that prayer desk, and I'll sit in this chair behind you and guide you through the service."

50

A NEW BEGINNING

JANUARY 22, 1946

With Gerald kneeling and his back to him wearing his purple stole, The Rev. Mr. Bryan spoke, "Now, my son, tell me what is troubling you. Please be as specific and thorough as you can."

For the next thirty minutes, the words rushed out as Gerald told the story of his desire to hurt those who put his family in the camps by becoming a spy for Japan and of his training to sabotage the work on the atomic bomb.

He described the many ways he and his teammates tried and failed to create chaos in the processes going on at Oak Ridge and of their finally developing a workable plan to destroy the mechanism that would detonate the test bomb at the Trinity test site in New Mexico.

He told of how getting to know and become friends with the people he came in contact with helped him to the growing realization that his hatred of Americans was as misguided as the hate that had been directed at his family. He knew he had to stop his teammates from achieving their goal.

Finally, he told of stabbing his teammate in self-defense and hiding his body in the woods and of all the lies he'd been telling to everyone since.

"Are you truly sorry for all these acts, and do you ask God's forgiveness?"

"Yes, I do."

"Do you vow to live the rest of your life avoiding such acts and instead caring for all you meet?"

"I do."

William placed his hand on his grandson's head. "In the name of God and His Holy Church, your sins are forgiven. Go in peace.

"And now for the advice I believe you are seeking.

"There is nothing to be gained by sharing these stories with your family or the authorities. You overcame your sin of treason by rejecting it before you did any actual harm. As for killing your teammate, you know it was self-defense. To confess it to the authorities would only cast light on your spying activities, for which it is unlikely you would get any understanding.

"I know you must live with the possibility of your actions coming to light on their own, but that seems unlikely. If that happens, you can count on the full support from all of us. Your mother's new work and her connections with the FBI might be helpful."

"Now, I have something to confess as well. There is something we've not told you tonight. Your mother asked me not to say anything, but I feel this is too important to keep from you.

"Hana is alive and living here near your family."

Gerald gasped and sprung from his chair. "Here? In Oklahoma? Is she okay? What is she doing? Can I see her?"

His grandfather put his hands on his grandson's shoulders. "Please sit, Gerald. I'll tell you the whole story as your mother has shared it with me."

"When you left the camp with no explanation, your family was upset and feared for your life. As soon as it was discovered that you were missing, they found Hana and told her. They knew you had become close but were unaware of how serious the relationship had become.

"Your loss to both Hana and your family brought them closer together as they coped with the harsh life in the camp.

"When word came to the camp about the bombing of Hiroshima and Nagasaki in early August of 1945, Hana was devastated. She felt sure her family had been killed. She went into a deep depression.

"Had it not been for your family, she might have taken her life. They got permission for her to move in with them. They took care of her until the camp was closed in October of 1945.

She went with them back to San Francisco. Without her parents' support, she was unable to continue her studies. Together, they survived the difficult time until they came here."

"We helped them find places to live when they got here. Hana asked to be near your family but wanted her own apartment. It is my belief that by living with them, she could not come to terms with the hurt of losing you."

"She has found work in a ladies' clothing store. We do our best to respect her independence while keeping an eye on her well-being. From time to time, she comes for a meal or a visit.

We are concerned about her. The sparkle in her eyes that your family loved, died with her parents. It has not returned. She seems rudderless.

"Tomorrow, your mother is going to tell her that you are here. Then, she can decide what she wants to do. I pray that she chooses to come to you.

"We'll see what tomorrow brings."

"Now it's time for bed. Tomorrow, you begin a new life in so many ways."

He led his grandson by his shoulder to the stairs.

ACKNOWLEDGMENTS

As with most things worth doing, having a good team makes the job easier and the results much better.

My sincere thanks to those who assisted me in the process of bringing this book to publication:

- My wife, Pat Freeman, an excellent proofreader.
- The members of my critique group.
- The Beta Readers.
- Janie Mills, my editor, and a delightful person with whom to work.
- My publisher, Frank Eastland, and his professional team at Publish Authority.
- Special thanks to Steve Okamoto from Foster City, California. Mr. Okamoto provided the author with invaluable fact-checking about life at Tanforan and Topaz[1].

---

1. Mr. Okamoto was five weeks old when his family was transported to the Tanforan Assembly Center. Fortunately, they did not have to be taken to the internment camp at Topaz. Steve's father was teaching Japanese to Naval Intelligence at the University of Colorado in Boulder, and they were able to join him there.

Mr. Okamoto provided the author with invaluable fact-checking about life at Tanforan and Topaz.

Mr. Okamoto was the Vice-Chairman of the Tanforan Assembly Center memorial committee responsible for erecting a memorial statue and grounds on August 27, 2022, on the site of the former race track that was converted to the assembly center.

ABOUT THE AUTHOR

Sollace Freeman, known to most as Mike, began his career as an author in response to the isolation forced by Covid.

He is retired from forty years of ministry in the Episcopal Church, thirty years as a chaplain with the US Navy, and six years as an international volunteer disaster relief responder.

Executive Order No. 9066 is his second published novel following the 2021 release of *If You Can Keep It: The Loss of a Vision.* He has begun work on a third book exploring the hidden and ruthless world of illegal ivory and wild animal smuggling.

When not traveling in their motor home, he lives in Gainesville, Georgia with his wife Pat and a ten-year-old "fur baby," Sassy the Shish Tzu. They have three children and seven grandchildren.

For more about the author, visit GainesvilleWriter.com.

THANK YOU FOR READING

If you enjoyed *Executive Order No. 9066*, we invite you to leave a review online and share your thoughts and reactions with friends and family.

Publish Authority